Other Books by Kassandra Lamb:

The Marcia Banks and Buddy Mysteries:

To Kill A Labrador
Arsenic and Young Lacy
The Call of the Woof
A Mayfair Christmas Carol
Patches in the Rye
The Legend of Sleepy Mayfair (Fall, 2018)

The Kate Huntington Mystery Series:

MULTIPLE MOTIVES
ILL-TIMED ENTANGLEMENTS
FAMILY FALLACIES
CELEBRITY STATUS
COLLATERAL CASUALTIES
ZERO HERO
FATAL FORTY-EIGHT
SUICIDAL SUSPICIONS
ANXIETY ATTACK
POLICE PROTECTION (2019)

The Kate on Vacation Novellas:

An Unsaintly Season in St. Augustine
Cruel Capers on the Caribbean
Ten-Gallon Tensions in Texas
Missing on Maui

Unintended Consequences
Romantic Suspense Stories:

(written under the pen name, Jessica Dale)
Payback
Backlash
Backfire (2019)

PATCHES IN THE RYE
A Marcia Banks and Buddy Mystery

Kassandra Lamb
author of the Kate Huntington Mystery Series

Published by *misterio press LLC*

Edited by Marcy Kennedy

Cover art by Melinda VanLone, Book Cover Corner

Photo credit: silhouette of woman and dog by Majivecka (right to use purchased through Dreamstime.com)

Patches In The Rye is a work of fiction. All names, characters, events and most places are products of the author's imagination. Any resemblance to actual events or people, living or dead, is entirely coincidental. Some real places may be used fictitiously. The towns of Mayfair, Florida, Buckland Beach, Florida, and Collinsville, Florida, and Collins and Buckland Counties are fictitious.

ISBN 13: 978-0-9974674-7-5

CHAPTER ONE

I stared up at the large white house, a mini-mansion really, and swallowed. Buddy and I climbed the steps to the broad, pillared porch. The buzz of an electric trimmer, wielded by a gardener manicuring an already pristine lawn, reminded me of a swarm of angry bees.

The noise covered the sound of the doorbell as I pushed the button beside the door. After a moment, I debated if I should knock.

Not yet. If the former Navy Chief Petty Officer actually answered his own door—with a place like this, he might have servants—it would probably take him awhile. I didn't want to make him feel rushed.

I was daydreaming, trying to jive the non-commissioned officer rank with the fancy house, when the door flew open, banging against the inside wall so hard the glass panels around its frame rattled.

And suddenly I was staring at a substantial amount of cleavage, tucked into a snug pink top. Long legs in tight jeans were already moving before the owner of the cleavage seemed to register that someone was standing in her way. She veered slightly to the side, but still came close to bowling Buddy and me over.

I caught a glimpse of her face as she barreled past us, mumbling,

"Sorry." Long, straight blonde hair, red-rimmed blue eyes, tear tracks on fair cheeks, an overall impression of beauty and youth.

I turned to stare after the teenager, my mind conjuring up a sordid explanation for why she was running away from my client.

"Sorry." This time, the word was delivered in a rumbling male voice coming from the open doorway behind me.

I turned back with a plastered-on smile, then had to lower my gaze to make eye contact with the man in the doorway. "Roger Campbell?"

"Yeah," he said. He wore a blond buzz cut, a faded Navy tee shirt and a dark green throw over his legs. "And you just met my sister, Alexis."

Watch those assumptions. My mother's voice. Even inside my head, she was annoyingly right most of the time.

Campbell whirled his wheelchair around. "Come on in."

He led Buddy and me down a long wide hallway, dim rooms on either side, with blinds mostly closed to protect dusty antiques from the Florida sun. A formal parlor, a dining room, and a library with shelves and shelves of books that made me salivate.

It was on my bucket list to someday own a home big enough for a separate library.

The hallway opened into a sparsely furnished area, a great room. No rugs or coffee tables cluttered the space. A tan leather sofa, matching loveseat, end table, and overstuffed armchair lined half the perimeter of the expanse of hardwood floor. A large, flat screen TV hung on the wall opposite the sofa.

The room would have been attractive—spacious with a lived-in air— if the dark wooden blinds covering the many windows weren't completely closed. Instead it resembled a giant cave, with only a few scattered lamps casting a feeble glow.

In one corner, a round oak table was surrounded by three chairs, with an open gap where one would expect a fourth to be. Roger's place at the table, no doubt.

That was confirmed when he maneuvered his wheelchair around in that spot until he was sideways to the table. He gestured toward the nearby loveseat.

A beer bottle sat on a placemat at his elbow. He nodded toward the bottle. "Want one?"

Another fake smile. "No, thank you." I perched on the edge of the loveseat and signaled for Buddy to lay down at my feet.

"I'm Marcia Banks." I'm sure he'd been given my name, but it seemed polite to introduce myself. "And this is Buddy, my mentor dog. He'll be helping to train whatever dog we pick for you."

This preliminary visit was a new addition to the process that Mattie Jones, the director of the agency I trained for, hoped would help the trainers assess what kind of dog would be most appropriate for new clients.

"Do you have any preferences regarding breed?" I asked to get things rolling.

Campbell shook his head without meeting my gaze. His mind seemed to be elsewhere.

"Can you tell me how you sustained your injuries?"

Suddenly his blue eyes, darker than his sister's, were focused on me —two mini laser beams. "Can't. Classified," he said brusquely.

I nodded, even though I knew that was probably horse hockey. If the operation where he'd been injured was truly secret, he would have given me the cover story, not said out loud that it was classified.

I caught myself reaching back to twirl my long ponytail of auburn hair around my fingers, a sure sign that I was more nervous than usual. Dropping my hand back into my lap, I said, "I'm not being nosy. I need to assess what kinds of things are triggers for you, what might set off a flashback, such as loud noises."

I'd be training his service dog to help with physical needs, such as picking up objects dropped on the floor, but our dogs were mainly trained to help veterans cope with PTSD and other psychological symptoms related to their service.

He gave me a grim smile. "I was on an aircraft carrier. I'm used to loud noises."

I opted to give up on this tooth-pulling process. We had a waiver of confidentiality from him and I suspected Mattie had a detailed report on his symptoms by now, although it wouldn't say much about the operation in which they were sustained, even if it wasn't classified.

I'd come back to that question another time, if necessary.

I launched into my spiel about how the process would proceed, that I'd pick a dog and bring it over to make sure they hit it off, before starting the expensive training process. Then it would be several months before he heard from me again, at which point I'd set up some times to meet and teach him how to work with the dog.

He was barely listening, looking at the door periodically and glancing at his watch.

Sheez, what's with this guy? snarky me said inside my head. I hid a proud smile. Ms. Snark, as I thought of that part of myself, was getting so much better at not blurting out her thoughts.

I went back to my spiel. Campbell glanced at his watch again.

I tried to mentally slap a hand over Ms. Snark's mouth, but I was too late. "Am I keeping you from something more important?"

He had the good grace to blush a little. "Sorry. I guess I'm preoccupied."

Duh, Ms. Snark said internally.

He used his elbows to push against the arms of the chair and sit up straighter. "Mar-see-a." He emphasized each syllable of my name. "Where'd you get that name?"

From my parents, like most people, Ms. Snark said inside. I imagined putting duct tape over her mouth.

I dug deep for another fake smile. "My mother thought that was more unique and melodic than Marsha, even though it's spelled M-a-r-c-i-a."

He nodded, and I went on, describing some of the things I would train his dog to do.

Again he was distracted, staring at the opening to the hallway. From where I was sitting, I could see an edge of the front door's frame. He would have a full frontal view.

I cleared my throat.

His head swiveled back toward me. Again he shoved himself more upright. "Sorry. I'm just worried about my sister."

This time my small smile was more genuine. "I gathered that."

I have a masters degree in counseling psychology and, although I've never been in practice, I use the skills I'd learned to get clients talking. This time, however, I wasn't sure I wanted to know what drama was behind his sister's precipitous exit.

"It's only me and Alexis now…"

Crapola. Apparently, he was going to tell me anyway.

"Both our parents are dead." His voice was hoarse. "And I think I'm losing her."

I stifled a sigh. "How so?"

"She's dating this guy who's too old for her, and he's got a criminal record. We used to be really close, but now we fight most of the time, usually about him."

"How old is he?"

"Twenty-six."

A year younger than Roger Campbell himself, if I was remembering his age correctly. But still way too old for Alexis. "How old is your sister?"

"Twenty."

Wow. I'd have guessed sixteen or seventeen. Did her youthful appearance make her brother more protective of her?

My older brother had never been particularly protective. When we were kids, he was the one I most often needed protection *from*. But we got along fine now. When Ben's oldest picked on his younger brother at family gatherings, I'd roll my eyes at Ben and smirk. If no one was watching, he'd stick out his tongue at me and then grin.

Elbows on the chair arms, Campbell leaned forward a little. "Do you happen to know any private investigators? I want somebody to look into this guy."

The abrupt change of subject surprised me, the word *investigator* making my heart beat faster.

"I'm sure there's more dirt there." He grimaced. "Besides the sealed juvenile record I was able to find." He looked at me with a hopeful expression. "I'll pay good."

The corner of my brain that constantly worries about money perked up. An image of my past due electric bill flashed into my mind's eye.

I tried to tamp down both my excitement and my avarice. *I am not a private investigator,* I told myself.

"No, I don't know anybody, but my boyfriend might." I kind of hated that term for an almost forty-year-old divorced cop, but for lack of a better word. "He's a police detective."

Campbell frowned but then shifted his expression to a smile. "Would you ask him?"

"Sure."

"That would be great." The smile was still there, but his eyes didn't look all that happy.

He paid closer attention to the rest of my spiel after that.

"I'll be in touch, once I've found a suitable dog." I pushed myself to a stand and Buddy rose too, giving his body a small shake.

"Don't get up. We can find our..." Heat crept up my cheeks as I realized my blunder.

The ends of Campbell's mouth quirked up and his eyes sparkled with amusement. It was the first genuine expression he'd exhibited. "I'll let you see yourself out."

Once on the porch, I paused and lifted my face to the Florida sun, already intense even in early March. Its warmth chased away the slight chill running through my body.

~

"Happy anniversary," Becky trilled in my ear when I answered her call.

"Thanks." My tone was less than enthusiastic.

"So what are you two doing to celebrate one year of dating?"

"I'm eating a poptart and reading a client's file. Will's chasing bad guys."

"Oh sweetie." Becky's voice deflated.

"Yeah, well. Goes with the territory." Will had recently transitioned from the sheriff of a small rural county to a detective in a much larger county's sheriff's department, primarily so that he could move closer to me. He considered it a lateral career shift and was happy to be solving crimes again rather than attending eternal meetings with county commissioners.

But it had its downside. He no longer controlled his own schedule. So our plans to celebrate the anniversary of our first date had gone by the wayside when a string of armed bank robberies threatened to put Marion County on the map, and not in a good way.

Tired of my pity party, I changed the subject. "How's little Buster or Betty Boop doing?"

"Behaving his/herself lately. No more morning sickness."

I brightened a bit. Some good news tonight at least. "That's great."

"So can you meet me for lunch tomorrow?" Becky asked.

I slumped in my kitchen chair again. "Can't. I'm dog hunting."

"You still gotta eat." Her voice sounded borderline desperate.

"I'll probably be running all over central Florida, and once I get this dog rolling with their training, I'll need to start another one." Normally I liked to have one dog about halfway through their training before starting another, but multiple recent events had disrupted that pattern, and had left my bank account on life support.

"I could go with you," Becky was saying. "I'm dying of boredom down here."

I got that. It was one of the many reasons I'd resisted moving in with Will when he was still sheriff of Collins County, the position Becky's husband Andy now held.

"You know that's a bad idea, Beck. You'll come home with a half dozen puppies."

A deep sigh. "Yeah. I've got no willpower where cute is concerned." A pause. "So when can you get together?" The whine in her voice was unmistakable, and out of character.

"Soon, I hope. I–" A mind-boggling idea blossomed in my brain, stalling my tongue. I knew instantly that it had been percolating ever since Roger Campbell had asked me about private investigators.

And I also knew that pretty much everyone who cared about me would hate it.

"You still there?" Becky said in my ear.

The doorbell rang before I could answer her. I jumped up and headed for the living room. "Hang on. Someone's at my door."

I peeked out my front window. A stranger in jeans and a tee shirt stood on my porch. Shafts of bright light from the setting sun lit up the cleared field across from my house. One sunbeam spotlighted the giant bouquet of multi-colored roses in the man's hands. A green panel truck, parked at the curb behind my car, sported *Belleview Florist* on its side in pink frilly letters.

"Will sent me flowers," I told Becky as I threw open the door.

The guy said my name, mispronouncing it as Marsha, of course. I nodded, too pleased by the sight of the roses to bother correcting him. Grinning, he relinquished the bouquet and trotted to his truck.

"Is there a card?" Becky asked.

"Yeah." I read it silently as I stepped back inside the house, then found it difficult to get the words past a lump in my throat. "He says he'll make it up to me."

"Why so glum?" Becky asked.

"Not glum, guilty." I sighed. "I'm the reason he took this job, remember? I should be making it up to *him*."

Becky spent the next five minutes trying to convince me that Will had made his own choices regarding his career and I had nothing to feel guilty about. It was a nice try, but I wasn't buying it. I knew darn well that in the meeting-each-other-halfway aspect of relationships, he'd gone seventy-five percent of the way and I was barely at twenty.

And if I implemented my new bright idea for making more money, I'd be backsliding to about ten percent. I glanced at the pile of unpaid bills on my coffee table and grimaced.

CHAPTER TWO

With morning coffee close at hand, I sat at my kitchen table perusing Mattie's list of donated dogs currently being fostered by agency staff members or volunteers. All the dogs were too young and still being trained in the basics by their foster parents.

I started calling the rescue shelters in central Florida. Mattie has an understanding with many of them allowing us to take a dog on a trial basis. But none of them had a dog that met our criteria.

I remembered the young woman I'd met at the Buckland County shelter last summer. Buckland Beach was on the east coast, two hours away, but I was getting desperate. I called their number while I tried without success to recall the woman's name.

I was in luck. The chirpy young woman who answered the phone said that yes, *she* remembered me. "Jake Black's friend. He's been in several times, since... all that happened. He and his wife now foster some of our kittens."

Jake Black was a former client—not really a friend *per se*—and "all that" referred to the two times his service dog Felix had been sent to the Buckland shelter when Jake and his wife were arrested, first for robbery and then for murder. One of those times Buddy had been in the house with Felix and had also been hauled away. I never wanted to relive that horrible Saturday afternoon when I was desperate to get to the shelter before it closed, and would be closed for the next two days. I'd felt like child protective services had taken my kid away from me.

"I'm sorry but I can't seem to remember your name," I said.

She giggled. "I'm not sure I ever gave it to you. Stephie, um, Stephanie Wilson."

My brain conjured up an image of her young face, smooth and round, with big brown eyes and a halo of frizzy dark hair.

I told Stephie I was searching for a dog for a new client and gave her the criteria.

She thought for a moment. "I may have just the guy for you, a Heinz 57. But he's not quite that tall."

A Heinz 57, a mix of many breeds. Not a bad thing. Mutts were often healthier than dogs who came from more limited gene pools.

"How much shorter than twenty-four inches?"

A beat of silence. "Maybe two, but he's muscular, weighs about sixty pounds. And he's really well-mannered and eager to please."

I considered the fact that Roger Campbell was in a wheelchair. His file had revealed that he'd fallen off of an airplane wing during a maintenance inspection and landed hard on the aircraft carrier's deck, sustaining "severe and most likely permanent injury to his spinal cord."

You can bet Ms. Snark had some things to say about that *classified* mission! But the ignoble way he'd sustained the injury didn't make him less of a hero to me. Anyone who was willing to serve our country in the military is a hero in my book.

What *had* bothered me a little was his general discharge, under honorable conditions—a discharge that sometimes, but not always, meant the recipient was a troublemaker.

"You still there?" Stephie said in my ear.

"Yes." Since Roger Campbell would be wheelchair-bound for the foreseeable future, a shorter dog should work fine. Might even be better. "Any aggressive behaviors or fears?" I asked.

"None that we've seen. And he knows all the basic commands—come, sit, lie down, stay."

"Can you hold him for me? Until I can get over to the coast."

"Um, I guess so. For a few hours."

"I'll be there in two."

I figured the dog was a long shot, but Mattie would reimburse me for the gas. And I'd remembered Stephie had expressed an interest in learning to be a trainer.

My bright idea was beginning to solidify into a half-baked plan. If I had help with the training, I'd have time to explore a possible new career.

Two hours later, I was eyeing the dog dubiously. "Looks like he's got some pit bull in him."

"We don't think so." Stephie was trying to hand me his leash, which I was passively resisting by keeping my hands at my sides.

"Our vet said he's probably half American Staffordshire Terrier, with a conglomeration of a few other breeds thrown in. Amstaffs are cousins of pit bulls, but they have somewhat different personalities."

I was still skeptical. "Aren't they dog-aggressive, like pits can be?" A dog that reacted much to other animals, either overly friendly or aggressive, would be too easily distracted to be a good service dog.

"Sometimes," Stephie said, "but this guy's fine with other dogs."

I arched an eyebrow at her.

"Come on. I'll show you." She turned and led the dog away. Short of being rude, a mortal sin according to my mother, I had to follow.

Stephie opened the gate to a fenced enclosure. She turned the mutt loose in it. He bounded away and started sniffing clumps of grass. "I'll be right back."

I was getting to know the boy—he was adorable, white with tan patches and an intelligent face—when Stephie returned with two other dogs in tow. Both were smaller than the Amstaff, one some kind of terrier mix half his size and the other a Chihuahua, who was snapping at the terrier. Stephie was struggling to keep them apart.

I went over and helped her with the gate. Once inside, she let the dogs off their leashes. The Chihuahua went after the Amstaff, stopping just shy of his nose and putting on her best snarling and snapping routine. The terrier stood by the gate, barking, hair standing up on his back.

The Amstaff cocked his head at both of them. They could have been inanimate objects that someone had wound up and set loose. Indeed, he might have reacted more to such objects, as toys. These nuisance dogs he ignored.

"What's his name?" I tried to sound gruff, like I was still resisting the idea.

Stephie grinned. She knew I was hooked. "We've been calling him Patches."

It suited him. And it was a good name for a service dog—short and simple, easy to call out quickly to get his attention.

I turned to the young woman. "Did you ever call Mattie Jones about becoming a trainer?"

Her cheeks turned a light shade of pink. "Yeah. She said I'd be a good candidate, but then I got busy with the fall semester and never followed up. I go to Buckland Community College."

"Will you have time for training if I ask you to train under me?"

Her blush deepened and she nodded her head, dark curls bouncing. "I'll make time."

"I'm two hours away."

That gave her pause, but only for a moment. "I can probably get over there for a good chunk of time at least three days a week."

"That should work. I need to take the dog on a two-week trial basis, see if he's going to work out."

"I think the adoption director will go along with that."

"I'll clear the training with Mattie," I said.

We both nodded and grinned at each other.

〜

Will made it home for a late dinner. Fully aware of my limited culinary skills, he'd stopped for pizza along the way.

Now, by "home" I mean my house, even though it technically wasn't Will's home. When I'd resisted living together—the next logical step in our relationship—he had bought the fixer-upper next door to me and made the job change to the Marion County Sheriff's Department.

Every time I thought about those changes he'd willingly made, my chest felt light and warm even as my gut twisted a little with guilt. I didn't deserve a guy who would go to such lengths to be close to me when I wasn't willing to commit past breakfast the next morning.

So now we did this odd combination of living together but not, often eating together and sleeping together, usually in my kitchen and bedroom respectively.

I didn't feel particularly guilty about our "conjugal visits" as Becky laughingly calls them. We'd both been married and divorced, hardly blushing virgins. Although I still hadn't told my rather old-fashioned mother, a pastor's widow, that Will lived right next door now. With fingers crossed behind my back, I'd told her he'd moved closer to me and our relationship was going well. Which was the truth, just not the absolute whole truth.

Between bites of pizza and trying to act nonchalant, I asked him about good private investigators in the area.

"Why do you need a P.I.?"

"It's for a client."

His blue eyes sparkled and a grin stretched across his rugged face. "Phew! You had me worried for a minute."

My stomach clenched. I knew Will was *not* going to like my half-baked plan. Would it be the final straw for him?

I was five-seven, curvier than was fashionable, with freckles on what I thought was a rather plain face. My only really good feature was my long dark hair with its red highlights. I seriously doubted I'd ever attract another man like Will.

But... I desperately needed money. Events beyond my control last summer had both cost me money and slowed down my training schedule, and the occasional online psych classes I'd been teaching for a local college had disappeared when they'd hired more full-time faculty.

Plus a year ago, I'd totaled my car in a close encounter with a palm tree. Again, not my fault. At the time, a guy was standing behind the car about to blast me with a shotgun.

Now I had car payments and higher insurance premiums. The insurance company was skeptical of the shotgun story.

I held my breath, as Will thought for a moment. If he did know a good P.I. maybe that would be a sign that I shouldn't do this. At any rate, I was trying not to tell him what I was contemplating, until it was real.

Dropping a thin strip of pizza crust on his paper plate, he put his hands behind his neck, elbows sticking out, and stretched to loosen tight muscles.

I almost swooned as said muscles rippled in his tanned arms.

Leaning his chair on its back legs, he finally said, "Can't think of any. Know a few bad ones. I'm sure there are some good ones around, but I haven't crossed paths with them yet."

Keeping my gaze on my plate, I asked, "Um, how does one go about getting a background check on someone, and how much does it cost?"

I felt more than saw Will jerk a bit in his chair across from me. The chair's front legs hit the floor with a thud.

A beat of silence. I was afraid to look at his face.

"There are online companies that do them." His voice was neutral, maybe too neutral. "For one worth having, they run about fifty to a hundred. Why do you need a background check on someone?"

"A client seems a little weird."

"Same client?"

Sure, I'd call Campbell "a little weird."

"Yes."

"I could run it for you." He sounded more normal. "But don't tell anyone about it, and it would be illegal for you to openly use the info against the person."

I was a tad surprised by the offer. Usually Will was pretty by the book.

I crossed my fingers under the table. "That's okay. Since I've already told you it's a client, I really can't say his name now. Confidentiality and all that." Actually, I didn't even know the name of the young man my client wanted investigated.

I made myself meet his gaze and managed a smile. "If I find something bad, Mattie will probably reimburse me. And if I don't, it will be worth it. I'll feel more comfortable working with him."

He returned my smile. "Good to see you being so careful."

I felt like a worm, until I decided that maybe I should run a background check on Campbell after all, as well as his sister's boyfriend.

I relaxed. Now I *was* telling the truth. Again, not the whole truth, but hey....

And my plan felt more like two-thirds baked now. All I had to do was get Roger Campbell to go along with it.

The next morning, I knocked on the Campbells' door, then stepped well back, gesturing for Buddy to follow suit. He cocked his head, giving me his patented what's-up expression.

"To avoid flying sisters," I whispered to him.

I glanced at my car, parked at the curb in the shade of a live oak tree. I'd left Patches in the backseat until I could assess the situation with Roger Campbell.

He answered the door and gave me a pleasant enough smile. "Ms. Banks, come on in."

"Please, call me Marcia." I stepped over the threshold and looked around. The house was quiet. Maybe his sister wasn't home.

His smile widened. "Okay, and I'm Roger."

"Are you ready to meet your potential service dog?" I said with an exaggerated smile of my own.

"Sure." His tone wasn't completely enthusiastic, but it wasn't hesitant either.

Even after I'd shelled out fifty bucks for an online background check of this guy, I still had reservations about him. Why, I couldn't quite pinpoint. The only thing I'd come up with was that he'd made no move to interact with Buddy the last time we'd been here.

It was as if the dog didn't even exist, which pegged Campbell as not much of a dog person. But then again, he had been distracted.

He didn't have to love dogs, but he had to at least like them. So I'd designed a little test. I gave Buddy the release signal—hands crossed at the wrists, then opened wide—a gesture one was not likely to make accidentally.

"I'm going to leave Buddy here while I get Patches. I've released him from duty so it's okay to pet him." Buddy gave a tentative wag of his big black tail.

I paused for a moment before turning back toward the front door.

Roger Campbell patted the lap throw over his thighs. "Come here, boy."

Buddy trotted over, and Roger held out his hand in a loose fist for the dog to sniff it. Then he patted Buddy's shoulder, before moving his hand up to scratch behind an ear.

Buddy's tail was waving like a conductor's baton.

Okay, enough of a dog person to know how to interact with a strange dog. Most of my tense muscles relaxed.

I went out to my car to fetch Patches.

After dog and man had gotten to know each other—with some sniffing and ear scratching—I gestured for both Patches and Buddy to lie down, my hand parallel to the floor and moving straight down. I added a verbal, "Lie down," for Patches's benefit. He hadn't quite made the connection yet to the hand gesture.

"So what do you think?" I asked.

Roger smiled at the dog, a good sign. "He's a handsome fellow, and he seems pretty bright."

"I think he's going to work out fine. I'll work on some preliminary tasks this week and get a better feel for how trainable he is."

He gave one slight nod of his head, then asked, "Did you find out about a private investigator?"

I shifted mentally to that subject. "My boyfriend didn't know anyone he was willing to recommend."

Roger's gaze dropped to his knees. His face slowly turned red. Suddenly, he smacked the arms of the wheelchair with his hands, making me jump.

Buddy looked up at me, worry in his eyes. I shook my head slightly.

Roger started cursing a blue streak.

I cringed a little inside. I'm no prude, mind you, but my mother was really strict about swearing. My friends know it makes me uncomfortable and try to resist cussing around me.

Thus the phrase, "cussed like a sailor." For once, I was grateful for Ms. Snark's commentary. I relaxed some.

Until he smacked the chair arms again. "A man needs to be able to protect his family."

I took a deep breath, debating now if I should mention my two-thirds baked plan. Something about this whole scenario felt off.

But Roger went there first. Dark blue eyes boring into mine, he said, "I heard you're a pretty decent detective yourself."

I feigned surprise. Actually, that wasn't too hard since I *was* somewhat surprised by his statement. "Where'd you hear that?"

"Retired vets' grapevine. I heard you helped Jake Black out of a fix last summer."

I gave a slight nod and let out a slow breath, thankful that he hadn't heard about my first attempt at detecting, which hadn't ended nearly as well.

"Could you check out my sister's boyfriend for me?"

I gave a small self-deprecating shrug, which I'd practiced several times in the mirror that morning. "I guess I could try."

Roger wheeled over to a small desk in a corner of the room. He pulled a checkbook over in front of him. "How's a thousand dollars as a retainer sound?"

Like a bunch of overdue bills getting paid off, Ms. Snark commented internally. I reminded her that I was going to keep the money in my savings account until I was sure I'd earned it.

"That's fine," I said out loud, trying to keep my expression serious. Excitement bubbled in my chest. "I'll need more information."

Thirty minutes later, I left the Campbell residence with a dog to train, a check to deposit and a decision to make about how and where to start in my role as private eye.

My other quandary was how to explain to Will that I was once again sticking my toe in the detecting pool, this time quite intentionally, and that I might be considering—not a career change *per se*, but a career addition.

CHAPTER THREE

I headed home to meet Stephie Wilson for her first training session with Patches.

By the time I'd gotten to the turnoff for Mayfair, I'd decided how to begin my investigation.

"My investigation," I whispered to myself and a frisson of excitement ran through me.

First, I needed to talk to Alexis Campbell. Maybe she would tell me, another woman, things she wouldn't say to her brother.

Maybe she wasn't even all that hung up on this guy and only kept seeing him to get under Roger's skin—an act of rebellion against the older brother who'd taken on the parent role. In which case, it wouldn't take much dirt to accomplish Roger's goal of breaking them up.

Aha! Ms. Snark said.

Aha, indeed. I'd just put my finger on what was bothering me about this whole set-up. I doubted Roger Campbell would be happy if I came back and told him that the young man his sister was dating was squeaky clean, despite his juvenile record. And unless I found something pretty awful, I wasn't real comfortable being a party to interfering in someone's love life.

There's a reason why juvenile records are sealed. The majority of kids with such records are never arrested as adults. Either they get better at not being caught, or they straighten up and fly right, as my mom would say.

My earlier excitement gone, I mentally smacked myself for not thinking this through better. As the first case in my budding new career, this one kind of stank. I sighed. I'd made the commitment, so I'd at least give it a try to see what I found out.

Stephie was there when I pulled up in front of my house. I glanced down the street. Will's truck was gone.

Good. I hoped to get Stephie set up to start training Patches and get out of there again before he got home.

I gave her a tour of my house, which took all of three minutes, then led her and the dogs out back where I usually trained. The temperature was a comfortable seventy-two. Perfect training weather.

"I'd like you to work with Patches on two basic commands today," I said, "*Come* and *lie down.* He needs to learn a gesture command for each as well as the verbal one. That allows for the most flexibility." I demonstrated the lie-down gesture. Buddy dropped to the ground.

Patches did not. He stood there, tail wagging, expectantly watching me.

I smiled a little in spite of myself. This dog seemed so eager to learn.

"He's kind of shaky on *come.* Couple that word with a pat on the thigh," the gesture I knew Roger already used as that signal. "Give him a treat when he comes promptly and no treat if he dilly-dallies."

She looked confused by my old-fashioned words, one of my "motherisms" as Will had dubbed them. I'd picked them up as a kid, a defense against my mother thinking some slang word from my generation was "inappropriate." If I talked like her, I was safe.

Unfortunately, those supposedly safe speech patterns, along with the unusual pronunciation of my name, had gotten me teased by other kids. Todd, my ex, had also made fun of the way I talked, but Will thought my motherisms were cute.

Stephie's face cleared and she nodded, her curls bouncing. "Right. No rewards for dilly-dallying."

I think I'm gonna like this kid.

That brought me up short. Since when did a twenty-something become a kid to me?

I handed her a packet of treats and gestured toward the open yard.

Settling myself and Buddy at the small table on my tiny deck, I glanced at my watch. Ten of eleven. As a detective, Will worked irregular hours, but hopefully this would be a more normal nine-to-five day.

Trying not to get antsy, I watched Stephie for twenty minutes. She seemed to know what she was doing when it came to training basic commands. And she had a good manner with the dog, firm but kind.

Patches rarely glanced our way, and when he did, Stephie immediately said his name and he would return his attention to her. Definitely not an easily distracted animal.

I nodded to myself. It looked like both the dog and the young woman were going to work out fine.

Stephie called out, "Come," patting her thigh, and Patches romped right to her. "Good boy," she said and gave him a treat.

I rose from my seat and walked over to them. "Do you feel comfortable working alone for a little while? I need to run an errand."

A flicker of anxiety in Stephie's eyes and then it was gone. "Sure. We'll be fine."

"Good. Feel free to take a break if you or the dog gets tired." I gestured back toward the deck.

Stephie nodded. "I brought my lunch."

A twinge of guilt that I hadn't offered her something. My mom frowned at me in my mind's eye.

Stephie's face had clouded up. "Am I doing okay?"

I gave her a big smile. "You're doing great."

She grinned back at me.

With Buddy in tow, I headed for the house. On my way, I dropped the sign that said *Training* over the fence between my property and Will's. It signaled that he shouldn't come over without calling first to make sure he wasn't interrupting at a crucial moment.

And today it served the dual purpose of keeping him from finding out what I was up to.

Thirty minutes and a quick stop for a fast-food burger later, I was back in Roger Campbell's neighborhood on the western edge of Belleview, just south of Ocala. I parked my car, and Buddy and I went for a stroll. The white Ford Focus that Roger said his sister drove was nowhere in sight. He'd told me she was a student at the University of Florida, but that she only had morning classes on Fridays. I hoped she would come home soon.

She pulled up ten minutes later, and Buddy and I casually strolled past as she was gathering textbooks and an oversized tote bag from the passenger's seat.

"Hi, Alexis," I called out. "Good seeing you again."

She yanked her head out of the car and looked my way. "Do I know you?"

"Well, we weren't formally introduced. I'm Marcia Banks. I'm training your brother's service dog."

"Oh." Her expression relaxed. "Is this him?"

"No, this is my dog, Buddy. I'm afraid you missed meeting Patches earlier today." I was hoping she didn't ask what I was doing back here now, because I didn't really have a good story to cover that. "Say, can we chat for a few minutes. I like to get to know family members a bit, those who will be living with the dog along with his veteran handler."

She glanced toward her house, then shrugged and shifted the textbooks from one arm to the other. The strap of her tote chose that moment to fall off her shoulder, almost making her drop a book.

"Here, let me help you with those." I grabbed the teetering book and lifted the tote bag off her arm. "Is it okay to put these on the porch for now and maybe you can walk with us for a couple minutes?"

I wanted her away from her brother. No way she'd open up with him around.

Alexis seemed a little nervous but she went along with the plan. After we'd dumped her things by her front door, she strolled down the sidewalk with Buddy and me. "May I pet him?"

I appreciated her asking even though he wasn't wearing a service vest. "Sure."

She lowered her fingers for Buddy to sniff, then scratched his ears as we strolled along. "I hope this service dog you're gonna train for Roger helps him be more independent."

"It should," I answered, then shut up to see how she would fill the silence.

"I really want to move out, get my own place. But I can't do that now, not when there are certain things he can't do on his own."

"You see, it's really helpful to know that."

Her lovely face blanched. "Please don't tell him I said I want to move out. I haven't, um, talked to him about it yet."

"Oh, I won't." I crossed my fingers behind my back. I wouldn't tell Roger about that. But anything she said about her boyfriend I'd likely repeat to her brother.

Mark that in the P.I. con column. I wasn't totally comfortable with lying and also wasn't particularly good at it.

"So why do you want to move out?"

She grimaced. "We fight all the time. Roger doesn't get it that I'm an adult now."

That was pretty much what I'd expected her to say, but the candor of her next comment surprised me.

"He can't stand my boyfriend Shawn. And he won't listen when I tell him he's got it all wrong."

"How long have you been dating Shawn?"

"About five months. We met shortly after my father..." She paused, bit her lower lip. "After my dad died."

Dang, their father died that recently! I hadn't meant to prod a fresh wound. That helped explain Roger's protectiveness.

I was feeling a tad protective now myself. This young woman's innocence and openness was refreshing, but it made me scared for her out in the big, bad world.

"Where'd you and Shawn meet?"

"At his family's horse farm. I answered an ad for part-time stable help."

I almost blurted out, *You have to work? I thought there was family money.* But I caught myself. The fancy house didn't guarantee that liquid funds were readily available.

"You're working and going to school," I said instead. "That's a lot on your plate."

Alexis chuckled. "Oh, I didn't get the job. I love horses, so I thought that job would be a great way to be around them. But Shawn figured out pretty quickly that I didn't know beans about the things a stable hand has to do. He didn't hire me, but we hit it off and he asked me out."

"Which farm is his family's?" Ocala was right in the middle of horse country.

"Clover Hills."

I knew the name, had passed the green and white sign a few times, dangling between two white pillars on either side of a wide drive. Miles of pristine white fencing and green fields, flat as pancakes, stretched in both directions from the entrance. I remembered thinking that the owners must be from up north. No native Floridian would have called the place anything *Hills*.

So Shawn's family was well-to-do. He probably wasn't after Alexis's money then. *Unless* the horse farm wasn't making a profit. I made a mental note to check that out, after I figured out *how* to check that out.

Look at you! Thinking like a real detective, Ms. Snark said. I ignored her.

"Have you met his family?"

"Oh yeah. I go over there, whenever I can get away..." She glanced back at her house. "So I still get to hang out with the horses, but without having to get dirty and smelly." She grinned. It lit up her already lovely face. "I adore his mom. She says I'm a good influence on Shawn."

We had reached the end of the block. I stopped and turned toward her. "Oh, does he have need of a good influence?" I said it with a joking note in my voice.

She smiled again and giggled, shaking her head. Silky blonde hair slid over her shoulders, which were clad in a blue knit top that matched her eyes. "Not now, but I understand he was a 'bit of a hellion' in the past." She made air quotes. "That's how his dad describes it."

"How does Shawn describe it?"

"He said he got into some scrapes in high school, and in college he drank too much and cut classes a lot. He almost flunked out. But he straightened himself out toward the end of his junior year."

"What's he doing now?"

"He helps run the farm. His dad wants to retire soon. He's kinda on the old side, fifteen years older than his mom." Alexis glanced nervously toward her house down the block. "Do you have any more questions about Roger? He'll be wondering where I am, and I've got a ton of schoolwork to do tonight. I better get started on it soon."

Somehow I doubted she was nervous about getting her schoolwork done on a Friday afternoon. How tight a rein was Roger trying to maintain on his twenty-year-old sister?

I turned us back toward the house. "Anything else you can tell me about your brother that might be helpful?"

She snorted softly. "Besides the fact that he's overprotective and paranoid?"

I gave her a half smile. "Yes."

Her face now serious, her fingers absent-mindedly stroked Buddy's head as we walked. "Roger tends to get down sometimes, depressed, I guess."

"Okay, that's definitely helpful. I train my dogs to pick up on anxiety and offer soothing. I'll work on picking up on signs of depression as well."

She turned toward me as we neared her front walk and gave me another light-up-the-world smile. "That would be great. I worry about him." She gestured again toward the house.

I glanced up and saw a curtain move. Roger was watching us.

"Well, I better get to it," she said. "Nice meeting you, Marcia."

"And you, Alexis."

"Call me Lexie. Everybody does."

Startled, I blurted out, "Everybody but your brother?"

Her face took on a pinched look. "He used to, until he decided to take on the daddy role." Her voice was bitter, tinged with sadness.

"Well, I'll work on training the best service dog ever for him. Then he can be independent, and so can you."

Her smile came back and she threw herself at me, despite Buddy being between us. For a moment, we all teetered in an awkward but enthusiastic hug. "That would be so wonderful, Marcia. Thank you."

And then she was dashing away up the walk to gather up her books. She gave a little wave and entered the house.

I looked down at Buddy. He cocked his head to one side, as if to say, *What was that?*

"My reaction exactly, boy."

He and I walked to my car and headed for home. I couldn't wait to get on my computer and order a background check on Shawn Davis. And since it was Roger Campbell's money I was spending, I'd order the deluxe version for a hundred bucks.

I wanted to know all about those high school "scrapes."

Becky called as I was driving home. Bestowing blessings on the inventor of Bluetooth technology, I answered.

"What's up, Beck?"

"Um, I'm not sure." Her voice sounded funny.

Adrenaline shot through me. "Is something wrong with the baby?"

"No, not that, but... I went into town with Andy this morning. I needed a few things and didn't feel like driving to Polk City. You know I'm getting pretty big now. Well everybody was nice and friendly before, and most folks still are. But my big ole baby bump got a few funny looks today. And one woman blatantly snubbed us as we were walking down the street."

The adrenaline subsided. It left a sick jittery feeling behind. Andy was a light-skinned black man who'd recently won the sheriff's election in the small town of Collinsville, after Will had opted not to run for re-election. You might think electing a black man with a white wife would be a sign of the demise of bigotry in rural Florida, but it was really about the lesser of two evils. Without Will in the race, a much darker-skinned black *woman* was their only other choice.

"What happened?"

"I had my arm looped through his and we were talking and laughing. I didn't even notice her until she was almost in front of us. She made this harumphing sound. Andy looked up, smiled and turned us around sideways so she could go past. He even tipped his hat and said, 'Good morning, Miss Shirley.'"

I groaned inside.

"She downright glared at my belly and then stepped off into the road to go around us. I don't get it." Becky's voice hitched. "She's been nice to me before."

"The old battleaxe," I muttered. "Sweetie, Miss Shirley is at least mid-eighties. Her generation's attitudes aren't necessarily shared by others." What I didn't want to tell her, if she didn't already know it, was that Miss Shirley single-handedly supervised the town's rumor mill. By sundown, half the population of Collins County would be believing that Andy and Becky were half-naked and doing it right there on the sidewalk.

Even pregnant, Becky was drop-dead gorgeous, and she had a real knack for picking clothes that were both graceful and accentuated her curves. That thought produced another, a hunch. "What were you wearing?"

"Jeans and a new maternity top I ordered from Rosie Pope's Maternity in New York. Why?"

"So it's the modern kind of top that snugs around the baby bump instead of billowing out to hide it."

A half-beat of silence. "Oooh." Then a soft chuckle.

I chuckled too, although my insides were far from relaxing. "Her reaction was probably more about your fashion statement than anything else."

She laughed again, a soft melodic sound, and I visualized her running a manicured hand through dark, thick curls, a smile spreading across her heart-shaped face.

"So maybe I'll save that top for trips to Orlando," she said. "It's really cute, with big pink hibiscus flowers all over it."

"Or to Mayfair. Edna'd probably get a kick out of it."

That got yet another laugh. Edna Mayfair was my octogenarian neighbor and friend who had a penchant for wearing muumuus with flowers on them in colors that were rarely found in nature. She pretty much defined the word *feisty* and still ran the Mayfair Motel, with no plans for retiring anytime soon.

The sick, jittery feeling hadn't completely dissipated. I wasn't at all sure that Becky's wardrobe choice was the only thing that was setting Collinsville residents' teeth on edge about their new sheriff and his family.

"So how are *you* doing?" Becky asked.

I took a deep breath. "I'm considering a career shift."

"Say what?" she squealed in my ear.

"Not a complete career change. More like a career addition. I'm tired of being strapped for money all the time."

"So what are you considering adding?"

"Private detecting."

Silence. I could hear her dishwasher making soft churning noises in the background.

"How's Will feel about that?"

"I haven't told him yet."

"Uh, oh."

"Yeah, I know. He's not going to like it. But it actually pays decent money. Someone has given me a thousand-dollar retainer to check into a person's background."

"It may be decent money," she said, "but it's a job that can get dangerous, as you well know."

I swallowed a sigh. "Beck, it's not just the money. I'm…" I faltered, not sure how to express what I was feeling. "I'm excited about life, for the first time in a long time." For the first time since last summer when I'd helped Jake and Janey Black figure out who was trying to frame them for robbery and murder.

"I won't stop training dogs, but I'd rather do that at a more leisurely pace, instead of working seven days a week and *still* not making ends meet."

Another beat of silence. "Okay, but you better not get yourself in trouble," she mock scolded. "You're gonna be a godmother in a few months."

"Don't worry," I said and left it at that. I still wasn't sure how I felt about being a godmother. I knew Becky wasn't particularly religious. To her, it was more a way of making me an official part of her child's life.

I wasn't all that into organized religion either, but I had been raised by an Episcopal priest—yes, they can marry. I'd been taught to take the role of godparent seriously.

Becky changed the subject to how much her feet were swelling lately. We talked for a few more minutes and then signed off as I was driving past the new Victorian-style Mayfair Motel.

Edna's great nephew, Dexter, was on the front porch, dressed in his usual cool-weather attire of plaid flannel shirt and blue jeans. He waved and yelled out, "Hey, Marcia."

I waved back but kept going, praying I had beat Will home.

Made it with fifteen minutes to spare.

Will had the weekend off, which was both wonderful and annoying. I loved spending so much time with him, but there was no opportunity to continue my investigation.

We'd finally had our delayed anniversary celebration, a delightful dinner at the same French restaurant in Belleview where we'd had our first date.

Several times I'd almost gotten up the nerve to tell him about the investigating gig, but I'd chickened out. Once was on Sunday, over dinner, but I couldn't bring myself to spoil the pleasant evening—or at least, that's what I told myself.

On Monday morning, Stephie arrived for a training session. I gave her a new assignment, to work with Patches on *sit* and *stay*. "He's pretty good with both," I said, "but he has to be excellent. Then we can start teaching him the cover command. Did you read up on that?"

Stephie bobbed her head, her dark hair even frizzier than usual. The cold front that had come through on Saturday was now being overpowered by moister tropical air from the south. The temperature would make it to eighty by this afternoon.

I should have stuck around but I was anxious to resume my investigation. "I need to run an errand. Will you be okay on your own for an hour or two?"

Stephie's face fell but she quickly covered her disappointment with a game smile. "Sure, we'll be okay."

My heart squeezed in my chest. I vowed that after today, I'd focus more on training both Stephie and Patches.

Guilt partially appeased, I grabbed Buddy's leash and patted the pocket that contained the background report on Shawn Davis. "I'll get back as quick as I can."

The background check company had definitely earned their hundred bucks. They'd found the sealed juvie record, but they'd also reported he'd been arrested in his junior year of college, when he was no longer a minor.

Young Mr. Davis had been charged with aggravated assault. The charges were later dropped.

I very much wanted to know what that was all about.

CHAPTER FOUR

I had looked up Clover Hills Farm, located west of Ocala, on the other side of I-75. They advertised "fine Paso Fino horses for riding and showing." I'd heard of Paso Finos but had never ridden one.

I was horse crazy as a kid, as so many girls are. I even had a pony of my own for a while. My grandparents had bought him for me and had paid the monthly board payments. Then I'd outgrown the pony and discovered boys.

Such a cliché, Ms. Snark commented.

I didn't honor that with a response.

I'd called ahead, asking if they currently had any riding horses for sale. The woman on the phone confirmed that they did. "I have an appointment in a little while." Her voice was cultured with only a hint of a twang that I couldn't place. "But my son Shawn can help you."

Perfect! I'd thanked her and signed off.

Now, as I pulled into the driveway under the green and white sign, I caught Buddy's eye in the rearview mirror. He was stretched out across the backseat, head resting on his front leg.

"Keep your eyes and ears open for anything strange," I said.

He raised his head and cocked it to one side, as if to say, *What are you up to?*

I'd seen the same expression in Will's eyes last night over dinner, when I'd been making bright and nonsensical small talk, too wired to be quiet but also too scared of his reaction if I told him what really had me so excited—a possible new career as a P.I.

It wasn't only that I needed to make more money. I still loved the dogs, but the training process had some pretty tedious parts to it. Like this early stage of reinforcing the basics that I was turning over to Stephie.

Dumping on her is more like it, Ms. Snark said.

I shook off the guilt and parked in front of a large, low building. Buddy and I got out.

The double-wide doors, under the slight peak of its roof, were rolled back, as were the doors at the other end of a long aisle. Silhouettes of several horses' heads stuck out of stall doors along the sides, and that of a man carrying a bucket and walking away from us.

We jogged over to the doorway. I stopped to let my eyes adjust to the dimmer light inside the building. When I could make out more than dark silhouettes, I called out to the man, "Hello."

He turned. "Hi. Can I help you?"

We walked toward him. As we approached he gave Buddy a skeptical look.

"Don't worry," I said. "He's very well behaved."

"Still, some of our horses don't like dogs."

As if on cue, there was a loud thud against the door of the stall we were walking past. It was one of the few that did not have the top half of the door open.

The man surprised me by grinning. "Don't mind Diablo. He doesn't like anybody."

I peeked through the crack between door and post and saw a black horse, about fifteen hands. He was beautiful, with a flowing black mane that rippled like silk as he tossed his head and stamped one front hoof.

And he was glaring at me. I quickly broke eye contact.

"He's our stud. Gorgeous and he knows it. He produces spectacular foals, but he's got a major 'tude problem."

I let out a little laugh. "Um, I called and talked to Mrs. Davis. She said you had several riding horses for sale and I could stop by this morning to look at them."

"Sure, I'll go see if she's back yet."

"Uh," I fluttered my eyelashes, "I'd rather talk to you." My flirting skills were pretty rusty so I probably looked like I had something in my eye.

But he graciously held out his hand. "I'm Shawn, her son."

"I'm, uh..." I hesitated, wondering if I should give a false name, "Mary... Hanks."

"These are mostly show horses at this end of the barn." He waved his hand around. "Follow me and I'll show you the riding stock, unless... Were you planning on showing?"

"Oh, no. I just want to ride again."

"Again?" he said as he led the way down the barn aisle.

"I rode as a kid and young teenager, until I discovered boys. Now I'm coming back around to animals."

He chuckled. "Boys didn't work out so well?"

I smiled. "Yes and no. But I'm definitely not obsessed with them anymore."

As he smiled back, hazel eyes shone in a tanned face, framed by blond hair that was slightly overdue for a haircut. "Animals are simpler to relate to than humans sometimes."

Shawn Davis was easily as handsome as Alexis Campbell was beautiful, but my gut said looks weren't the main attraction for either of them. He seemed to have the same down-to-earth, sweet nature as she did. Of course, that could be an act, meant to disarm young women into trusting him.

We'd reached the other end of the barn. Another black horse's head, smaller than Diablo's, stretched toward Shawn as he approached. He took something from his pocket. A flash of orange and the piece of carrot was gone, gently scarfed up from his hand by delicate black lips.

My heart ached a little. I'd forgotten how much I loved horses. "Is she as sweet as she looks?"

Shawn was rubbing the velvet nose. "How'd you know it was a mare?"

"The size of her head, I guess."

He glanced my way and nodded approvingly. "Yes, she's very sweet. The perfect lady's horse."

Under other circumstances the feminist in me would have taken offense, but I knew in horse parlance that meant the mare was gentle and on the small side—a horse that a woman could easily mount and handle, even if she wasn't an extremely experienced rider.

"Unless you were looking for something more challenging?" Shawn said.

"Oh no." I stepped forward and reached out to stroke her silky neck. She turned her head slightly toward me and big dark eyes stared into mine. Warmth spread through my chest.

"Would you like to try her out?"

I nodded, and he walked away, toward a rack of saddles.

"What's her name?" I called after him.

"Niña." He pronounced it the Spanish way, Nee-nya.

I remembered enough high school Spanish to recognize the word—it meant *little girl*. And it fit her.

"Um, not sure how she'll react to the dog," Shawn said as he returned with a saddle that looked like an English one, but with wider side flaps and bigger stirrups.

I led Buddy several yards away to a wide wooden post that rose to the ceiling.

"You can tie him there," Shawn called over.

I told Buddy to sit and stay, but I didn't tie him. I wanted him to be able to move out of the way if someone brought a horse in or out. Instead I took his leash off, so it wouldn't somehow get tangled in a horse's legs, and dropped it in a heap by the pole.

Shawn raised an eyebrow at me as I returned to the mare that he was now saddling.

"He'll stay there," I said. "He's been trained as a service dog."

Shawn switched eyebrows but said nothing as he cinched up the saddle.

I followed him and the mare out into the bright sunshine, trying to remember the carefully rehearsed segues for getting Shawn to talk about his past. But all I could do was watch the mare's shiny black rump and twitching tail and swoon.

I wanted this horse! And I knew darn well I couldn't afford her.

Again, someone or something in the universe was looking out for me. Shawn provided the segue. "I know someone who's getting a service dog."

"Oh, who?"

"My girlfriend's brother. He was in the Navy and got injured. Now he's in a wheelchair."

"Oh my! That must be really hard on him, and on your girlfriend."

Shawn shrugged. "I have trouble feeling sorry for him. He's such an as...uh, jerk." He glanced at me and turned a little pink.

Your mama taught you well, Ms. Snark said inside my head.

At least about not cussing in front of the customers, I agreed silently.

We had stopped outside the gate of a small corral. Shawn flipped the side panel of the saddle up to check the girth.

"How's he a jerk?" I said, realizing I was about to lose the opportunity to find out more. As much as I wanted to ride this horse, I also wanted to do what I'd come here for, to find out about Shawn Davis.

"He keeps trying to break Lexie and me up."

"Why's that?" I hoped I sounded like a curious busybody rather than an interrogator.

Shawn shrugged. "He found out about some things I did when I was younger."

I tried to look shocked. "Those things couldn't have been all that bad. You seem like a nice... guy." I almost said *kid*, but I figured he wouldn't appreciate that.

He gave me a small smile that didn't reach his eyes. "Actually, I was quite the hellion—drinking, cutting classes, and that was in high school. Come on, I'll give you a leg up."

Reins looped over one shoulder, he cupped his hands down low next to the horse.

There was nothing to do but place my sneakered foot in his hands and let him boost me into the saddle.

I looked down at him as he adjusted my foot in the stirrup. "I still find it hard to believe that you were a bad boy. What turned you into the nice guy that you are now?"

He glanced up, squinting because the sun was behind me. Moving to the gate, he opened it and let it swing wide. I thought he wasn't going to answer me.

But then he said, "Something happened in college that scared the crap out of me."

As I maneuvered the horse past him, he slapped her rump. "Lean back," he called after us as Niña broke into something that only vaguely resembled a trot.

It jarred my teeth until I did as I was told and leaned back a little. Suddenly it was as if I were in a rocking chair, being gently rocked.

I squeezed my knees slightly, and Niña picked up speed, sailing around the packed dirt path at the perimeter of the corral. Or maybe they called it a paddock in Paso Fino land.

"Loosen up your reins some," Shawn called out.

I did so and Niña stretched her neck and picked up speed again. I was sailing along with her, my body barely moving as I leaned back a little farther. I'd never ridden a horse with such smooth gaits.

After a few circuits of the paddock, I reluctantly pulled up on the reins. "Whoa, girl."

She dropped back to the trot that wasn't a trot and, in response to my slight shifting of the reins in that direction, pranced toward Shawn at the gate.

He was grinning. "She's what we call a push-button horse. You even think about what you want her to do and she'll do it."

I tugged gently on the reins and she stopped right by him.

My whole body ached with longing for this horse. I turned my head away as I dismounted, so Shawn couldn't see the tears pooling in my eyes. I knew I wouldn't be able to afford her.

"How much is she?"

"Six thousand."

My head jerked around. "Dollars?"

He nodded. "That's the usual legal tender." The words were a bit snarky but the tone was gentle. "Pasos aren't cheap. You could get one that's older for less, but ours are all two and three year olds that we've raised and trained ourselves."

I was trying to talk sense to myself. *I didn't come here to buy a horse. I came to get information.*

My brain was half listening, but my heart was daydreaming about long rides in the woods and fields around Mayfair.

Buddy would make a great trail dog.

"You can take some time to think about it," Shawn said, again his voice gentle. He knew I'd fallen for her. "We don't start advertising our spring sales until next month."

I nodded, not sure I could trust my voice.

He took the horse's reins and led her, with me still on her back, toward the barn. "Diablo's her grandsire," he said, "but her grand dam and dam were gentler souls."

Was he talking to give me time to get myself under control? If so, he was a perceptive guy. Again, I reminded myself, that didn't mean he always used that perceptiveness to be kind, like he was now. Psychopaths could be quite savvy about others' emotions and use them to manipulate people.

Buddy was lying down right where I'd left him in the barn. "He is well trained," Shawn said admiringly.

"Thank you."

The dropped assault charge no doubt was related to whatever "scared the crap" out of him, but short of letting on that I'd already checked him out, I couldn't think of a segue to ask more about it.

I said I'd be in touch, then tore myself away before I broke down.

As I drove back out the long driveway, I realized I had more questions now about Shawn Davis than I'd started with. But two things I knew—one, despite my best intentions, I liked him.

And, two, I loved that horse.

I was within a hundred feet of the end of the drive when a pale blue sports car turned in. Since the macadam was only about a lane and a half wide, the polite thing for that driver to do would be to wait for me to get to the wider section at the end.

But this driver didn't do that. Instead, he raced toward me, forcing me partway onto the grass and almost sideswiping my car.

Excuse me. *She* did that. As the car whizzed by, I caught a glimpse of a twenty-something redhead with a pissed off expression on her face.

CHAPTER FIVE

I eased my car forward as I watched in the rearview mirror. The sports car tore up to the buildings and stopped with a screech of tires. Then the redhead was out of the car and running toward the barn. She was built like a Barbie doll, wearing skinny jeans and a red top that looked like it was painted on.

Shawn Davis met her halfway and gestured sharply toward her car, as if he wanted her to get in it and leave. She was yelling at him. Suddenly he grabbed her arm and dragged her toward the barn. She shook him off, but then followed him.

I made a quick K-turn and drove back to the barn. Once stopped, I leaned over and pretended to be looking in my glove box. Instead I was slipping my cell phone inside of it.

"Stay, Buddy. I'll be right back." Leaving all the windows open, I exited the car and jogged to the barn.

They were in the aisle at the far end, hissing and snarling at each other in hushed voices.

I moved in their direction, pausing here and there to glance behind hay bales and saddle racks, as if searching for something.

Shawn saw me first. His eyes went wide.

"Hey, did you see my cell phone anywhere?" I called to him.

The woman turned around. The light was dim but I got a decent look at her face, memorizing her features—blue eyes, narrow cheeks, sandy eyebrows a shade lighter than her carroty hair.

She was about Shawn's age. A former girlfriend perhaps?

She scowled at me, not appreciating the interruption.

"Uh, I haven't seen a phone anywhere," Shawn called back to me. "But I'll keep an eye out for it."

I moved a little closer, keeping up my mock search. When I was about five feet from Shawn and the redhead, I shrugged. "Maybe I left it in my doctor's office earlier."

I turned away, still glancing here and there for the wandering phone, and walked slowly back the way I'd come.

The redhead resumed her hissing at Shawn. All I could make out were the words "money" and "pay," both said emphatically.

Out in the driveway I jogged quickly to my car and dug in my purse for paper and pencil. I jotted down the plate number of the pale blue car.

I didn't know who the redhead was, but I had every intention of finding out.

I called Stephie as I started out again. She assured me that she and Patches were doing fine.

"Good, then I may make another stop before coming home."

"No problem," she answered cheerfully. Perhaps a bit too cheerfully.

Guilt made my empty stomach do an uncomfortable little flip.

I pulled into a fast food drive-thru and grabbed a chicken wrap to tide me over, so I could stop in Belleview on my way home to give Roger Campbell a progress report.

Again, we were almost bowled over as I stood on the Campbell's porch, this time with my finger poised to press the doorbell button.

Lexie Campbell stopped one inch short of smashing into my nose. "Oh, sorry." She dipped her head, but not before I saw the red-rimmed, swollen eyes. She ducked around me.

Buddy and I turned and followed her down the steps. "What's wrong?"

She shook her head without slowing down. I picked up my pace, Buddy trotting beside me.

I drew up next to her and let out some exaggerated huffing and puffing. "Come on, give an old lady a break here."

That got me a sideways glance and a small smile, but she did slow down. "You're what, thirty?"

"Thank you. A couple years past that." Almost three, but close enough. "What's going on?"

She shrugged. "Just another fight with my brother."

Out of the corner of my eye, I studied her slumped shoulders and dejected expression. Somehow this didn't seem like a "just another fight" reaction.

"What started it?" I asked.

"I asked him for some money from my trust fund." She stopped and turned toward me. "It's my money," she said defiantly. "I have a right to use it anyway I want."

I had a funny feeling about how she wanted to use it. "Shawn called you a little while ago, didn't he?"

Her mouth dropped open. "How'd you know that?"

I pushed my advantage. "Who's the redhead, and why is she demanding money from him?"

Lexie dropped her head and scraped the toe of her sneaker against the sidewalk. "He's being blackmailed."

That was not what I'd expected. I'd been thinking he'd gotten the redhead pregnant and she either wanted abortion money or child support.

"Blackmailed by whom, and for what?"

She tossed blonde hair over her shoulder. "He doesn't know who."

Hmmm. "Who's the redhead?" I asked again.

Her head jerked up. After a beat, she answered, "Someone he barely knew back in college."

"What's he being blackmailed for?"

"I can't tell you that."

I softened my face and gentled my voice. "Look, Lexie, I'm trying to help here. But I can't do that if I don't have all the info."

"Trying to help? I thought you were the dog trainer."

"Well, yes. But I feel for you and Shawn." I crossed my fingers behind my back. It was true, but not the whole truth, and I dreaded the day when this young woman found out what I was really doing.

"It's not my story to tell. I appreciate your concern, but we'll be fine." She turned and walked away.

It was telling that she'd hardly given Buddy a glance.

I opted not to talk to Roger after all. I wanted to process what I'd just found out and get a few more answers first.

Instead I loaded Buddy back into the backseat and headed toward home. My phone rang and Will's name popped up on the Bluetooth screen.

I lowered my voice, channeling the sultry tones of my favorite singer, Adele. "Hey there."

"You okay? Your voice sounds funny."

I cleared my throat. "Yeah, I'm fine."

"You sure," he said, a barely suppressed chuckle in his voice. "You sound like maybe you're coming down with a cold?"

I stuck my tongue out at the Bluetooth screen. "I am fine." I enunci-ated each word.

A weird noise, a half snort that sounded like it had been swallowed before it could totally escape.

"Okay, so Adele I'm not."

He laughed out loud. "How's your day going?"

"Stephie's working on some basics with Patches, and I'm out running errands. What's up with you?"

"Unfortunately, I caught a new case." His voice sobered consider-ably. "I may be late tonight, if I get home at all."

"Okay." I was both disappointed and relieved. I'd been trying to figure out how to get him to tell me the easiest way to find someone via their license plate. But I was also thinking now I could spend all evening on my own "case."

"Does that mean you caught the robbers?"

"No. I've been reassigned to homicide."

"Really? That's great." I wasn't as enthusiastic as I sounded. I knew he'd wanted into the homicide division for a while now. But the transfer meant even more erratic hours.

We chatted for a few more minutes and then signed off with an exchange of "I love you's."

The words actually tripped off my tongue now without effort, unlike a few months ago. But my reluctance to confessing my love had nothing to do with Will and everything to do with my cheating ex-husband up in Baltimore.

I'd barely disconnected when the phone rang again. This time the name on the screen was Roger Campbell. Where I'd been blessing the convenience of Bluetooth a few minutes before, I was now cursing it. But I might as well get this conversation over with.

"Hey, Roger."

"Got anything to report?" No greeting, terse tone.

"Not much yet. I'm still getting to know the players. I met Shawn Davis. He seems nice enough, but that, of course, could just be surface charm."

"Harrumph," was the only answer I got.

"There do seem to be some things in his history that bear looking into further."

"Such as?"

"He was arrested on an assault charge but the charges were later dropped—"

The sound of a hand slapping something, most likely his wheelchair's arm. "I knew it! I knew there'd be something like that in his background."

"It was five years ago," I added. I was a little bothered by the idea of condemning someone for something that *might* have happened a half decade ago. "I'll see what else I can find out about it."

"Good. Keep me posted." He disconnected without saying goodbye.

I took a deep breath and blew it out. In addition to the many other reasons for feeling unsure about my role as novice private investigator, I was realizing I didn't like my client much.

Guilt squeezed my chest. It felt wrong to dislike a veteran, and one in a wheelchair at that. But bottom line, Roger Campbell was not a very nice person.

I pushed that thought aside as I turned off I-75 and settled back to enjoy the drive on the country roads to Mayfair.

The phone rang yet again. I groaned.

The Bluetooth screen read *Mom* this time. Could be good, could be bad, depending on her mood. Again, I opted to get it over with rather than having to call her back later. Not being able to reach me on her first try tended not to improve her mood.

"Hey, Mom."

"Hey yourself. Haven't heard from you in a couple of weeks." Mildly irritated tone.

"Sorry. I've been busy with a new dog, and I'm also training a trainer."

"Really." Her voice took on a more cheerful note. "That's pretty cool that Mattie trusts you to do that."

My throat tightened a little. "Yeah, and right now I'm letting her do a lot of the boring stuff at the beginning."

"So what else have you been up to?"

My mother could be a tad judgmental at times, but mostly she and I had a good relationship. And I could use a sounding board at the moment. I took a deep breath and said, "I'm, um, exploring another career option."

"Instead of dog training?" Her tone was incredulous. "But I thought you loved the dogs."

"I do, but it doesn't pay enough. I'm not going to stop training, but I might do something else too."

"Such as?"

I gulped in air, then took the plunge. "I'm checking out the idea of doing some private investigating."

Silence. Not even background noise.

"Mom, are you there?"

"Yeees." She drew out the word, as if buying time. "What kind of private investigating?"

"Oh, nothing too... intense." Yes, *intense* was a good word. Conveyed not dangerous without saying that *per se.* "Right now I'm doing an in-depth background check on someone."

Another beat of silence. "How's Will feel about this?"

"I, uh, haven't told him yet."

The sound of air being sucked in on the other end of the line.

"He's got a big case," I said quickly, as I turned onto Mayfair's Main Street. I crossed the fingers of both hands, which made steering a little tricky. "I haven't seen him much to talk about it with him, but I will soon."

I waved to Edna Mayfair, in sweats and one of her nephew's plaid shirts, raking leaves in front of the Mayfair Motel—both a fall and spring chore in central Florida since live oaks, one of the most common trees in the area, shed their leaves twice a year.

"Promise me you won't do it," Mom said, "if he thinks it's too dangerous."

My turn to be silent. That was a promise I was not willing to make. I chose my words carefully. "The kinds of cases I can get, that won't be unduly risky, is part of what I'm assessing right now. This one I'm on certainly isn't dangerous."

I doubted Shawn Davis would come after me for checking out an old assault charge.

Now the sound of air being blown out in a long sigh. "Marcia, you're going to be the death of me. Let me know what you decide to do."

"Oh, I will. And Mom, try not to worry. I'm a big girl. I can take care of myself."

She grunted and signed off.

What I hadn't told her was that I'd ended up in more than my share of dangerous situations in recent times, and I wasn't getting any money for dealing with them. If danger was bent on finding me anyway, then I was going to make it pay!

CHAPTER SIX

I had a productive but boring afternoon with Stephie and Patches. We'd gotten a good start on the beginnings of the cover task, in which the service dog literally turns and "watches the back" of his owner. Veterans with PTSD, or anyone who suffers from that disorder, often startle easily and feel uncomfortable if someone is behind them. This can even keep the veteran from going out in public. But knowing the dog will signal if someone is approaching really helps the vet to relax.

It is one of the hardest tasks to teach, however, because it has four distinct parts to it. The first part, getting the dog to automatically stop and sit every time his human stops moving, is the easiest step. Getting the dog to turn around before sitting is a bit harder.

And teaching the dog to watch for people approaching from behind and signal the owner with a tail thump and/or ear flick is quite tricky. Those two steps would be saved for the latter part of Patches's training.

After saying goodbye to Stephie and feeding the dogs, I made myself a sandwich for dinner and sat down at my laptop to do a little investigating.

I discovered it's not that easy to find out about a criminal charge that was later dropped. But the good news was there were several online services that matched license plate numbers to registered owners. The pale blue sports car belonged to a Marissa Andrews.

Unfortunately, the service did not provide a current address, which turned out to be somewhat harder to narrow down. An online search turned up two people by that name in the Ocala area and three in Gainesville to the north.

I considered calling the corresponding phone numbers but decided that would tip my hand.

Tomorrow, I needed to work with Patches at some point, since Stephie wasn't available. But first I would head north to see if I could find the Marissa who had visited Shawn Davis.

Florida license plates have the county where they were registered at the top. The pale blue sports car was registered in Alachua County, so I'd start with the Gainesville addresses. But it was quite possible that my Marissa now lived in Ocala, and her registration hadn't been changed yet.

It was also quite possible that, in this day of cell phones, she wasn't in any "phone book," online or otherwise, in which case I probably wouldn't be able to find her without Will's help.

The next morning, Will showed up on my doorstep. "I've gotta go in early, but I figured we could have breakfast together."

I'd already gobbled down a handful of cookies as a makeshift meal, but since I wasn't up for telling him where I was going so early in the morning, I had to delay my departure and go along with the breakfast idea.

Besides, he'd brought egg sandwiches and pastries from the newly reopened Mayfair diner.

Mayfair had been little more than a ghost town when I'd moved here three years ago, but through the concerted efforts of Edna Mayfair and the town's new Chamber of Commerce it was coming back to life. The diner reopening was one of Edna's success stories. The Chamber had big plans for attracting tourists to our "humble but quaint town," as the CC brochure called it. *Quirky* would have been my name for it, but that might not sell as well as *quaint*.

I got out the good china and napkins, i.e., paper plates and a roll of paper towels, and Will and I settled at my kitchen table.

"How are things going with this new client?" Will asked as he bit into his egg and cheese sandwich.

That was probably the best segue I was going to get, and I couldn't justify putting off telling him much longer. I took a big bite of my own sandwich, chewed and swallowed, buying time while I formulated my best approach.

"Fine with the dog, but he's asked me to look into something else."

Will arched his eyebrows and kept chewing.

"You remember I asked you about P.I.s?" He stopped chewing, but I forged on. "That was for him. When I couldn't suggest anyone, he asked me to check on something for him."

"Mar-ci-a..." He emphasized each syllable in an ominous tone.

"Look, it's not dangerous. He doesn't like his sister's boyfriend and he asked me to check into his background, that's all."

"And you're doing this out of the kindness of your heart?"

"No, he's paying me."

Will put his sandwich down on his plate. "I'm pretty sure P.I.s need to be licensed in this state."

"Well, yeah, I'll check into that. If I decide to keep doing this kind of stuff."

Will's eyes narrowed. "You plan to keep doing *this kind of stuff?*"

"Maybe." I focused on my sandwich, taking a small bite and chewing quickly. Anything to avoid his gaze. "I've got to do something else to make some money. The dog training just doesn't pay enough."

"And you're choosing investigating because it's so similar to dog training." Will's tone would've done Ms. Snark proud.

"No," I said, "because I enjoy it and I seem to have a talent for it."

"You have a talent for stumbling into trouble and meandering around until someone rescues you, usually me."

"That's not fair," I protested. "I helped Jake Black and his wife, and Rainey Bryant. And I helped *you* figure out about those bones." I gestured toward the front of my house, and the field beyond, where a thirty-year-old corpse had been uncovered last November.

Will's expression had softened some. One corner of his mouth quirked up. "One of the few times I didn't have to rescue you."

I opted to ignore that. "This grilled sour dough bread really makes this sandwich."

"Marcia, private eyes are glorified on TV, but their jobs are mostly boring. They spy on people for insurance fraud cases and run background checks through computer programs all day."

Will began wrapping the remainder of his own sandwich in the waxed paper it had come in. "And I don't know what the licensure laws are down here, but in New York, they have to go through a lot of training."

I covered my dismay at that information. Nodding, I said, "Okay, I'll put that in the con column. Say, how does a private citizen find out about an assault charge that was later dropped?"

"A private citizen doesn't. It's not public record until the person is either convicted or acquitted."

"But a private *investigator* could, couldn't they?"

"Not unless he or she had an in with a police department somewhere, someone who was willing to run the person's name through the system on the sly."

"I don't suppose you'd be that person for me, would you?" I gave him an exaggerated smile and batted my eyelashes, pretending I was joking.

"No." His tone was emphatic. "I am not going to jeopardize my job for this hare-brained scheme of yours."

"Okay, you don't have to get snippy about it." I scrambled for a way to get things back on a friendly note. "So P.I.s mostly spy on Johnny Scammer to make sure he's not doing calisthenics in his living room when he's supposed to have a back injury. That doesn't sound too dangerous."

Will's stiff shoulders relaxed. "No. Worst case, he'll chase you out of his bushes."

I faked a chuckle.

He faked a smile.

I tried to look innocent. "How well does that insurance stuff pay, I wonder?"

He blew out air. "Probably better than dog training."

For a moment I reveled in the fantasy of a decent income.

He pushed aside his wrapped sandwich and took my hand. "Sweetheart, I can solve your money problems. If we lived together, we'd only have one set of utility bills, and if we got married, I could get you on the department's health insurance."

I tensed, fighting the urge to pull my hand away. "Not exactly the most romantic proposal."

He frowned. "I've tried the romantic approach."

I sighed. "I know. I'm sorry I'm so gun-shy." The truth was my resistance was a borderline phobia. The thought of marrying again made me hyperventilate. Okay, make that a full-blown phobia.

He squeezed my hand. "Admit to me that you know we're going to end up married eventually." He'd tried for a teasing note in his voice, but the urgency under the surface belied that.

My heart pounded, and I wanted to run from the room. I wrapped my feet around my chair's legs to keep myself in my seat. Swallowing hard, I pushed out words. "I think that's a distinct possibility."

Will let go of my hand and flopped back in his chair. "I guess that's the best I'm gonna get for now, huh?"

I smiled and patted his hand. "I do love you."

He stood and picked up his sandwich. "I know. I've gotta go." He leaned down and kissed my forehead, then started for the living room.

"Hey, what about your pastry?"

He paused in the kitchen doorway, was still for a beat, his back to me. "You can have it. Turns out I wasn't as hungry as I thought I was."

He looked back over his shoulder. "Stay out of trouble."

While grabbing Buddy's leash and my purse, I apologized to Patches for neglecting him. He gave me an inscrutable look from his crate, settled his chin on his paws and heaved a sigh.

If luck was with me, I'd find the right Marissa Andrews by lunchtime and could get some training in this afternoon.

During the hour-and-a-half drive up I-75 to Gainesville, I tried to focus on my investigation. What else could I do to find out more about Shawn Davis?

But my mind kept coming back to Will's proposal, like a tongue seeking out a sore tooth.

I wasn't sure if I should be pleased or pissed. Was he really suggesting that I should marry him just to solve my financial problems?

And what did that last interchange mean? Had my news about a possible career adjustment made him lose his appetite for his danish... or for me?

The next thing I knew, I was fantasizing about living with him and letting him pay all the bills, while I trained one dog at a time, at a much more leisurely pace than I did now. I worked pretty much seven days a week. Even if I had some social event to attend, I'd try to train for a little while before or after it. The thought of not having to work that hard was luring.

I mentally yanked myself out of the daydream as I took the exit for Gainesville off I-75. The commitment phobic part of me—which was most of me—much preferred the idea of becoming an investigator as a means to improve my finances.

I took it as a sign when I pulled to the curb in front of the second address on my list, a townhouse in a decent neighborhood on the southwest side of Gainesville, and spotted a pale blue sports car in the driveway. *And* a redhead was washing it.

I'd decided on a more direct approach this time and found myself wishing I had a business card to present to Ms. Andrews.

I'd also planned to use Buddy as an ice breaker, but now I thought better of it. He loved baths and might think the hose and bucket of sudsy water were for that purpose. He would, of course, sit quietly at my side once I told him to do so, but it could be a distraction.

Leaving the car running with the fan on, I got out and walked over to the bucket. "Marissa Andrews?"

She glanced my way as she sprayed the car with a garden hose. "Who wants to know?"

"I'm Mary Hanks, private investigator." Yeah I know, the fake name was pretty lame, but I figured I could always pretend later that the person had misheard me. "I'm doing a background check on Shawn Davis."

Her back stiffened, but otherwise she didn't react. "Who?"

"Oh come on, Ms. Andrews. I saw you with him. And you saw me." I ran my fingers through my own auburn hair. Being a redhead, or even having red highlights like mine, made one stand out in a crowd.

She dropped the hose on the ground and turned toward me, hands on her skinny hips. "Okay, so I know him and he knows you and I saw you there. So what?"

"You seemed angry, and I caught the word *money* as you were arguing with him."

She smiled a nasty smile. "Haven't you heard? Money is the root of all evil."

"Yes, I've heard that," I said blandly.

She scowled at me for a couple of beats, then picked up the hose nozzle and went back to rinsing her car.

"Where did you meet him?" I asked over the hiss of the water.

She glanced my way. "I didn't *meet* him."

"Okay, where do you know him from?"

Another glance, but no comment this time. I let the silence stretch out.

She dropped the hose nozzle again and began drying the car, with what looked like a baby diaper.

I felt a twinge of guilt for my poor car. I ran it through a carwash every four to six weeks.

"Look," I said, "I know someone is blackmailing him, and you were there, yelling about money. Ergo, you are likely the blackmailer."

She froze for a second, then resumed her swirling of the diaper across the pale blue hood. "I have no idea what you're talking about."

"I'm not the police. I don't care if you're blackmailing him. I want to know what for."

She straightened and turned to me again. "Well, suppose I am blackmailing him about some deep, dark secret. It would be pretty dumb to tell someone that secret, now wouldn't it?"

"What if I promised not to tell anyone but my client?"

"Who's your client?"

"Sorry, confidential." I was doing a pretty good Sam Spade imitation, but I was starting to feel a little nauseous. Confrontation was not my favorite thing.

Another one for the con list, Ms. Snark commented. I mentally stuck out my tongue at her.

Real mature. A male voice.

Crapola. Now I had snarky me, my mother, *and* Will's voice inside my head.

Ms. Andrews seemed to be considering. "What will you do with the information?"

"Excuse me?"

"How will you use the information against Davis?" she said.

I gave that some thought. I was pretty sure this woman hated Shawn Davis. "It would probably cause him to lose the affections of the woman he loves."

The nasty smile was back. But she picked up another dry diaper, slapped it on the fender, and moved it to the side of the car, soaking up drops of water as she went.

I channeled Sam Spade again. "There was an assault charge against him a few years ago," I said in a gruff voice. "You know anything 'bout that?"

She gave me a funny look.

Okay, maybe I was laying on the *noir* a bit heavy.

"Maybe," she said. "I was the complainant."

I froze, not wanting to spook her. "Oh?"

She turned to me, hands on hips again, one holding the damp diaper. "Shawn Davis raped me at a frat party."

CHAPTER SEVEN

No! was my first gut reaction.

I didn't like this woman. I didn't like my client. I *did* like Lexie Campbell and, much as I'd tried to resist his charm, I liked Shawn Davis. I didn't want to believe ill of him, even though this was exactly the kind of dirt my client had hired me to find.

Shame burned my cheeks. How could I not believe her? What with *#MeToo* trending all over social media.

I intentionally gentled my voice. "What happened?"

"I don't know exactly." The words were spit out like bad seeds. "Which is why the district attorney 'declined to prosecute.'" She made air quotes. "I woke up and Davis was beside me in bed, passed out. My boyfriend said he found Davis on top of me." She looked away. "My clothes were messed up and there were signs I'd been…" her voice caught and she swallowed hard. "But no… he must have used a condom."

My chest ached. "What kind of signs?"

She looked at me, her eyes hard but glossy. "Bruises and other physical signs… that I'd been forced."

"I'm so sorry that happened to you." And I meant it, but something was niggling at the back of my brain.

I took a small notepad from my purse and scribbled my cell number on it. I tore it off and tried to hand it to her. "If you need to talk."

Her eyes turned harder still. "I don't need to *talk*," she spat out. "I need to make that s.o.b. pay!"

She crossed her arms across her chest. "I'm not supposed to be discussing this."

That brought me up short. "Why not?"

She glared at me and turned away, went back to drying the car. "I signed an agreement."

I pushed some but she refused to say another word. When she picked up the hose and acted like she was going to spray me, I decided it was time to leave.

In the car, I watched her out of the corner of my eye as I slowly put my seatbelt on.

She had dropped the hose and turned away from the street. It looked like she might be holding a phone to her left ear.

She moved her head a little and put her right hand over her other ear. Yup, she was talking on the phone.

She glanced around, saw my car still sitting at the curb, and ran for the house.

"Very curious," I said out loud to Buddy.

He lifted his head from his paws and cocked it to one side.

The first thing that came to mind when I'd heard the phrase, "signed an agreement," was a non-disclosure clause in a settled lawsuit. That probably came to mind because the current President of the United States was embroiled in a messy controversy over such an agreement, made with an alleged former mistress.

How does one find out about lawsuits? I pulled out my own phone and Googled "lawsuits Florida." And right there was a link, at the top of the list, on how to search court records online. One more click and I was hooked up with a service that would search Florida's records. They didn't even charge unless you wanted a copy of something.

Awesome!

Andrews was a common enough surname, and Marissa wasn't all that unique either. But there was only one lawsuit filed in that name in either Alachua or Marion Counties in the last five years. And sure enough it was against Shawn Davis, for damages due to severe emotional distress. A release of the suit had been filed three months later, and no further details were available.

It was time to pay Clover Hills another visit.

I debated. I really needed to do some training today, but I really *wanted* to keep investigating. I looked at my watch. It was early yet. I could squeeze both in.

As I drove us to the Davis's horse farm, Buddy snoozed in the back-seat and I plotted. I decided to start off again with the buying-a-horse ruse, until a good opening presented itself to confront him.

I glanced back at Buddy, glad to have him along, just in case Shawn turned out to not be such a nice guy after all.

Despite the disturbing nature of what I'd learned from Marissa Andrews, I was feeling better about this case. If Shawn Davis was a rapist, then it would be a good thing to get him away from sweet Lexie.

I wasn't sure if it was good luck or bad luck that the little black mare was still available. And Shawn was agreeable that I could ride her again.

Buddy and I stood back as Shawn brought her out of her stall and hooked her up in cross-ties. "She needs some brushing this time. She rolled in the dirt earlier."

I picked up a brush and started on one side as he did the other. "I really do like her," I said, mostly to get the conversation rolling.

Shawn grinned at me over her back. "She's a sweetheart."

"I'm trying to scrape together the money. I'm already working two jobs."

He nodded and ducked down to check her hooves. A minute later, he circled around the back of the horse, one hand on her rump. He was now facing me, hoof pick in hand.

"I'm training to be a private investigator," I said casually, as I ran the brush once more over the mare's sleek coat.

He froze for a second, and I found myself wondering how much damage a hoof pick could do if used as a weapon.

Then he gave me a crooked smile. "That's a rather unusual profession..."

I suspected he'd been about to add, "...for a woman." But he'd caught himself.

"Yeah, but it's pretty interesting," I said, as Shawn turned his back to me, leaned over and lifted the mare's back hoof. "I'm working on a case now that involves a five-year-old assault charge."

His back stiffened.

"There seems to be some blackmail going on, but I can't quite figure out who is shaking down whom."

The hoof pick clattered onto the cement floor. He straightened and whirled around, inches from me. "Who are you?" he pushed through clenched teeth.

I took two steps back from his glaring face. The mare moved restlessly, picking up on our tension. I stroked her neck, then ducked under the cross-tie, in case I had to run for it.

Buddy, who had been sitting off to the side of the wide aisle, stood and growled low in his throat.

A part of my brain noted that he was breaking training, but at the moment, I was glad he was willing to defend me.

For now though... I held out my hand and signaled for him to lie down again. He complied.

"Who are you?" Shawn repeated.

I opted to ignore the whole name issue, now wondering if I should have given my real name to start with. "I'm working for Roger Campbell."

His eyes narrowed even more. "Get off our property!"

"Wait, Shawn. At this point, I probably have enough dirt on you to break you and Lexie up. But I want to hear your side of the story first, before I give my final report."

He glared at me for another couple of beats, then deflated. His shoulders sagged and he dropped his head to stare at the straw-strewn floor. "Come on, let's go outside." He reached to unhook the cross-tie from the mare's halter.

I jumped back a little.

He gave me a grim smile. "Contrary to what you have probably heard, I am not a violent person."

I stepped back so he could put the mare in her stall. My throat closed at the realization that I wouldn't get to ride her today. Indeed, I'd probably never see her again. I didn't believe in love at first sight between humans, but between me and this horse, it was real.

I shook my head as I followed Shawn out of the barn. *Focus on the task at hand, Banks!*

I patted my thigh and Buddy fell into step beside me. I rubbed his ears for comfort.

Shawn stopped at the paddock and crossed his arms above the top rail. He stared straight ahead. I joined him, leaning sideways against the fence, facing him and debating what to say to get things rolling. Buddy flopped down in the dust at my feet.

The silence worked better than anything I could've come up with.

Shawn cleared his throat. "I was in a fraternity at the University of Florida. It was one of the wilder ones, but I tended to hang on the periphery. I like to think I was already starting to mature a bit, outgrowing my 'youthful indiscretions.'" He made air quotes.

He turned toward me slightly. "I was totally out of control in high school. Good grades always came easy to me, and I got bored." He shook his head. "No, that's a lousy excuse. I've also been known to blame it on my mother's leniency. She let me get away with a lot growing up. I'm her only child, and my Dad's a lot older than her. But as a youngster, I was basically a good kid."

He took a deep breath. "The bottom line is that something snapped when I was in high school. I got tired of being the good kid and decided to see what happened if I broke the rules. The answer was not much. I'd get in trouble and my mom would bail me out. She'd convince the powers-that-be to let me off with a hand-smack. Sometimes there would be a hefty donation to someone's favorite cause."

He turned away again to stare into space. "Then my junior year at UF, the fraternity had a party. As usual, most of us got pretty hammered. And as usual, there were a bunch of girls there, invited by various brothers. I didn't usually have much to do with the girls, but I did get drunk that night. I was sitting on the sofa in the frat house living room feeling sick. The next thing I remember is waking up next to a girl who's yelling at me, and two guys, one brother and a friend of his who wasn't in the fraternity, are dragging me out of the room."

I nodded. That jived with the little bit that Marissa Andrews had told me.

Shawn turned to me. His eyes were shiny with unshed tears. "I swear I never intended her any harm. I don't remember what happened, but I must have seen her there and thought, in my drunken state, that she was okay with having sex with me. I didn't even realize she was passed out."

Something occurred to me. "Whose bed did all this happen in?"

"Mine. I shared a room with the other guy, the brother who pulled me off of her. Gerry Fields. Marissa was his date for the evening."

"And his friend?"

"I don't remember his name. He came to a lot of our parties."

"So you were arrested," I prompted.

"Yeah, but there was no..." he glanced my way, his cheeks turning pink, "you know, no DNA. She had some bruises on her so they charged me with regular assault at first. I think they were hoping to find more evidence and be able to change that to sexual assault instead. Some of my hair was on her clothes, but my lawyer argued that she was lying on my bed and could have easily picked it up from there."

"And the charges were eventually dropped."

"Yes, but I didn't exactly get off easy. Our fraternity was banned from campus for a year, and I was thrown out. The guys who had supposedly been my friends avoided me, or worse, bullied me when they got the chance.

"And worst of all was my parents' reactions. My mother was horrified that I'd done that, and my father was furious."

He was staring off into the distance again. I was pretty sure he wasn't seeing the green field of hay on the horizon.

"I'll never forget the expression on my father's face. I thought he was going to have a stroke. He put his foot down. No more bailing me out. I even had to get a legal aid lawyer."

I was grateful for the information, but also a little surprised that this guy was divulging so much to a virtual stranger, and one who had deceived him at that.

He glanced my way and must have read my thoughts on my face. "Yeah, I know. I blab too much. My dad says it's one of my many faults."

His father sounded like a piece of work, as my mom would say.

Again, I could see the attraction for Lexie Campbell. The same open candor. Meeting each other probably felt like finding a safe harbor.

Kind of like you and Will. Mom's voice.

Most of the time, I answered her.

Shawn had fallen silent.

I prompted him. "Then Marissa sued you…"

"That was six months later. My folks had calmed down by then and they were worried about the reputation of Clover Hills if it all came out. So they settled with her for a hundred thousand dollars. It came out of their retirement savings, and my father's never let me forget that I'm the reason he's still working at seventy."

"Who's blackmailing you now?" I asked.

He did a double-take. "Boy, you have found out a lot." Then he shook his head slowly. "I don't know who it is. I get these text messages. A techie friend of mine tried to trace them but he couldn't, so he said they were probably from a disposable phone. Whoever it is threatens to expose me and ruin my parents' reputation if I don't pay each month."

"How much?"

"A thousand a month. It's one-third of my take-home pay."

I paused for a moment, digesting the idea that this man made in a month almost half of what I make training a service dog for six months.

"I'm a trainer," Shawn said, his face flushed again. I guess he felt the need to justify his salary. "Our only trainer at the moment, although we hire consultants sometimes."

I shook my head slightly. "I'm in the wrong business."

His blush deepened. "I suppose P.I.s don't make that much."

I let that go. I had no solid idea yet how much I could make as an investigator.

Note to self. Google that before this goes much further. That and what the requirements were for licensure in Florida.

"I'm confused," I said. "I saw you and Marissa fighting the last time I was here, and I overheard her say something about money. I assumed she was your blackmailer."

"I don't think it's her. Yes, she was yelling at me when you saw her, but she was saying that money couldn't make up for what I'd done to her, that she'd make me pay another way for the pain she'd been through."

I processed that. I certainly didn't want to minimize Marissa's pain. And even drunk, Shawn should be held accountable. But it sounded like he was truly remorseful, and apparently that event had straightened him out.

Yet Marissa was coming back five years later screaming for more retribution. Something didn't totally add up here.

I stared at the side of Shawn's face as he stared off into space. Was I being naive, buying this guy's story? I needed more corroboration.

"I'd rather you not tell Roger Campbell all that," Shawn said. "I mean most of it's in the police records anyway, but he'll just use it to try to ruin my reputation, and he'll take my parents down with me. Lexie already knows the whole story."

I gave a noncommittal nod. "This Gerry Fields. Do you know where he lives?"

"He's still in Gainesville. Last I heard, he and Marissa were living together."

Very interesting!

~

The address Shawn had given me was that of the house where Marissa had been washing her car, but there wasn't enough time today to go back to Gainesville. I headed for home.

I pretty much had the country roads leading back to I-75 to myself. There was only one black truck, or it might be a SUV, farther back. I let my mind wander, trying to mentally juggle the next day's schedule to fit in some sleuthing.

I merged onto the highway and moved into the center lane, accelerating to bring my speed up to that of most of the traffic. In other words, five miles over the speed limit. If you try to do the speed limit on I-75, you'll get run over.

Even though I was moving with traffic, the guy driving the black SUV in the far left lane seemed to take exception to me. He started coming over, until there wasn't much more than a coat of paint between his fender and my side mirror.

There was an eighteen-wheeler to my right, so I had nowhere to go. I hit the brake and the SUV surged forward.

I was trying to calm my racing heart and glancing in the rearview mirror to check on Buddy, when the SUV was suddenly beside me again, his back passenger's door within inches of my front fender.

"What are you doing?" I yelled, even though obviously he couldn't hear me. I wondered if perhaps he couldn't see me either, since his side windows were tinted way past the legal limit in Florida.

Body tense and heart pounding, I laid on the horn and braked again.

He slowed to stay with me and edged over still farther.

Within seconds, I would be jammed between his side door and the undercarriage of the truck on the other side. Fiercely praying that it was the right move, I pushed down on the accelerator.

My car shot through the narrow opening between SUV and truck like a bullet from a gun barrel. I kept my foot down, racing to get ahead of the truck and pull over before this guy had a chance to trap me again.

He was obviously nuts, some kind of road rageaholic whom I'd unwittingly offended.

I whipped in front of the truck and tapped my brake to bring my speed back down some. On the horizon, about a mile away, a Florida Highway Patrol trooper had pulled over some speeder. I didn't want to be his next catch.

The truck's brakes squealed. The front of its cab loomed in my rearview mirror.

On second thought, maybe I'd better not slow down too quickly. Better a speeding ticket than being smashed by a truck.

The black SUV appeared in the middle lane, pulling past the front of the truck. It raced up next to me and moved toward the side of my car again.

I instinctively swerved to miss him, my front right tire rumbling on the ridged pavement at the extreme edge of the roadway.

My stomach had taken up residence in my throat and had been replaced in my abdomen with a brick of dread. This guy was trying to kill me. I had a dizzying moment of *déjà vu*, flashing back to last summer when a guy in a pick-up truck had intentionally rammed the back of my car. But that had been at a much slower speed.

I tried accelerating again, to get past the SUV. It kept up and the back passenger door tapped my front fender.

Now I was fighting to keep my car under control. Obviously he wanted to force me off the road. But if I hit the gravel shoulder at my current speed, who knew what would happen?

My seatbelt and air bag would probably keep me alive, but I was more worried about Buddy. His safety harness could only handle so much jerking around before he would have internal injuries.

My foot moved to the brake, as I glanced in the rearview mirror. The truck had backed off but was still too close. If I suddenly braked, it would likely hit us.

I tapped the brake once, twice. The SUV's back fender was now parallel to my front end. As I tapped my brake the third time, it swerved over as if pulling in front of me. But it was nowhere close to being clear of my front bumper.

Metal scraped against metal.

My options were limited—stay where I was and get sideswiped at high speed, brake hard and get run over by a truck, or go off on the shoulder at high speed and pray I didn't flip over.

I prayed, braked hard and spun the wheel to the right.

CHAPTER EIGHT

My car's back end fishtailed in the gravel, but miraculously I managed to keep all four tires on the shoulder. If we'd gone off into the sandy soil next to it.... I shuddered.

I'd lost track of the SUV. When I got my car stopped, I jerked my head around in all directions, expecting some madman to come running toward me. I wouldn't have been surprised if the SUV had pulled off and then backed up to ram me.

But the black vehicle was gone. Instead the state trooper was running toward me, his hand on his holster, which made my already racing heart skip a couple of beats.

I released my seatbelt and opened the door, putting my hands out first before exiting the car. "That guy ran me off the road!" I yelled.

Still thirty feet away, the trooper angled to one side to see past me. "Who else is in your car, ma'am?" he called out.

"Just my dog!"

His body relaxed some, but he kept jogging toward me, his hand no longer on his holster. "Are you okay?"

"Yeah, I think so." I wasn't hurting anywhere but I was wondering what my body would feel like tomorrow morning. "I need to check my dog."

He nodded, and I opened the back door and ducked my head in. Once I'd determined that Buddy was okay, I lingered for a minute, stroking his black silky ears. Sensing my distress, he rested his head on my shoulder as he'd been trained to do, offering comfort to soothe anxiety.

I rubbed my cheek against his fur. Meanwhile, I was trying to decide how much to tell the officer. Now that the risk to life and limb was gone, worry had settled in. What would be Will's reaction to my near miss?

He was with a different force, the county sheriff's department—I doubted he monitored routine traffic reports from Florida Highway Patrol. But if the report was filed as a possible attempted assault....

You're going to keep this from him? my mother's disapproving voice in my head.

I shoved both her admonition and the decision about what to tell Will aside for now.

When I pulled my head back out of the car and straightened, the first thing I saw was the eighteen-wheeler that had been following me, now pulled off on the shoulder beyond the trooper's cruiser and the car of the hapless speeder.

And the trucker was talking to the FHP trooper. The decision of what to tell him had been taken out of my hands.

Cars were whizzing by us, so I opted to leave Buddy in the car with the windows rolled all the way down. I trotted over to the two men.

"There was mud or somethin' on the license plate," the trucker was saying, his voice excited. "I couldn't see the number." He grabbed for my arm. "Are you okay?"

I normally don't like strangers touching me, but in this case I was tempted to throw myself into his arms. "Yes, thanks."

"You're sure the SUV was deliberately tryin' to run her off the road?" The trooper asked the truck driver.

The trucker nodded, pulling off his orange UF Gators' baseball cap and swiping a flannel-clad arm across his forehead. "Either that or get her to slam on the brakes so I'd run her over. That was some quick thinkin', miss," he said to me.

"Lemme finish up with this other guy," the trooper said. "Don't go anywhere. I need both your names and contact information for my report." He jogged off.

The truck driver, who looked to be in his late thirties, walked over to my car. He took a couple of pictures with his cell phone and then stooped down to examine the fender.

"It's scraped up but it should be driveable." He took a close-up of the fender.

I groaned inside. My insurance company was going to drop me for sure.

"Want me to email these pics to you?"

Of course, I could take my own photos, but I didn't want to seem ungrateful. I gave him my email address and thanked him.

He touched his hat brim. "Happy to be of service, ma'am. A lot of truckers are all about their schedules these days, but my daddy was a trucker. He always told me that we should be the 'knights of the road.'" He made air quotes.

I gave him a small curtsy. "Thank you, Sir Trucker."

~

It dawned on me as I pulled up in front of my house that I wouldn't be able to *not* tell Will what happened. Duh, he'd see the dents and scratches on my fender.

And maybe sooner instead of later. His truck was in front of his house. If he was home this early, that probably meant his case was resolved. He'd be taking a nap and then coming over in a little while, most likely ready to celebrate if he'd made an arrest.

Might as well distract myself with some training.

I decided to try out the go-get command, just to see how quickly Patches was likely to pick up that task. Telling Buddy to stay in the living room, I took Patches into the kitchen.

Luck was with me. Someone had played catch with this dog in a previous lifetime.

I rolled a small ball across the kitchen floor several times, saying, "Go get the ball." Patches ran, picked it up, and trotted back with it each time.

Then I showed him an empty pill vial. It had two small pebbles in it to make it rattle. I shook it, showed it to him again and said, "Pills."

Patches eagerly watched the object in my hand, most likely not caring what it was as long as he got to chase it.

I rolled it across the floor. "Go get pills."

Of course, he did just that, trotting back and dropping the vial at my feet. I gave him a treat from my pocket. We repeated the process several times, with me emphasizing the word *pills*.

I placed both the ball and the pill vial on the floor. Hooking a finger through Patches's collar, I led him back across the kitchen and then let go of his collar. "Go get pills." I pointed to the vial.

He swiveled his head around, trotted across the room, and brought back the ball.

I sighed. *Did you really think you would get off that easy?* Ms. Snark commented.

He dropped the ball at my feet and sniffed my closed fist, which contained a treat.

I kept it closed. "Go get *pills*."

He cocked his head at me.

Hmm, how to convey this?

I picked up the ball with my other hand. Feigning throwing it, I said, "Go get *pills*."

Patches, of course, took off to chase the phantom ball. When he got to the other side of the room, no ball. He sniffed around.

"Go get *pills*," I said again and held my breath.

He looked at the pill vial—if dogs could shrug I'd swear that's what he did. Then he caught the vial up in his teeth and brought it to me.

Eureka! I gave him the treat from my hand, plus a bonus treat from my pocket.

We did the whole thing again, and again. He kept bringing the ball as his first offering, but then would trot back over for the pills when I said, "go get pills," a second time.

Finally, on the seventh try, he brought the vial first. That earned him another two treats and a vigorous ear scratch.

I repeated the whole process another dozen times, until Patches was bringing the vial every time I asked for the pills. Then I made myself do it another six times for reinforcement, hoping that he would remember the difference between ball and pills next time.

At four-thirty, I put Patches in his crate with a grain-free chew stick and jumped in the shower.

Sure enough, at five, Will was at my door with a platter of grilled steaks and a bottle of wine in his hands, and a grim expression on his face.

I ignored the expression as I put the platter in my oven to keep the steaks warm while I made a salad.

I was slicing tomatoes, my back to him where he sat at the kitchen table. He cleared his throat.

I pretended I hadn't heard him.

"Mar-see-a," he said slowly, drawing out each syllable.

"What?" I gave him my best innocent look over my shoulder.

"What happened to your car?"

I turned back to the tomatoes. "Some idiot wandered over into my lane on I-75." Chop, chop went my knife. "But I managed to get slowed down and off on the shoulder okay," I added in a cheery voice. "The bozo didn't even bother to stop." Chop, chop. "But an FHP trooper was giving some guy a speeding ticket. He took my info and said he'd file a report." Chop. Chop.

"Did you get the guy's plate number?"

I shook my head, staring down at the tomatoes that were now diced almost to mush. I pulled some spices out of the cabinet, and a bag of nacho chips from my snack cabinet. I would pretend I'd intended to make salsa all along.

"Does this have anything to do with your little investigation?" Will asked.

My chest tightened. *Little?*

Then a chill ran through my body, washing away the anger. Could it be that the driver of the black SUV wasn't a nutcase after all? Could he have been quite sane, and quite determined to get me to stop investigating Shawn Davis? Maybe the blackmailer—who didn't want me killing his golden goose by exposing Shawn's secret to the world.

"Not that I know of," I managed to get out. My eyes stung. I didn't want to fight with Will tonight. He deserved a celebration after bagging a bad guy. And I wanted to forget about everything for a few hours.

I grabbed an onion from my produce bin. It had sprouted but it wasn't particularly soft. I chopped off the sprouts and started dicing the rest. Soon my eyes were watering copiously, a great cover.

I dumped the diced onion and mushy tomatoes into a small bowl and blindly added spices.

The nacho chips went into a larger bowl, and I used one to scoop up a taste of the salsa. It wasn't bad, all things considered.

After wiping my eyes with a dish towel, I popped a couple of potatoes into the microwave and brought our pre-dinner snack to the table.

Will frowned, but he poured the wine without further comment.

We munched and sipped until the microwave dinged, announcing the potatoes were done.

Will continued to eat in silence after I'd served the steak and potatoes. When the last bite of his meat was gone and his potato was scraped down to the skin, he put down his fork and sighed.

Somehow I knew it was *not* a sigh of contentment.

"Who'd you piss off?" he asked.

The chunk of buttery potato in my mouth turned to sawdust. I managed to swallow it down.

"No lectures, okay? I really thought this would be a safe investigation. All I had to do was see if there was any dirt in this kid's background and turn over the info to my client...." I trailed off, poking at the remainder of my steak with my fork.

"But?" Will prompted.

"But the dirt I found turned out to be an aggravated assault charge during his college days, a rape accusation without enough evidence for the district attorney's office to prosecute."

"Wait a minute," Will said. "Aggravated assault, not sexual assault?"

I nodded. "The girl was passed out cold, and he was pretty drunk too. He doesn't remember what happened. But there was bruising, messed-up clothing."

Will sat forward. "Thus the aggravated assault. She was incapacitated, unable to give consent, and there were signs that something violent had happened."

I nodded again. His voice was sounding more normal. Maybe we wouldn't fight after all.

"So why didn't they prosecute?" Will asked.

"Two other guys said they pulled Shawn off of her, but she couldn't testify to what happened, and there was no, you know..." The pastor's daughter in me took over, blushing. "No DNA."

"He was too drunk to perform?"

"Apparently."

Will frowned. "Most ADAs would decline to prosecute that kind of mess. They didn't even have a she said/he said. They had a these-other-guys said."

I snorted.

"So turn all that over to your client," Will said, "and be done with it."

When I didn't answer, his frown turned into a scowl. "What's the problem?"

I sighed. "The problem is that I don't like my client, but I do like the sister, Lexie, and her boyfriend, Shawn."

Will slowly shook his head. "Marcia, investigating doesn't have anything to do with who you like or don't like. It's about gathering the facts, the evidence."

"I know that," I said in an exasperated voice. "But I can't help how I feel. I want to find out what really happened, for Shawn and Lexie's sake."

He leaned back in his chair and ran a hand through his hair. "So why would a five-year-old rape case get somebody stirred up enough to run you off the road?"

"That's a very good question." I hesitated. Should I tell him about the blackmailer? That felt like a confidence that I shouldn't share without permission.

Although I was being paid to share it with Roger, wasn't I?

I was so confused. I got into this to make some extra income, but if I wasn't going to do what my client wanted me to do, I couldn't in good faith keep his money.

And now I'd have a repair bill for my car. I put my head in my hands and groaned.

"What's the matter?" Will asked.

I lifted my head and shook it slightly. "I just thought of a bill I need to pay soon."

His mouth pinched together into a thin line. "Mar–"

I held up a hand. "Please don't propose to me again. I'm confused enough right now about what I should be doing."

He narrowed his eyes at me. "Sorry the fact that I love you is such a burden."

I blew out air. "You know that's not what I meant."

I watched his face as he visibly reined in his anger, swallowing and willing his expression to relax. Finally he said, "What's next in your investigation?"

"I have the address of one of the guys who said Shawn had assaulted this woman. He lives in Gainesville, with the victim."

I hated using that word. I knew the more PC term was *survivor*, but honestly I didn't feel like Marissa Andrews had survived all that well. She seemed to be firmly stuck in the past.

Don't judge until you've walked a mile in their shoes.
Yeah, you're right, Mom.

"I'm off tomorrow," Will was saying. "I'll go with you."

"I don't need you to do that."

"I think you do." His tone was terse. "You've ticked somebody off. And whether you like it or not, I love you and I don't want anything to happen to you."

He pushed himself to a stand. "When do you want to leave tomorrow?"

For half a second, I considered telling him not until the afternoon, and then going to Gainesville by myself in the morning. But he'd never forgive me for that.

"Nine-thirty, I guess."

He nodded. "I think I need to go to bed early. Still catching up from forty-eight hours of pretty much no sleep." He was trying to sound normal, but I could tell that he wasn't over being ticked off at me.

And since I wasn't sure whether or not I was ticked with him, I let him go. "Okay. Thanks for the steak and wine."

He leaned down and kissed me on the forehead, a gesture I usually found endearing. But tonight it smacked a little too much of father rather than lover.

I gave him a fake smile. "See you in the morning."

As the front door thudded closed behind him, it dawned on me that having him along tomorrow wasn't a bad idea.

Reality was sinking in. There was a distinct possibility that someone had tried to kill me, to stop me from poking around in the past. But even if I did what Will had suggested, stopped investigating and turned it all over to Roger, how would the guy in the SUV know that I'd done that? He might very well still think I was a threat.

And the truth was I didn't want to stop investigating. The attempt to ram me and Buddy into a tractor trailer's undercarriage was now pissing me off, and it had me wondering if there were other secrets that Mr. SUV didn't want me to uncover.

CHAPTER NINE

I didn't sleep well. Surprise, surprise.

At six-thirty, I finally gave up and pulled on the previous day's clothes to take a walk. Maybe the cool morning air would help clear my head so I could make some decisions.

Buddy tried to turn left, toward Will's house, at the end of my side-walk. "No, we're going this way, boy."

He gave me his what's-up look, trotted over and licked my hand.

And suddenly I felt like bursting into tears. Why were my feelings in such a muddle? Why was I risking my relationship with Will in order to play detective? And now maybe I was risking my life as well.

Why was I doing this whole detective thing anyway? The investigating was fun, but I didn't like having to report to someone and follow their agenda. I wanted to be able to help the people I thought deserved my help, not the ones who were paying me.

So maybe I should be pickier about what cases I took and from whom. Okay, I could do that. But that still left me conflicted about this case.

Buddy stopped and sniffed a clump of wild flowers, lifted his leg and peed on them.

"Kinda what I feel like I'm doing to Shawn and Lexie," I said to him. He cocked his head at me, then trotted on to the next bush.

"I know. I made this mess and now I've got to figure out how to get out of it."

The insatiably curious part of me wanted to see the investigation through, even if I wasn't getting paid for it. And I felt bad for Lexie and Shawn. Between her disapproving brother and his mysterious black-mailer, I didn't see a rosy future for them.

But if I wasn't going to investigate for money, then I should be calling Mattie to get another veteran assigned to me, so I could get the process rolling with another dog.

By the time I met with a new veteran and got a dog picked out for him or her, Patches would probably be moving into the middle phase of training, he was that bright and eager to learn. I needed to get back into the pattern of working with two dogs at once. Then I could make ends meet.

Barely, Ms. Snark pointed out.

I'd been wondering when she would show up to kick me while I was down.

Hey, she objected, *I'm only telling it like it is.*

She was right, unfortunately. Dog training just didn't pay enough. I needed another part-time job that paid better. But what other talents or skills did I have?

My brain had gone around in circles as Buddy and I had gone around our favorite ten-block route, down Main Street past the motel and then east on Mayfair Avenue, out to Highway 25 and back around to the Mayfair Methodist Church.

As we approached the motel again, a voice hailed me over noisy barking. Edna Mayfair was out walking her Springer Spaniels, Bennie and Bo, before starting her work day.

"How's it goin', Marcia?" Edna said as we drew closer. Today's muumuu was chartreuse, with turquoise flowers. It made my eyes hurt. She wore a grey sweater against the morning breeze, but she'd already turned in her winter moccasins for flip-flops, her official declaration that spring was here, regardless of the still chilly nights and cool mornings.

Her black and white pups were trying to turn themselves inside out in order to get loose from their leashes and come play with Buddy.

I solved their problem by turning him loose. He trotted over and tolerated "the boys" jumping and nipping at him. Then they went after each other, tumbling over and over several times.

Laughing, Edna let go of their leashes. She wasn't much of a disciplinarian with them, which was probably why they still acted like puppies at age three.

The pair took off through the tall grass in the field across from the motel. Buddy trotted after them at a more sedate pace. I swear he was shaking his head, like the big brother amused by his immature siblings.

Big brother, echoed in my head, drowning out whatever Edna was saying to me.

What if Roger, the big brother, was Shawn's blackmailer? Had he actually found out about the rape accusation before and had been milking Shawn, threatening to expose him?

But then why would he hire me to find dirt if he already knew about Shawn's big secret?

The pieces were struggling to fall into place.

Edna cleared her throat. She was looking at me funny. "You okay, Marcia?"

"Yeah. Sorry, I'm just a little distracted this morning. What did you ask me?"

"I said I was wonderin' if you and Will had made it official yet?"

"Made what official?" I was half paying attention to her, while struggling to recapture the puzzle pieces that were now threatening to float away on the morning breeze.

"Why, your engagement."

My mouth fell open. I quickly clamped it shut. "What makes you think we're getting engaged?"

"Well, isn't that the next step?"

I gritted my teeth. Edna was feisty, and sometimes nosy, like now, but she was a good soul and I didn't want to snap at her. Well, I wanted to, but I knew I shouldn't. She meant well.

"We're not engaged."

"Yet," she added with a grin and a twinkle in her eye.

Grrr.

"So what have you been up to?" she asked. "Besides makin' Will crazy."

I plastered on a smile. "Not much. Just started a new dog." I wasn't in the mood to tell her about the investigating gig, and I knew the mention of a dog would distract her.

It worked. She asked me a bunch of questions about Patches as we watched the dogs play in the field.

"Well, I'd better be getting back and start working with him," I finally said and whistled for Buddy.

Edna nodded. "Yup, the work day's a callin'."

I gave her a genuine smile this time. "Take care."

My smile quickly evaporated as I turned away and realized the pieces of my puzzle had indeed scattered on the wind—maybe not to the four corners of the earth, but definitely to the four corners of Mayfair.

I had no clue what I'd been on the verge of discovering earlier. The only part I could remember was thinking maybe Roger was involved in the blackmail.

I shook my head. That was crazy.

An hour and a half later, I was still in a muddle over most aspects of my life, but I was feeling pretty good about Patches. We'd worked on the go-get task and the beginnings of the cover task. The dog was now consistently picking up either the pill vial or the ball, depending on which I asked for. And when I'd walked him around the backyard, he'd sat automatically every time I stopped moving. The next step was a bit trickier—I'd tackle it soon with Stephie—getting him to turn around before sitting.

At nine-fifteen, Will arrived on my front porch with another bag of egg sandwiches, plus an apologetic look on his face.

I held up my hand before he could say anything. "Let's pretend last night didn't happen. As a matter of fact, I'd just as soon pretend all day yesterday didn't happen."

"I don't know. They were pretty good steaks."

"Yes, they were." I gave him a hug. "Thank you for the steaks, and for breakfast, and for putting up with me."

"You're welcome, and I'm sorry I haven't been more supportive of your new career."

"I can't blame you for being frustrated with me." After all, I was pretty frustrated with myself. "But this is what I like best, when we're a team, working together."

He smiled, exposing his sexy dimples. I stood on tiptoe to kiss one of them.

He moved his head and found my lips instead. I melted against his warm chest.

I was seriously considering a different kind of "together" activity when my stomach growled loudly.

He broke the kiss and grinned down at me. "Last one in the kitchen has to pour the other one's coffee." He took off, with me behind, laughing and trying to jostle past him.

And that was the beginning of a lovely morning. I left my car at the junction of State Road 40 and I-75, since I was planning to go see Roger Campbell later with a progress report. Buddy and I climbed into Will's shiny new pick-up. It was the first vehicle he'd bought in Florida, since Collins County had previously provided him with a county car as sheriff.

The white truck had leather seats and a surprisingly smooth ride. The backseat was half the size of the front and was *not* leather, but Buddy didn't seem to mind.

As we drove to Gainesville, I filled him in on the blackmail. If we were working together now, he needed to know it all.

He listened attentively without comment, then stared ahead at the road for a couple of minutes. "Do you think this Gerry character is the blackmailer?" he finally said.

"I don't know. Shawn seems convinced that Marissa is not." I considered telling Will about my wild theory that Roger might be the blackmailer. But it was just that—wild.

"Gerry lives with her," I said instead. "I can't imagine him being the blackmailer without her knowing about it."

"Who says she doesn't know about it?"

I shrugged. "I guess she could. Maybe she found out about it and that's what triggered her outburst at Shawn. She wanted to let him know that money wasn't enough to make up for what he did."

Will gave a slight shake of his head. "It seems like something had to have happened recently to stir it all up for her again. I've worked with sexual assault vics before. Their emotions can certainly stay intense, even for years, but the scene you described... it seems like her feelings are more raw, as if the wounds were fresh."

My heart warmed in my chest. This was one of the things I loved about this guy. He might be the big rugged lawman on the outside, but he got emotions better than most of the men I'd known in my lifetime.

"Maybe it's because she feels justice was never served, since the charges were dropped." Another thought struck me. "Or maybe she's gone into therapy recently and is only now getting in touch with her anger." I'd done some therapy myself and knew how it could stir things up, in a good way ultimately once you got those things resolved, but in the meantime, it could be pretty rocky.

My heart softened toward her. She hadn't been very pleasant with me, but I'd been asking about her connection to the man accused of assaulting her, which certainly would have felt extremely *un*pleasant to her.

I also didn't know what other psychological baggage she might be carrying. Mom's-voice-in-my-head was right. I had no right to judge how well or how poorly she had "survived."

We pulled up in front of the house with the pale blue sports car in the driveway.

I turned on the truck seat to face Will. The serious mood I was trying to set with my somber expression was somewhat diminished when Buddy licked my ear. I struggled not to laugh.

When I had myself under control, I said, "Look, I'm really glad you're here, as my backup. But I think I should talk to this guy alone. If–"

Will interrupted. "I'm thinking the same thing. I've got no evidence that he's committed any crime, so I can't interrogate him as a law enforcement officer, and if I go in and pretend to be a private citizen and he admits to something unlawful–"

"Like blackmail."

He nodded. "Then a defense attorney could make a case for entrapment."

I was thinking more along the lines of, if I'm going to be an investigator, I needed to do this myself, but Will's reasons were sound too.

And I was really loving how we were finishing each other's sentences.

Will's forehead was wrinkled with worry lines. "But what if this guy's the driver of the black SUV?"

I'd given that some thought. I pulled out my phone and typed in a text message to him—*Help.* I didn't send it but rather held the phone up to show him. "I'll keep the phone in my hand inside my pocket. First sign of trouble, I'll hit send."

Will nodded.

I took Buddy with me this time.

But all the worrying and planning was for nothing. Gerry Fields wasn't home.

Marissa stood on her porch and threatened to call the police if I didn't stop harassing them. I resisted the urge to hold out my phone and invite her to call the cop sitting out at the curb.

Of course, she had reason to be mad at me. Once again, I was stirring up old pain. But she'd already seemed upset when she'd first opened the door—eyes swollen, face splotchy.

"Are you okay?" I asked sympathetically, even though she'd just threatened to sic the law on me.

Her face started to crumble, then slowly it hardened into a mask of anger. It was a rather fascinating metamorphosis to observe.

"Go away!" she yelled.

We went.

Will took us back to my car.

He and I kissed for a while in his truck. Buddy politely pretended to sleep in the backseat.

Will finally broke off with a gasp for air. "Whoa, we better stop before we get arrested."

I wrapped a hand around the back of his neck and tried to pull his head back down.

But he resisted with a laugh. "How would it look if a Marion County detective got picked up for lewd and lascivious behavior? Besides, I've got some stuff I need to do today on the bedrooms." He was remodeling his house, a former worker-bee cottage from the pre-Disney-World days when the Mayfair Alligator Farm was the hottest tourist attraction in central Florida.

I mock pouted. "Don't use up too much energy. I've got plans for you this evening."

Wiggling his eyebrows and grinning, he leaned over and opened my door. "I'll keep that in mind."

I hopped out of the truck and reached into the pint-sized backseat to unhook Buddy's safety strap from the seatbelt. He jumped out.

Will waited until we were in my car and I'd started the engine. Then he waved and drove off.

I sat there for a moment, contemplating my next move. I had planned to go see Roger Campbell with an update, but for some reason I was now resisting that idea. I decided instead to pop in on Shawn Davis again.

A little black filly named Niña could have had something to do with that plan.

~

Shawn was gracious about letting me ride the mare again.

"I really am trying to come up with a way to buy her," I said.

"It's okay. We get this a lot, folks coming back to look at a horse multiple times. They're expensive animals. People want to be sure."

He brought the mare out of her stall and led her all the way to the end of the barn before putting her in cross-ties.

"She's going into heat," Shawn explained, "and it would make Diablo nuts if he picked up her scent."

As if on cue, a thump came from the other end of the barn.

We groomed Niña together, and Shawn began tacking her up. "Do you have a saddle?"

"No." My chest tightened. Owning a horse again would mean far more expenses than just her purchase price, as we'd found out the hard way when my grandparents gave me my pony. Board, tack, feed—it was not a cheap hobby.

My throat hurt. Why was I torturing myself by riding this horse? I was never going to be able to buy her.

But torture myself was exactly what I was going to do. Shawn led the filly out and around the barn the long way.

I looked around for Buddy. He'd been sitting off to the side of the aisle when we were grooming and tacking up the horse.

Now he was farther down the aisle, scratching at the cement floor in front of a stall.

I hadn't told him to stay, but I was still kind of surprised he'd wandered off on his own. "Come on, boy," I called out.

He looked at me and whined. A thump came from the stall.

It was Diablo's, and apparently Shawn's efforts to keep Niña's scent from reaching him had been for naught. Another thump, louder. Buddy let out a woof.

"Buddy, come here," I said, my voice stern.

Reluctantly he came, glancing back over his shoulder.

As we followed Shawn and Niña to the paddock, I gave some thought to how I should deal with Buddy. More and more he was acting like a pet and guard dog, rather than a service dog. And yet he continued to do what I needed him to do as a mentor dog. He was great at demonstrating the service dog tasks to my trainees. And on those rare occasions these days when I put his red service-dog vest on him, he still behaved accordingly.

We'd reached the paddock. I shook my head to rid it of other thoughts. I'd decide how to deal with Buddy later. Right now, I was going to enjoy what might be my last ride on Niña.

At the gate, I held my hand out parallel to the ground and lowered it. Buddy obediently laid down. "Stay," I said.

Shawn led the mare into the paddock, and I mounted. Then we were sailing around the packed-earth circle along the fence—once, twice, three times. I felt lighter than I had in a long time.

I started to pull her up, but she snorted and shook her head. She was having as much fun as I was.

"Wanna take her for a longer run?" Shawn called out.

I nodded, slowing the horse to a fast walk.

He opened the gate and pointed to a freshly mown hayfield. "It's safe to run her there. No sandy mounders."

I stopped Niña beside him. "Sandy what?"

"Sandy mounders. They're little gophers, indigenous to Florida. They dig their burrows and push the dirt out around the entrance, making a little sandy mound."

Hmm, just when I thought I knew my adopted state, I learned something new about Florida.

"Not as dangerous as the bigger gopher holes up north," Shawn was saying. "But still not a good thing if a horse's hoof lands right on the mound and sinks into the weakened ground."

"Are you from up north?" I asked.

"West Virginia. We came down here when I was nine. Go on." Shawn grinned up at me. "Try her out at a full gallop."

I grinned back and nudged the horse's sides with my heels. "Come on, Buddy," I yelled.

Sailing was no longer the appropriate analogy. Now we were flying. I laughed out loud, the wind snatching the sound away. Buddy raced alongside of us, woofing with excitement.

Finally I slowed the horse and we trotted, excuse me, gaited our way back to Shawn.

He was grinning from ear to ear.

"You love doing this, don't you?" I asked.

"Yeah." His face fell. "Hopefully, I'll get to keep doing it."

"What do you mean?" I dismounted and patted Niña's now sweaty neck. She wasn't breathing all that hard though. They kept her in great condition.

Buddy trotted up to me. His tongue was lolling out of the side of his mouth. He looked happy.

He'd definitely make a great trail dog. I shoved that thought aside.

Shawn shook his head, his expression forlorn. "My parents weren't very happy with me, you know, before..." He trailed off, shook his head again. "My dad, in particular. If all that mess comes up again, makes it into the news... He's about to retire. He told me that if I kept my nose clean he'd turn this place over to me. If not, he'd sell it and I'd have to find a job."

"Don't worry, I'm not going to tell anyone." Not even Roger Campbell, I decided in that moment.

Shawn fell into step beside me as we headed back toward the barn. "Doesn't matter now. The blackmailer's probably about to expose me. I was supposed to leave the monthly payoff in an empty stall last night. I left a note instead saying I wasn't going to pay anymore."

He turned to me, his eyes pleading. "You said you're a private investigator. Could you—"

His words were cut short by a scream.

CHAPTER TEN

Barking ferociously, Buddy took off for the barn.

"Wait, wait!" A signal that meant stop whatever you're doing and wait for more instructions.

It didn't work this time. Buddy kept going. I ran after him, continuing to yell, "Wait!"

He finally stopped just outside the barn entrance, whining and looking back at me with a pain-filled expression.

He'd witnessed an attack on his original owner, Jimmy Garrett. Was Buddy having some kind of flashback? Could dogs have PTSD?

I caught up with him, Shawn hard on my heels.

Together we entered the barn, Shawn holding Niña's reins, me hanging onto Buddy's collar. It took a few seconds for our eyes to adjust to the gloom of the barn after the bright sunlight.

A slim, middle-aged blonde stood in front of a stall, her hands covering the lower part of her face. She was whimpering.

As we ran toward her, she turned and met Shawn's gaze. Then she whimpered again and crumpled to the ground.

Dropping Niña's reins, Shawn ran to the woman.

I let go of Buddy's collar and pointed to the far side of the aisle.

Some of the tension inside me relaxed when he obediently trotted over there and sat down. "Stay," I said, and made a beeline for the stall door, beyond curious as to what would make a grown woman faint.

The upper half of the door was open. Suddenly a black horse's head lashed out of the opening. Eyes wide, whites showing around dark irises, Diablo shrieked out a loud whinny.

I jumped back, then held out my hands, palms out. "Shh, shh. It's okay, boy."

The horse looked at me, his teeth bared in a hideous grin-like expression.

"Shh, shh," I repeated, approaching slowly. "It's okay," I said in a softer voice. "You're okay."

Diablo's eyes rolled around in his head, from me to Shawn and back again.

But Shawn was occupied with trying to revive the woman lying on the barn floor. He chafed her hands. "Mom, wake up. Please, wake up."

"It's okay," I said again to the freaked-out horse. I held out a hand, palm up, as if I were offering a carrot. I fervently wished that I had one.

Diablo snorted and moved forward a bit, sniffing at my hand.

"I'm sorry, boy," I said gently. "Wish I could deliver on the promise."

The horse snorted softly again. I took a chance and reached out with my other hand. He let me take ahold of his halter.

"That's a good boy, Diablo," I crooned. "You're such a good boy."

I took a step closer, one hand on the halter, the other slowly stroking the horse's long nose. I risked taking a peek into the stall.

Then wished I hadn't. The pile of rags in the far corner looked inno-cent enough, until my brain registered the blood on them.

"Did you notice anything unusual before the body was discovered?" Will asked, as if I were a regular witness to a homicide rather than his girlfriend.

I bristled. "No." Then I glanced across the aisle of the horse barn to Buddy, sitting obediently in front of a rack of saddles.

"Buddy was sniffing and whining in front of the stall door," I said.

Shawn had removed Diablo from the stall, now a crime scene. And the coroner had declared there was blunt force trauma to the head that was not consistent with a horse's hooves. In other words, the guy was probably already out cold when he was put in Diablo's stall.

The horse people among us had breathed a sigh of relief that the stallion wouldn't be blamed. That included Shawn's mother, who was now quite conscious and kept saying, "I have no idea how this happened in our barn." Her voice had a slight West Virginia twang.

But the situation had already progressed far beyond her feeble attempts at damage control. Before the deputies had arrived, Shawn had admitted to me that he knew the victim.

"It's the other guy." His voice had sounded strangled.

"What do you mean?" I'd said.

"The other guy at the party. Gerry's friend. The one who said I'd attacked Marissa."

Now, Will turned to Shawn. "And you recognize the victim?"

Shawn nodded, his Adam's apple bobbing in his throat as he swallowed hard. "After I got the horse out of there, I went to check on the guy, hoping he was still alive."

He turned a little green, and I instinctively took a step back, ready to flee if he started tossing his cookies, as I knew mine wouldn't be far behind.

But he swallowed again and continued. "I don't remember his name. He was a friend of my college roommate."

Eyebrows in the air, Will glanced my way. His jaw was clenched.

He asked Shawn, "What do you remember about the guy?"

"I didn't know him very well. He came to parties at the frat house sometimes."

Will looked at me again, silently inquiring.

I nodded slightly.

I didn't think his expression could get any grimmer, but somehow it did. His baby blues icy, he took my arm. "Mr. Davis," he said over his shoulder as he began to move me away, "please give your statement to my partner."

Partner?

A roly-poly man stepped forward. While Will still wore the jeans and chambray shirt he'd had on earlier, his partner was dressed in a cheap mud-colored business suit.

He offered Shawn his hand. "Detective..." He introduced himself but I didn't catch his name as Will nudged me farther down the wide aisle of the barn.

I hereby dub him Mr. Brown, Ms. Snark said. It fit him. Everything about him was brown—hair, eyes, suit, tie. Even his shirt was tan. He looked like a whiskey barrel with a head, legs and arms.

My preoccupation with his partner caused me to miss the first part of what Will was saying. "...roommate is the guy we went to see this morning, Gerald Fields?" His voice was a low hiss.

"Yes. The one who wasn't home," I whispered back. I wondered if he wasn't home because he was busy murdering his friend.

"I've got some more info on him," Will said. "I'll explain later, but you need to leave this alone."

When I didn't answer, he added, "Completely alone!"

"I'm not sure I can. I think I may have stirred up this hornet's nest."

"That's quite possible, but that doesn't mean you have to *keep* stirring."

Again, I didn't say anything. A rational discussion didn't seem likely, given Will's current mood, but I wasn't willing to make a promise I might not be able to keep.

"Sorry your day off got screwed up," I said instead.

Will waved a hand in the air, dismissing my feeble attempt to distract him. "I ran this Fields guy through the system. I don't have time to go into all of it now, but let's just say he's not a model citizen."

"Okay," I said cautiously.

"So this has gotten way too dangerous for amateurs. Just go home and train your dog."

I stared at him, my teeth clenched, my mind trying and failing to come up with any appropriate words.

"I mean it, Marcia. Stay out of this now. It's a police matter."

He let go of my arm and walked away.

I stared after him, trying to figure out what I felt.

I wanted to be mad at Will, but somehow I understood. We'd both assumed that my dabbling in private investigating was rather tame, despite the bozo who'd tried to turn me and Buddy into roadkill. But now my "little" investigation had led me right into a murder scene and entangled me in Will's professional life in a way that complicated things considerably for him.

I looked down at Buddy. "Is it me, or does Will seem a bit stressed out?"

My dog cocked his head at me, seemingly unimpressed with my attempt to lighten the mood.

The worst part was that I wasn't sure I could step back as Will wanted me to. I knew Shawn had been about to ask me, right before his mother screamed, to investigate what really happened at that frat party. And now it looked like he'd been set up for the murder of one of the players in that party scene.

A part of my brain wondered if Shawn could be the murderer. I shook my head. If he knew a dead man was in Diablo's stall, he wouldn't have told me the blackmailer was supposed to come last night, and that he'd left a note refusing to pay any more money.

I stopped halfway to my car and turned around. I wanted to ask Shawn some questions, like how long he'd been paying blackmail. I'd gotten the impression that it had been a few months.

"Better wait on that," I muttered to myself. Will would not appreciate it if I went back in there and tried to get Shawn aside.

And since when did Will have a partner? He'd been with the Marion County Sheriff's Department for six months now, and he'd always been a lone wolf. I tucked the partner question away, to use next time I needed to change the subject with Will.

I really, really wanted to talk to Gerry Fields now, but I didn't dare go see him before the police did. That would most definitely shoot Will's blood pressure through the roof.

So, with nothing better to do, for the time being I followed instructions and went home.

~

I was running around my backyard, being chased by a werewolf named Gerry, when something warm and fluttery on my forehead jerked me awake.

Jimmy Kimmel was interviewing somebody on the muted TV, and Will was standing over me, a chagrined look on his face. "Sorry. Didn't mean to startle you."

I gave him a small smile. "I tried to wait up."

He sat down next to me on my sofa. "Because you wanted to see me or because you were curious about what I found out about Gerry Fields?" His tone was teasing.

Relief made me lightheaded. He was back on an even keel.

We were back on an even keel.

"Some of both," I said, rubbing my tired eyes. I grabbed the remote and turned off the TV.

Will sighed. "Seems he's been on our Vice Unit's radar for a while. They think he's running an online prostitution ring."

I stared at him, no longer the least bit sleepy. "Whoa!"

"Yeah." He scrubbed a hand over his stubbled face. "We still can't find him. His girlfriend claims he was gone when she got up this morning and didn't come home all day. And he's not answering his phone."

"What's this about a prostitution ring?"

"He's got a secret website, hidden behind another site that's supposedly for his legitimate business. People can order up whichever gal they want and he sends them to their house, or business or whatever."

I shook my head. "That's pretty dangerous for the women."

"He's got a couple of muscle guys. With new clients, they go with the girls and wait outside. Trouble is Vice is about to run a sting on Fields, to get the evidence they need to put him away. They want us to back off our investigation."

"I would think murder trumps a vice charge."

"Well, it would, if we had any evidence that he's the killer. But we're just trying to question him about his friend. Vice is pretty pissed at us that we've driven him underground."

"How can they believe that, when he was gone early this morning, before the body was even discovered?"

Will looked at me, his eyebrows arched. "Because I went there with you this morning. I had to tell them, and my partner *and* my supervisor, about all that. Almost got me pulled off the case."

"I'm sorry," I said.

"Not your fault. We had no idea this would happen."

"But again, we went there *before* the body was found."

Will blew out air. "And that's the only reason I'm still on the case. Because it wasn't a case yet when I got involved, if only as chauffeur and bodyguard."

"So if Gerry Fields isn't your main suspect, who is?" I braced myself, knowing what the answer would be.

"Your boy, Shawn Davis. We found his note in the stall. Apparently the dead guy was the blackmailer."

"Well, at least that part of the mystery is solved."

Will narrowed his eyes at me. "And you're done with this particular mystery, remember?"

That seemed like a question I was better off not answering. I changed the subject. "Can I borrow your truck tomorrow, so I can take my car to the body shop for an estimate?" I was impressed with how innocent my voice sounded.

Will's mouth fell open. "You've got to be kidding? You don't exactly have a great track record with vehicles. Last count was one totaled and one banged up," he held up two fingers, "twice."

"Well, how else am I going to be able to get it to the shop?"

"I'll take you, but I can't do it tomorrow. The next morning probably I can."

I'd had an ulterior motive for asking—I wasn't at all sure that whoever ran me off the road wouldn't try again, and my dented, scraped fender might as well be a bull's eye painted on the car. But my I-75 assailant wouldn't be watching for a white truck.

Will was staring at me—I'd waited too long to answer. "You're planning to go investigating tomorrow." A statement not a question.

I shook my head, even as I slipped my hand under my thigh on the sofa, so he couldn't see me cross my fingers. It wasn't a lie if you crossed your fingers, right?

"I need to go see Roger Campbell and tell him I'm off the case." That was partly the truth, at least. If Shawn was about to be arrested for murder, I certainly didn't need to be digging up more dirt on him. And I wasn't willing to do so anymore.

Will pushed himself to a stand. "The answer is still no. Call him. It's safer. And I need my truck tomorrow to do some investigating of my own." He looked down at me. "I'm the real detective, remember?"

"Ouch."

He smiled a little and gave a slight shake of his head. Then he reached out a hand. I took it, and he pulled me up, close in front of him, and wrapped his arms around me.

I leaned into his shoulder and breathed in the smell of him—a hint of stale sweat and the remnants of his woodsy aftershave, left over from this morning.

"I need a shower," he muttered as he pulled the scrunchie off my ponytail and buried his face in my hair.

"Nope, you smell wonderful to me."

CHAPTER ELEVEN

My car problem got solved the next morning in an unexpected way. I went out front to check my mail and found my next door neighbor, Sherie Wells, in her mint green terrycloth robe, watering the hanging plants on her porch.

"Good morning, Marcia," Sherie called over in a cheerful voice. Even in a bathrobe, she held herself tall and proud. The word *regal* came to mind. Her shiny dark hair, streaked with gray, was already pulled back in a tight chignon. I marveled once again at the smoothness of her brown skin. She was mid-sixties, retired, with four kids and a half dozen grandchildren, but the goddess of aging had been kind to her.

We chatted for a few minutes, and she filled me in on the latest news of her youngest daughter, Sybil, who was finishing up her nursing program in Ocala. She was the only one of the Wells' offspring I knew well, since she had been living with her mother when I moved here.

"I'm so proud of her." Sherie beamed. "I'm proud of all my kids. They all finished college."

I smiled back at her. "No small feat." It was quite impressive, but even more so was the fact that Sherie and her husband had overcome the many obstacles in the paths of black kids in the 1960s and had both gotten their teaching degrees, despite their humble origins. Sherie's father-in-law, Pete Wells, had been the maintenance supervisor of the Mayfair Alligator Farm, and Sherie's father had worked for him.

Thoughts of Pete Wells gave me an idea. "Hey, do you still have that old car in your garage?"

Sherie turned slightly toward me, watering can dripping. "Daddy Wells's old Bonneville?"

"Yes. Does it run?"

She nodded. "I turn it on and take it to the store every few weeks, to keep it going."

"Could I rent it from you for the day?"

"Heck no." She smiled. "But you can borrow it."

It was a 1974 model that had once been gold-colored, but the finish had now worn down to a dull dark tan. The black vinyl-covered top looked like it had leprosy, with splotches of peeling skin.

According to Edna Mayfair, Pete Wells was spinning in his grave that the car had not been better cared for after he took ill in the late 1990s. Before then, he'd kept it polished and waxed. But for the last couple of decades it had resided in the garage—really a lean-to he'd tacked onto one end of the house—in a state of benign neglect.

I thanked Sherie before she could change her mind and ran back inside to get Buddy and my purse.

I wanted to get the conversation with Roger Campbell over with, before I lost my nerve.

～

On my way to Belleview, I rehearsed my plan again in my head. I could justify two hundred dollars in expenses, not counting the damages to my car. Including travel times, I had twenty-five hours invested. At twenty dollars an hour, a rate that seemed reasonable to my mind, that was another five hundred dollars—the exact amount of my deductible on my car insurance.

But I hadn't written any of that down. I'd finally gotten around to checking out Florida's licensure laws for private investigators. They were stricter than I'd assumed they would be. No wonder Will had been so upset with me when he first learned what I was doing. Technically, I'd been breaking the law.

I didn't want anything in writing regarding why Roger had given me that thousand-dollar check. I could just give him his money back, but that left me poorer than when I'd started. And I had done what he'd asked. If he insisted, I would give all but the expenses back. But I was going to try to keep most of it.

In Belleview, I stopped at an ATM first and withdrew three hundred dollars cash from my savings account.

"About time," Roger said when he opened his front door. He spun his chair around and wheeled it down the hall.

Buddy and I stepped inside, and I nudged the door closed with my heel. We followed Roger to the great room.

"I have a final report for you."

He pulled his wheelchair alongside the round table and picked up a mug. He didn't offer any of what was in it to me.

Buddy and I stayed near the doorway to the hall. I didn't intend to linger any longer than necessary. "I found the dirt you were looking for on Shawn Davis, the dropped assault charge I told you about. But Lexie already knows about it. I couldn't find anything else. I don't think there's anything else *to* find. I think he was an out-of-control teenager who finally grew up. He seems like a responsible young man now."

Roger slammed his mug down on the table. Amber-colored liquid sloshed out.

I jumped. Buddy growled low in his throat.

I put a restraining hand on his head and he quieted. Again, he was breaking training, but I wasn't sure I cared. I was glad to have him with me.

Roger Campbell, even in a wheelchair, was a little scary.

He sneered. "So he's won you over."

Without answering, I took a couple of steps closer, curiosity winning out over caution. I wanted to catch a whiff of the man's breath.

He stared at his mug, then picked it up again and downed its remaining contents.

I thought I smelled liquor as he set it back down again, but I couldn't be sure.

Now he was staring at me, an expression spreading across his face that could best be described as grim satisfaction. Something flashed in his eyes and was gone.

The light is dim. I'm imagining things.

"I want my money back," he said in a flat voice.

I matched his tone. "There was no money-back guarantee if you didn't get the results you wanted. I dug up what was there. I had two hundred dollars in expenses–"

"Where's the itemized account of those expenses?" He held out his hand, palm up.

"I haven't written it up yet. I'll email it to you." I crossed my fingers behind my back.

"Humph." He curled his upper lip. "Amateur."

My stomach and jaw both clenched. I'd had a talk with myself on the way over, about how I needed to stay civil with this guy since eventually I'd have to train him to utilize Patches effectively. But there was a limit.

"I never pretended to be anything but," I said in a firm voice. "You were the one who insisted I try this. If I haven't lived up to your expectations, than perhaps those expectations were too high," I paused, returning his glare, "for an *amateur.*"

He held my gaze for a beat, then looked away.

I slipped a hand into my pocket and wrapped my fingers around the bills there.

But before I could pull them out, he waved a dismissive hand at me. "Never mind. I don't feel like fighting over a grand."

Relief and amazement flooded my chest, in equal measure. My stomach relaxed.

A nasty grin spread across his face. "I hear your responsible young man is about to be charged with murder."

I went rigid, but I managed to keep my voice even. "Where did you hear that?"

"Cops came around lookin' for Lexie, with questions 'bout her lover boy." His words were starting to slur. "Said they were investigatin' a murder at Clover Hills."

After dating Will for a year, I knew the police wouldn't have said that. At most they would have admitted to investigating a "suspicious death." It wouldn't be officially ruled a homicide until after the autopsy, which was probably happening today.

It was more likely that they would have ducked questions about why they were there. But I hadn't listened to the news this morning. It was possible the death had been reported on TV and Roger had put the pieces together.

He was still staring at me and grinning—enjoying baiting me, no doubt.

I needed to end this before I said something I would regret. "Well, if Shawn does end up arrested, you'll get your wish about breaking him and Lexie up."

Roger's expression shifted to something darker. I couldn't tell if he was angry or sad. "No, that stupid girl will probably vow to wait for him."

I started backing us toward the door. "I gotta go."

Roger turned his chair and wheeled toward Buddy and me.

I held up a hand. "That's okay. We'll let ourselves out."

We got out of there as quick as we could without downright running.

Once in the car, I paused to mentally regroup. Again, I was left with the feeling that something was off about this man. What was that strange expression he'd had on his face for a few seconds?

Insight blossomed. Roger Campbell was a control freak. Probably always had been. It had no doubt made him a good aircraft mechanic, meticulous. It might also explain his general discharge, if he had conflicts with authority over how things should be done.

And now his injury and the resulting PTSD and disability had spun his life out of control, and he was trying to control the only thing he had left, his sister. He had no reason to dislike Shawn, other than the reality that Shawn was a threat to his influence over Lexie.

I almost felt sorry for Roger.

My mind flashed back to my thoughts the other morning—the ones that had scattered to the wind while talking to Edna about my non-engaged status.

It *was* kind of crazy to think Roger was the blackmailer, since he didn't particularly want Shawn's history to stay in the past. But did he already know about the dropped assault charge when he'd hired me?

He'd mentioned Shawn's sealed juvie record the first day I'd met him. If he'd found that, then surely he'd found the dropped charge as well. He had a computer. He could have ordered a background check as readily as I had.

I banged the heel of my hand against the steering wheel, as mad at myself as I was at him.

Buddy's head jerked up. He let out a soft woof.

"Sorry, boy. It's okay."

Roger hadn't hired me to find the dirt. He'd hired me to stir it up. He'd wanted me, the amateur, to blunder around, opening old wounds that would cause trouble for Shawn.

Had he been able to find out what the dropped charges were about? Did he already know about the frat party when he'd hired me?

I looked at my watch. I still had almost three hours before Stephie was due for our afternoon training session.

On impulse, I headed north toward Gainesville. Somehow, Marissa Andrews and that frat party were the key to all of this. I didn't know how, but I was going to find out.

~

An hour later, I was parked down the street from Marissa Andrews's house. What I would give to trade the muddy-mobile for that blue beauty in her driveway.

Now that was a P.I.'s car!

Of course it wouldn't be any easier to blend in with that one than with the Bonneville. If Marissa went out, it would be hard to discretely follow her in this tank, to see if she'd lead me to Gerry Fields.

But I didn't dare approach her again, when Will had so adamantly told me to butt out. No doubt if I talked to her, word would get back to him.

A few minutes later, that dilemma was solved, although how to blend in while tailing someone in the muddy-mobile was still an issue.

Marissa, dressed in a little black dress that left some things to one's imagination but not much, exited her house and climbed into the sports car. She didn't seem to be watching for a tail as she went right to her destination, at ten miles an hour over the speed limit most of the way.

I had to give it to the muddy-mobile—its eight cylinders had no trouble keeping up.

Marissa had led us to a slightly shabby section of town. She stopped in front of a small bungalow that had seen better days. Someone had made an effort to dress it up with some fresh plantings along the front walk, but the peeling paint and sagging roof said its owner didn't have much money. Or it was a rental with a neglectful landlord.

I drove on past and parked farther up the street, then grabbed my phone from the passenger seat and made a note of the address.

I hunched down and turned to peek over the back of the bench seat. Buddy sat up. I signaled with my hand for him to lie down again.

Marissa had beeped her horn. A girl exited the house and headed for the sports car. She'd apparently been playing dress-up with her big sister's clothes. Her dress, a tight lavender sheath with a slit to mid-thigh, sparkled in the sunlight.

As she neared Marissa's car and I got a better look at her, I upped my estimate of her age, from twelve to maybe fourteen. She had Asian features and her dark hair was swept up on top of her head in an elaborate style that, along with the dress, made no sense this time of the day.

If it had been evening, I'd say that they were going to the theater—the girl was obviously too young to go clubbing.

Marissa pulled away from the curb. I ducked down.

Just as her car cleared my front fender, my phone pinged on the seat next to me. I grabbed it up to quickly check the text. I needed to give my quarry a bit of a head start anyway.

Two words on my screen, in all caps. *GO HOME!*

A white truck pulled past me. The driver was staring straight ahead, his rugged jaw clenched. I couldn't see his eyes clearly, but I was sure they were an angry, icy blue.

Crapola!

CHAPTER TWELVE

It didn't take me long to put these particular pieces together. Marissa had lied to the detectives. She not only knew about Gerry's illegal activities, but she was an active participant. She and the girl had been headed to meet a john.

I shuddered at the memory of the girl's young face.

Then I shuddered again at the thought of what Will would have to say when he got home tonight.

I pointed the muddy-mobile toward Mayfair. "I guess we're done playing detective for the day," I said to Buddy in the rearview mirror.

He cocked his head to one side and let out a soft woof. I was pretty sure it meant, "Now look what you've gotten us into."

At home, Stephie was already there, pacing in front of my house.

"There you are," she said with relief in her voice, as I climbed out of the muddy-mobile.

I glanced at my watch. It was only ten of one, the time we were supposed to start the training session.

Stephie blushed. "Sorry, yeah, I'm early." Now she sounded totally flustered.

"What's going on?"

Boy, that masters in psych really pays off sometimes, Ms. Snark commented internally.

I mentally told her to shut up, but she was right. The fact that Stephie was upset was quite obvious.

"I left early from my shift at the shelter."

That info did little to enlighten me. "Did something happen there?" I leaned into the backseat to unhook Buddy from his safety strap.

He bounded out of the car and over to Stephie for a pat.

She petted him absentmindedly, still looking upset. "I got into a fight with another volunteer."

"A fight?" I led the way up my walk.

"An argument. I was telling her about some of the stuff we were doing and she said you...." She trailed off, looked away.

I opened my front door. Dumping my purse on the sofa, I let Patches out of his crate. "Heel." He immediately fell into step beside me, Buddy trailing behind.

Snuffling sounds. I looked back over my shoulder.

Stephie was standing in the middle of the living room, crying.

I turned back toward her. "For Pete's sake, just tell me what's wrong."

"She said you didn't know how to train dogs and I was wasting my time." Stephie's shoulders shook. "But already you've got him...." She pointed to Patches, opened her mouth as if to say more, but a sob came out instead.

I signaled the dogs to lie down and motioned her to the sofa. Shoving my purse aside, I sat down. "Why does she think I can't train dogs? And why are you upset about it?" It wasn't like we were BFFs. Why was she taking a slur against my training so much to heart?

"I dropped one of my classes, so I'd have more time to train with you."

I stared at her as guilt socked me in the gut. I hadn't been taking this young woman's desire to become a trainer seriously enough.

Stephie's brown doe's eyes were red-rimmed and a bit swollen. This wasn't her first crying jag of the day. "I jumped into this too fast. I always do that."

That makes two of you, Ms. Snark said. I ignored her.

"You're not sure you want to be a trainer now?" This conversation was making my head spin.

"No, yes, I want to be a trainer...." She looked away again.

Realization finally dawned. *Boy, you are slow on the uptake today*, Ms. Snark commented.

"But you're not sure you want to train with me."

Stephie nodded, her expression miserable. "You've been so nice to me. How can I doubt—"

I held up a hand to cut her off, since her words were twisting a knife in my already twisted stomach. I hadn't been that nice to her—I'd taken advantage of her.

"What did this other volunteer say exactly?"

"That you don't know what you're doing because you don't use a clicker."

Aha!

I leaned forward a little. "You've trained your own dogs, right?"

She nodded.

"Did you use a clicker?"

"Well, no. But I was only teaching them to sit and lie down and such."

"Same here. I never used one either when I was training my own pets. Do you know what the clicker's for?"

"You pair it with food treats, and after a while it becomes the reward. And it can be used to get the dog's attention."

"Yes, that pairing tends to happen, but initially the click is used to mark the behavior you are rewarding, so it's clearer to the dog which behavior will get him a treat next time."

Stephie nodded again, her face brightening some.

"Mattie's kind of old-fashioned. She uses 'good boy' or 'good girl' to mark the behavior, followed by a food treat."

Her eyes lit up. "That works as well?"

"Always has for me. But you can use the clicker system if you want," I added, giving Stephie that option as Mattie had with me. "And no matter what anyone says, there's more than one *right* way to train."

"That's okay," she said. "I just need to remember to say 'good boy.'"

"As quickly after the behavior as possible." I shoved myself up off the sofa. "And then eventually we use the food treats only intermittently."

Stephie jumped up and gave me a big smile. "Got it." Her face sobered a little. "But what about getting the dog's attention?"

I put a hand on her shoulder. "By the time we're done with him, Patches will know that when he's wearing his vest, he should be paying attention to his owner *all* the time. And if he does get distracted...." I held out my hands at hip level, palms down.

Both dogs jumped up and touched my palms with their noses, one on each side of me. "It's the first thing I teach my dogs. It means *You're on duty so pay attention.*"

Stephie grinned again and threw her arms around me.

Startled, I froze for a second before returning her hug. A warmth spread through my chest. I was beginning to really like this young woman.

Which was good, because I had just internally vowed to stick to training her and my dogs from now on.

That vow lasted thirty-six hours.

Thirty-six hours of only seeing Will from a distance, if that much. Both evenings, his house was still dark when I went to bed, but one morning he waved at me as he was climbing into his truck.

We'd exchanged a few text messages, the first one from me, a simple *I'm sorry.* I didn't know what else to say. I'd screwed up.

This morning, we'd had a short phone conversation, during which he'd asked if I was behaving myself.

"Yes," I'd said, but then stuck my tongue out at the phone.

He chuckled. "Real mature."

"I don't know what you mean," I said in my snootiest voice.

"I know you just stuck your tongue out at me."

"Maybe you don't know me as well as you think you do." I wasn't sure where that had come from, but he was starting to get on my nerves.

"Are you pissed?" Will's voice was mildly incredulous. "At me? After you're the one who stuck your nose into my case."

The pressure building inside increased. "I didn't stick my nose anywhere. I only followed Marissa Andrews for a little while. I was curious about where she was going all dolled up, that's all."

"Yeah, well you would've stuck your nose in if I hadn't stopped you."

I took a deep breath, reined in my temper. "I would not have approached her, and I didn't realize you had her under surveillance."

Will blew out air. "Unfortunately, we've only been able to watch her intermittently. We've got two other cases now."

Where did she go anyway?"

"No place all that interesting. She and the other gal went inside some guy's house. Then Marissa came out a few minutes later and went home."

My throat tightened. "Did you get him? Is she okay?"

"We didn't *get* anybody. We're trying not to blow Vice's case, since we only want to talk to her boyfriend about Jason Burrows's murder."

A small part of my brain registered the victim's name. Good to know.

But the rest of me felt sick. I realized my mouth was hanging open. "You left that girl in there?"

"What girl?" Will said. "Marissa?"

"No! The one she dropped off." My voice was rising, despite my best efforts to keep my cool. "You left an under-age girl in some pervert's house just so Vice wouldn't be pissed at you?"

A beat of silence. "Oh, you mean Amy Chen. She's twenty-two."

My mouth fell open again. "You're kidding."

"Nope."

"Never mind. Sorry I yelled."

"No problem. I can see how you'd mistake her for a kid from a distance. I'm sure that's part of her appeal for the johns."

"Oh gross."

Another half beat of silence. "Yeah, it is." His tone was much more serious than earlier.

His partner said something in the background. I couldn't make out the words.

"I gotta go," Will said. "We've got a lead in one of our other cases."

"Okay. Good luck. Love you."

The briefest of pauses. Then in a warm, low voice, he said, "Love you too."

Stephie arrived shortly after that, and we decided to take Patches out for his first public appearance in his red service dog vest.

I put Buddy's vest on as well, so it would be clear that we were training. Everyone in Mayfair knew to walk on by with a nod when they saw those red vests, rather than stop to chat as they would if it were only me and Buddy *sans* vest.

It wasn't too hard for Stephie to keep Patches focused during the first stretch, from my house to the corner by the motel. Only once did he stop to sniff a piece of trash by the side of the road.

"Leave it!" Stephie said.

Patches backed away from the paper, a candy wrapper crawling with ants. And I said a prayer of thanks to his previous owner, whoever that may have been. They might have neglected to get him microchipped and that had resulted in him becoming a stray. But they had taught him "Leave it," which meant "whatever it is, no matter what, drop it and back away," an essential command to keep a dog from eating something potentially harmful.

"Good boy," Stephie said, holding out her hand for him to touch her palm, then giving him a treat.

Good boy, I echoed in my head, but the real test would be when other pedestrians came along to distract him.

And here came the first one. Charlene Woodward, Mayfair's fortyish postmistress and sole mail carrier, was walking briskly in our direction.

Her uniform hung loosely on her thin frame, and I wondered fleetingly if she'd been sick lately. A sack of mail was slung over her shoulder and an unhappy expression marred her usually friendly face.

Normally I'd ask if she was okay, but not this early in Patches's training. I nodded and smiled, expecting her to walk past.

Instead, she stopped in the middle of the sidewalk, about twelve feet in front of us. "Marcia, don't tell me you're training one of those monsters for some hapless veteran."

Ms. Snark replied before I could stop her, "Okay, I won't tell you."

Stephie froze on the sidewalk. "Monster?"

CHAPTER THIRTEEN

Patches was pulling forward on his leash, his tail whipping back and forth at the thought of someone new to pet him.

"Deal with the dog," I said to Stephie under my breath. "I'll take care of her."

Stephie used the nose-to-palm signal to get Patches's attention again, told him to sit, and rewarded him with a treat.

I nodded my approval, then turned my attention back to Charlene. Her mouth was hanging open, no doubt in reaction to my rudeness. But I wasn't inclined to apologize.

"Hi, Charlene," I said in a fake cheerful tone. "Meet my new trainees, Stephie and Patches. Patches is the dog. He's an American Staffordshire Terrier, sometimes called an AmStaff."

Her upper lip curled. "Looks like a pit bull to me. I thought Florida outlawed them dogs."

"No, I don't think that legislation passed. And no, he's not a pit bull, although AmStaffs and Pitties are maybe third cousins." I think they're actually a little closer related than that—more like first cousins once removed—but I wasn't giving this woman any ammunition.

Charlene huffed and stamped her foot in its practical black oxford. "Well, I'm calling Marion County Animal Control."

"You're wasting your time, and theirs. They know me. If I'm training a dog, they know I've vetted it for aggressive tendencies."

Charlene glared at me as she pulled a clump of envelopes out of her mail bag. She stuck it out in my direction, but she didn't come any closer. "Here's your mail. Tell Will and Sherie that I'm not coming down your street as long as that dog is there."

I gritted my teeth to keep from saying one of the many retorts running through my mind, such as pointing out, not all that politely, that she couldn't refuse to deliver mail because of a dislike for someone's dog, not when said dog was properly restrained. And she definitely couldn't refuse to deliver my neighbors' mail.

I reined in my temper and said, "I can't take the mail now. I'm training."

"Fine. You can pick it up at the post office later." She returned the packet to her bag, turned on her heel and stomped away.

"Wow," Stephie said from beside me.

I glanced over. Patches was sitting quietly by her left knee. "Maybe I should have passed on him. His new owner's gonna be dealing with crap like—"

Stephie turned to me, her eyes flashing. "No. If we dog people give in to these prejudices, they'll never go away. First it was Dobermans and then Rottweilers and now Pit Bulls."

I looked down at Buddy, who's one-fifth Rottie. "She's right," I said to him. He cocked his head to one side.

But Stephie was too wound up to stop. "You know how many Pit Bulls and Pit mixes we get at the shelter? Twice as many as all the other breeds combined, and ninety percent of the time, the dog did nothing wrong. People got tired of the neighbors scowling at them, or their dog got accused of something it didn't do."

"Or they growled at someone," I said. "They're protective dogs—"

"But also sweet as can be," Stephie interrupted me again, "if they're not mistreated. Which makes them great family dogs and—"

I held up a hand and let out a little laugh. "Hey, we're both preaching to the choir here. And…" I pointed with my chin at Patches.

He was still sitting quietly at Stephie's side, his head swiveling around taking in the sights, but his butt hadn't budged from the sidewalk.

Stephie leaned down. "Good boy. You are such a good boy," she crooned as she rubbed his head and then gave him a treat.

"That's probably enough for now. I always like to stop working on a behavior when the dog has just gotten it right. Let that be what he remembers."

"Makes sense. Come on, boy."

"We'll work a while longer with him in my yard."

After Stephie left, I settled at my kitchen table with a glass of iced tea and a peanut butter and banana sandwich—my fave comfort food— and tried to sort out my emotions. I was still feeling a bit off-kilter from the run-in with Charlene, mainly because it was unexpected. Everyone in Mayfair had always been so supportive of my training efforts, and respectfully kept their distance when any dog with me was wearing a service vest.

I chalked the encounter up as something I couldn't control and opted to put it aside, focusing instead on how pleased I was with both Stephie's and Patches's progress.

I was also glad that Will and I had been able to talk more easily this morning, that we seemed to be back on solid ground. But…

I was not happy about being sidelined in the investigation. There was a restlessness in me, and a strong desire to find out what was happening.

I knew Shawn hadn't been arrested yet. Will probably would have told me that. And obviously other avenues were still being explored, thus Will's continued search for Gerry Fields.

Or was that only to find out what Gerry could tell him about Shawn and the victim?

Too often in books and movies, the cops latched onto a suspect and all their efforts then went into proving a case against them, not necessarily searching for the truth.

I shook my head. Will wasn't like that.

Swallowing the last bite of my sandwich, I reached for my phone to call Mattie. It was time to ask for another veteran to work with. Maybe if I had two dogs in training I'd be too busy to worry about other things.

The phone rang in my hand, making me jump a little. Caller ID showed Mattie's name. Laughing, I answered. "Hey, I was about to call you."

"The board got a letter." Her lack of preamble wasn't unusual, but her brusque tone was ominous. "From Roger Campbell."

My laughter died and my gut twisted. "Oh?"

"He said you took money from him to investigate something, and then didn't do it and wouldn't return the money."

My face flushed like it used to when I was a kid and my mother caught me doing something naughty. "Yeah, that's maybe twenty percent true."

"So you did take money from him?" Her tone was downright accusatory.

"Only after he insisted, when he couldn't find a P.I. that he trusted. And I did investigate. He just didn't like what I found."

"And you wouldn't return his money."

"I was prepared to return a portion of his retainer, less my expenses and the hours I had already put into the investigation." I was wishing now that I'd insisted on giving him the three hundred dollars.

The sound of air being sucked in and expelled. "And you didn't think this would be a conflict of interest?"

Actually, I hadn't given that much thought. "I guess I figured they were two separate things," I said lamely, then added, "And I went over there prepared to return everything but expenses if he'd insisted. But he dismissed the thousand-dollar retainer as if it were pocket change."

"And you didn't think to ask me first before making this little side deal?"

My throat hurt. Since when did I have to answer to Mattie about other aspects of my life, and why was she taking Campbell's side?

I took a deep breath. "Mattie, I'm sorry, but no, that didn't occur to me at the time. The guy dangled that retainer check under my nose and…." I was fighting the impulse to point out that if the agency paid better, I wouldn't be so desperate for money. I also didn't want to mention my speculation that Campbell had set me up on purpose to stir things up. I had no proof of that.

But while I was busy sitting on those impulses, something else slipped out. "Look, the guy turned out to be a jerk. And I'd rather not do the final training with him." I clamped a hand over my mouth. That thought had been in the back of my mind for the last couple of days, but now was definitely not the best time to bring it up.

Another intake and exhale of air, the sigh louder this time. "Which is why it's a conflict of interest. He's bucking to get you fired."

My face heated again, with anger this time. I wanted to shoot back that the agency couldn't fire me. I was an independent contractor, which was how they got around giving me benefits.

But I managed to rein in my tongue. If they cancelled my contract, the next nearest training group was in Jacksonville, over three hours drive from Mayfair, and they trained onsite.

I *really* didn't want to move to Jacksonville.

And, I realized, my anger was at Campbell, not Mattie. First he'd used me as a pawn in his little control game and now he was trying to get me fired, out of spite.

I took another deep breath. "I know this may not come across well right now, but I think he's a drunk. When I went to give him my final report Monday morning, he was drinking something that smelled and looked suspiciously like whiskey, and he was belligerent and slurred his words."

Another beat of silence, only this time there were keys clicking in the background. "I'm looking at his file." Her tone was more normal. "His counselor doesn't mention substance abuse problems."

"Maybe she doesn't know, or maybe the thing he wanted me to investigate has pushed him to start drinking."

"Which was?"

"I'm not sure I can tell you."

This time the sigh was so strong I wouldn't have been surprised if my grocery list had blown across the table. "Marcia, you are not a real P.I."

"Still..."

Silence.

I gave in. Why should I jeopardize my living to protect this jerk's confidentiality? "Campbell doesn't like the guy his younger sister is dating. He wanted me to find some dirt on him to break them up. I could only find some old stuff, from when he was younger. And I like the kid. He and the sister seem to really be in love."

More silence, except for a dull thudding sound in the background. I imagined Mattie banging her head against some hard surface.

"Not now, boy," she said, in a much gentler tone than she'd been using with me. My mental image shifted to her mastiff sitting next to her, his tail thumping on the floor.

"You stay away from him for now," Mattie said into the phone, her voice crisp. "Just finish training the dog. I'll check into the drinking issue and get back to you."

"Thanks, Mattie."

"You're not out of the woods yet." She disconnected.

I sat back in my chair. Air whooshed out of my lungs. Talk about mixed emotions. Of course, fear that I'd lose my training contract was dominant, but there was also relief. With any kind of luck, I'd never have to deal with Roger Campbell again.

And some guilt. I'd hated to squeal on him like that about the drinking, even if he had tried to get me fired, and possibly used me to stir things up.

It wasn't that unusual for veterans with emotional problems to try to self-medicate with booze or drugs, but that tended to rule them out as candidates for a service dog, at least from our agency. We felt an obligation to make sure the dog was going to be well treated.

Not all service dog agencies were that meticulous about screening the recipients of their animals.

Which brought me back to worrying about my job.

The restlessness was now unbearable. I *had* to do something.

Will had said he and his partner weren't always able to keep Marissa Andrews under surveillance. It was a long drive for nothing, if one of them already happened to be there. But if they weren't, I'd be helping them out by keeping an eye on her, wouldn't I?

And, I promised myself, no matter what, I would *not* approach her.

Besides, I could use the surveillance and tailing practice. If I lost my training contract, I might have to become a P.I. in order to eat.

I jumped up. "Come on, boy."

Buddy raised his head from where he'd been napping on the kitchen floor. He gave me a look that I could've sworn was long-suffering. Then he ambled to his feet.

Sherie was happy to lend me the muddy-mobile again, although she was curious as to why my car was still out of commission.

"Will's been so busy with a new case, we haven't had a chance to even take it to the body shop." I didn't mention that it was drivable, I just didn't want to be seen in it.

"I could go with you," Sherie offered.

That small gesture warmed my chest far more than it merited. Between the strain with Will and Mattie's displeasure—granted I had caused both—I was feeling somewhat friendless.

Note to self: Call Becky this evening.

I gave Sherie a big smile. "That would be great. Can you go tomorrow morning?"

"Sure. Say at nine."

I nodded, and she handed over the keys to the Bonneville.

An hour and a half later, I was on Marissa's street. I drove up and down it a couple of times, searching parked cars for any signs of official surveillance. No silhouettes in any of the vehicles and no white truck. Apparently they weren't watching Marissa at the moment.

Okay, I wasn't interfering with the official investigation. And all I would do was follow Marissa from a healthy distance if she left and report to Will if I saw anything helpful.

I parked as far away from the house as I could get and still see her front door. Her car was in the driveway so I figured she was home.

I settled in to wait, daydreaming about Marissa leading me to Gerry Fields and me calling Will to report that I'd found his witness for him.

An hour passed, and then another fifteen minutes. I was bored out of my skull and totally rethinking the whole investigating gig—Will was right about how tedious it could be—when a white sedan pulled up in front of the house.

A young woman got out. Another of Gerry's call girls?

She walked to the front door and rang the bell.

Thirty seconds ticked by. The young woman looked my way just as the door opened.

I sucked in air and my gut clenched.

It was Lexie Campbell.

CHAPTER FOURTEEN

Lexie didn't go inside. Instead, Marissa stepped out on the porch and closed the door behind her.

I let out the breath I'd been holding. At least Lexie wasn't in the lion's den yet.

The two women were talking, and from the body language, it didn't look like a friendly chat. I couldn't tell who grabbed who, but suddenly they were attached to each other, and Marissa was trying to back up into the house, dragging Lexie along with her.

I was out of the car and racing down the sidewalk before I'd had a chance to think. "Let go of her!"

Both women's heads spun in my direction. They broke apart and Marissa disappeared into the house. The door slammed.

Lexie ran down the porch steps and toward me, her face twisted. "Why'd you do that?" she screamed.

I grabbed her by both forearms, resisting the urge to shake her. "What did you think you were doing?"

"Getting her to help!" Her voice was high-pitched, bordering on hysterical. "If I could get her to say that there was no way she could know if Shawn… That it was a bogus charge back then, so why would he kill somebody over it." Her voice broke. She started sobbing.

"Aw, honey." I wrapped my arms around her. "It doesn't matter now what happened back then. Shawn's a suspect because he was being blackmailed."

Lexie practically collapsed in my arms.

"Come on." I half led, half carried her back to the muddy-mobile.

She stopped a few feet from it and stared at the Bonneville. "This is your car?"

"It's a loaner." I opened the passenger door. "Get in. We need to talk."

My own words were niggling at my brain. *It doesn't matter now what happened back then.*

Maybe it did.

"Why should I?" She tried to pull loose from me. "You're working for my brother."

I held on. "Not anymore. I gave him my final report."

"Oh, and what did you report?" Her tone was still hostile.

I let her go. "The truth. That Shawn had been in some scrapes in the past but I thought he'd learned his lesson and was now a responsible person."

Lexie clenched her fists and gritted her teeth. "Oh, I hate him!"

"Your brother?"

"Yes." She spit out the word. "He threw that assault charge up in my face a few months ago and I told him then that I already knew about it, and it didn't matter. And then he went and hired you to find even more dirt on Shawn."

My chest and throat tightened. I'd suspected as much, but she'd now confirmed it. Roger had used me. And he'd used his disability to fool me. That whole smacking-the-arms-of-his-wheelchair, helpless act had been a bit melodramatic, looking back on it.

Note to self: Screen potential P.I. clients much *more carefully!*

Ya think? Ms. Snark added.

I pointed to the muddy-mobile. Without further objection, Lexie got in on the passenger side.

By the time I got around to the driver's side, Buddy had stuck his head over the back of the seat. Lexie was rubbing his ears and he was licking her hand.

Hiding a smile, I climbed in. "Tell me everything you know about what happened at that party."

She stared at me for a beat.

I turned more toward her on the bench seat. "Look, I like you and Shawn. I want to help if I can."

Another half beat, then she nodded and started talking. Her account was pretty much the same as Shawn's.

I hadn't expected it to vary, since it had also come from Shawn originally. But I wanted a refresher, to see if I'd missed anything.

I had.

"Wait," I interrupted, "where was he again when he woke up?"

"Lying next to her."

"And the state of his clothing?"

"Both of their clothes were messed up."

"Did he ever say specifically how his were messed up?"

Lexie squeezed her eyes shut. After a second, she said, "I think he said his belt was unbuckled and his zipper was down."

"But his pants weren't pulled down?"

She shrugged. "I don't know. He never said that they were, just that his roommate and the other guy dragged him out of there and downstairs."

Would he mention if he'd had to pull his pants up first? Maybe, maybe not. But I had a more important question. "So where was the condom?"

"What condom?"

"Exactly. There was nothing they could get DNA from, so a condom was probably used. But nobody's ever said what happened to it. If it had still been there when the police arrived, they would have collected it as evidence and there would have been DNA."

"Maybe there wasn't one. He was drunk after all. Maybe he couldn't...." She stopped, her fair cheeks flushing to a becoming pink.

"Yeah." I flopped back against the car seat, processing. That was what Will had assumed. Certainly possible. But if he didn't even have his pants pulled down. I shook my head. We didn't know that, one way or the other.

None of this added up. Would someone as drunk as Shawn supposedly had been even have the wherewithal to use a condom?

Out loud, I said, "No DNA, no condom. So logic says that either there was no *completed* sexual assault." I didn't mention that even non-consensual drunken fumbling around would still be considered sexual assault, or at least some kind of sex crime. "Or there *was* a condom and somebody got rid of it for some reason."

Lexie bounced a little on the hard vinyl car seat. "And they wouldn't have gotten rid of it if Shawn had really been the one who attacked her."

Probably not, I thought but didn't say out loud. We didn't know who had called the police. Maybe Gerry and Jason had planned to clean up the mess and.... But wait, Marissa had told me that there had been physical signs that she had been forced. Somebody had done something to her that night.

I shook my head again, then noticed that Lexie's body had slumped on the seat. "I can't begin to tell you how...."

Doesn't this girl ever complete a paragraph without trailing off? Ms. Snark complained.

I patted Lexie's hand. "Relieved?"

She nodded. "I hadn't even realized until now that I didn't completely believe him."

"I would have had doubts too, in your shoes. I *have* had doubts all along...."

It was my turn to trail off. I'd been about to say, *but he didn't seem to be the kind of guy who would do that.* But wasn't that what people all too often said when they found out that a neighbor or a family member was a rapist?

What we'd figured out didn't totally clear Shawn, but the whole scenario seemed iffy. No one could bear witness to what happened, not even the supposed victim and perpetrator. And there were so many missing pieces, like why no condom. No wonder the DA's office declined to prosecute.

Lexie was staring at the cracked tan vinyl of the seat.

I put a finger under her chin and lifted it. "You don't need to feel guilty about anything here. You've stuck by him all the way."

"I guess." She pulled her chin free. "I still don't get why you freaked out because I was talking to that Andrews woman."

Because she's probably got contacts with human traffickers, and she could make you disappear. But I couldn't share that with Lexie. That info had come from Will, and he probably shouldn't have told me.

"It looked like she was trying to pull you into the house. She's dangerous."

Lexie frowned. "Why?"

"I can't tell you, but you need to stay far away from her, and her boyfriend. Let me take things from here, okay?"

She grabbed my hand. "You promise you'll find out what really happened?"

"I'll do my best."

For the second time that week, I found myself in an unsolicited hug.

"Give me your cell number," I said when she'd let go.

"Okay, but it's not working right now. I need to buy more minutes."

"Huh?"

"Oh, Roger got mad one day when he got the wireless provider's bill." She gave a little shake of her head. "Said they were robbing us. He cancelled the service and had me go buy us disposable phones. So now we've gotta get minutes added to them every so often. I forgot and mine ran out."

As I rummaged in my purse for my phone, I contemplated how a man could dismiss a thousand dollars he felt I hadn't earned with minimal argument but would go to all that trouble over an excessive wireless bill.

Wait, he actually *had* gotten what he'd wanted from me. Demanding the retainer back was *pro forma*, although I'm sure he would have accepted it if I'd given it to him.

I set up a new contact in my phone for Lexie and she plugged in her number. Then I watched her until she was safely in her car, doors locked and engine on.

As I pointed the muddy-mobile toward home, I immediately began kicking myself. What had I been thinking? I'd just recommitted to playing P.I.

Granted the restless feeling was gone, but it had been replaced by plain old icy fear—fear of the guy in the black SUV and fear of Will's wrath when he found out what I was up to.

I needed a sounding board. At the next stoplight, I called Becky.

With no Bluetooth in the muddy-mobile, I did the next best thing. I put the phone on speaker, turned the volume up and dropped it on the bench seat beside my thigh. I couldn't afford to be distracted. In addition to the normal heavy traffic on I-75, I needed to keep an eye out for black SUVs.

"Hey," I half-yelled when Becky answered, "How you doing?"

"I can't see my feet anymore, but other than that… Probably just as well. Andy says they're pretty swollen."

"Wait, you're what, six months? You shouldn't be that big." And swollen feet didn't sound good either.

"Why are you yelling? Do you have me on speaker?"

"I'm in a borrowed car with no Bluetooth. Did you have a sonogram yet?"

"Yup, this morning. And you know that debate about Buster versus Betty Boop?"

Excitement bubbled in my chest. I was about to find out if I would have a godson or goddaughter. "So which is it?"

"One of each."

I almost drove off the road. "You're having twins?" I screamed.

"Yup."

"Holy cow!"

"I used language a lot stronger than that when the doc told me."

"You're not happy about this? Hey, two babies for the price of one pregnancy. Instant family."

"Yeah, I guess. I... It just hasn't completely sunk in yet, and I am now officially on limited activity for the duration."

"Ugh." She'd already been bored before. Now she'd be climbing the walls.

"I promise to come down and visit soon."

"That would be great. So what's up with you?"

"Um, I'm not sure. Things are kinda confusing right now." I filled her in on recent events—the black SUV, the body in the horse's stall, Will's insistence that I butt out, our having barely gotten back to normal and now....

"I don't know why I said that, Beck. Why did I promise to 'take things from here?'"

A brief pause. "Because you believe in truth, justice and the American way."

"What? You think I have a Superwoman complex? I started down this path for purely selfish reasons, to make more money."

"But now you're doing it for free. And no I don't think you believe you're Superwoman. But you care about people getting a fair shake, and sometimes you care too much. It's gonna get you in too deep one of these days."

I paused for a moment, processing that.

"The guy in the SUV," I said, "he was probably a nutcase, or maybe he was drunk and didn't even realize what he was doing." I didn't really believe that, but I didn't want Becky to worry. I shouldn't have told her that part.

I looked in my rearview mirror. No black SUVs back there.

Becky said, "So why are you convinced the events at that party five years ago have any bearing on this murder? I mean other than the fact that the murder victim was blackmailing Shawn over it. Which does give him a pretty strong motive."

"I don't know. I just feel compelled to find out what really happened back then, even if it doesn't change things now."

Then it hit me. Shawn was pretty torn up about what he believed he'd done. "Maybe he'll still be convicted of murdering his blackmailer," I said, "but if I can find out what really happened at that party, there might be one less black cloud following him to prison."

She sighed. "Be careful, okay? And get down here as soon as you can."

"I will. I promise."

We signed off as I exited I-75.

I breathed my own sigh, this one of relief. No black SUV had tried to run me off the highway. Maybe the guy hadn't intentionally targeted me. Maybe it really was a case of someone having too much to drink with his lunch that day.

Or maybe the muddy-mobile had thrown him off.

Two miles from the turnoff to Mayfair, a black vehicle pulled out of a dirt road up ahead.

Or maybe not, Ms. Snark said.

The black SUV was coming toward me in the opposite lane.

Surely there are lots of black SUVs in Florida, I told myself. Even though I knew that white was by far the most popular vehicle color in the Sunshine State, and black was the least.

The SUV was coming fast. *People often go too fast on this straightaway.* My feeble internal reassurances were doing nothing to calm my pounding heart.

I slowed the muddy-mobile, but there was nowhere for me to go. The shoulders were only half a car's width—one third the width of the massive Bonneville—and they looked pretty soft, more dirt than gravel.

I clutched the steering wheel, my heart in my throat. Gritting my teeth, I vowed that if I had to endure another go-round with the black SUV, I was going to make sure I could identify the driver.

If I survive.

I tried to ignore that thought as I studied the approaching driver. I couldn't see much more than a silhouette. A big person, most likely a man from the breadth of the shoulders. I kept my eyes on him, waiting for him to get closer.

Was that the bill of a baseball cap?

My gaze dropped to the front of the oncoming vehicle, and suddenly I knew why it was black. From this distance, I could barely make out several scratches and buckles, from where dents had once been, in the fender and hood. Such damage would show up more readily on a white vehicle, making it more recognizable.

The front end of the SUV suddenly swerved into my path.

Instinctively I slammed on the brakes and cut the wheel to the right. I caught a glimpse of the SUV's driver out of the corner of my eye as he flashed by. He turned his head to one side, showing me his profile rather than his full face.

And then I was wrestling too strenuously with the big car to worry about him. Its right front tire was off on the soft shoulder and the back end fishtailed into the other lane. I remembered to steer into the spin and barely managed to keep the car from doing a complete three-sixty.

Buddy whined in the backseat. I prayed he was okay.

The car stopped, facing sideways across the country road. I looked around, expecting to see the SUV's brake lights as it approached the curve a half mile back.

Instead it was making a K-turn. The guy was coming back to try again.

Just because you're paranoid... Ms. Snark commented.

I struggled with the big steering wheel—power steering only helps so much when you're driving a tank—and got all four tires back on the pavement. I floored it.

The muddy-mobile coughed twice. *Please don't die on me now!*

The engine roared. I looked in the rearview mirror. A cloud of dark gray smoke erupted from my tailpipe, obscuring my view of the SUV.

I was doing seventy-five by the time I approached the turn-off for Mayfair. The smoke had cleared some behind me, but I still couldn't see the SUV. I slowed, made the turn, then hit the accelerator again. My eyes were more on the rearview mirror than on the familiar road.

I had to slow for the curve in front of the motel but then went as fast as I dared toward the houses at the other end of the street.

All I could think about was getting myself and Buddy safely locked inside my house and calling 911.

I spotted Will climbing out of his truck in front of his house.

"Change of plans," I yelled to Buddy in the backseat.

I flew past my own house and screeched to a halt in front of Will's. The muddy-mobile's engine coughed and died.

Will was staring at me, eyes wide, mouth hanging open.

I jumped out of the stalled car and ran straight into his arms.

CHAPTER FIFTEEN

I really could have used a quiet evening at home, snuggled safely in Will's arms. Instead I was sitting at a metal desk in a bullpen at the sheriff's department, looking at mug shots on a computer.

Will and another detective, not his new partner, were hovering behind me as I studied the monitor in front of me.

My mind wandered for a moment. I hoped Buddy was really okay after all the tossing around in the backseat. Those safety harnesses can only do so much. I'd run my hands over him multiple times, while Will returned the muddy-mobile, apparently none the worse for wear, to Sherie's garage.

The dog seemed fine. I'd left him with an extra chew stick.

Will coughed behind me, bringing my attention back to the task at hand.

I was ignoring the front shots, since I'd only seen a silhouette of his head and shoulders. I pointed to another of the profiles and said, "Maybe."

The other detective, a thirty-something hottie with a stubbled chin and dark, mysterious eyes, leaned over and clicked on that image to move it to a temporary file for further review.

The guy's name was Derek Mills and he was from Vice. It might have been a nice diversion, having him lean close, except he smelled like he hadn't had a chance to go home and shower recently.

"Sorry, guys," I finally said. "My eyes are starting to cross."

Derek lifted one corner of his mouth, the closest he'd come so far to a smile. "Let's take a break and then look through the 'maybe' file."

I stood up and raised my arms in the air to stretch my back. "Any coffee?"

Will snorted. "No, but there's some dark oily stuff that sorta smells like coffee."

"How bad is it?"

"Judge for yourself," Derek said, walking toward the coffee maker on a table along one wall. He picked up a carafe and poured what looked like ink into three mismatched mugs. "There's creamer and sugar if you want it."

I nodded. "One of each." He doctored a mug and handed it to me.

I took a sip. Even with cream and sugar, it was pretty wretched. But I made myself take several more sips, swallowing as quickly as possible so the taste didn't linger on my tongue.

"So what's happening with the sting?" I asked.

Will shot me a quelling look. Derek glanced his way and arched one dark eyebrow in the air.

"Had to tell her something to back her off," Will said.

Derek smirked at him. "Yeah, that worked."

"So are you guys going to take down this prostitution ring or what?" The sight of Amy Chen climbing into Marissa's car was still haunting me, even though I now knew she was a consenting adult.

"Gerry Fields is still in the wind," Will said.

"And until we locate him," Derek added, "we can't do much."

"Has it occurred to you all," I said, "that Gerry might have killed Jason Burrows and framed Shawn Davis for it? And that's why he took off."

Derek shrugged. "Far as we know, Burrows wasn't part of the prostitution operation. He and Fields were friends in college, but they'd drifted apart. Fields had no motive to kill the guy."

I put my mug down on the nearest desk and crossed my arms, trying to think of something else to say to defend Shawn.

"Come on." Will gestured toward the desk I'd been sitting at. "Let's get this done so we can go home. I'm beat."

Guilt unsettled my stomach, which was already unhappy about no dinner and the vile coffee. "I'm sorry this screwed up your evening off."

Will put an arm around me, I thought to steer me toward the computer again. He did that, but he also gave me a squeeze. "I'm just glad you got away from the s.o.b.," he whispered.

I went through the "maybe" file twice, mentally picking out three "likelies." I stared at each of those three again, then pointed to the one with the jowly chin and thick neck. "It could definitely be him."

"Not exactly an I.D. that would stand up in court," Will commented.

Derek cleared his throat. "His name is Brody Johnson."

I stared at the man's profile on the computer screen. The name Brody brought up images of sun-bleached hair and surfboards. This guy was no Brody.

"Or at least, Johnson is his current alias," Derek said from behind me. "His real name is Leonard Hoffman, aka Lenny the Plow. He's had multiple arrests for assault, been convicted twice."

I swiveled around to stare up at him, feeling the blood draining from my face. "Plow, as in he likes to plow people off the road?"

Derek nodded. "He's one of Gerry Fields's thugs."

Will suggested we get some dinner before heading back to Mayfair. My growling stomach seconded the motion.

As we walked out of the sheriff's department into the cool night air, I noted the tension in his body. He might be glad that I got away from Brody aka Lenny, but that didn't mean he was happy with me in general.

Once we were in his truck, I asked, "So what's the deal with your new partner?" I was hoping to forestall a lecture on how one shouldn't blurt out information about sting operations that one wasn't supposed to know about. And, to be honest, I wanted to distract myself from the reality that a convicted felon was trying to kill me.

"Joe Brown? He had another assignment tonight."

Laughter bubbled up. I imagined Ms. Snark slapping her knees and roaring. "That's really his name, Brown? How'd you end up with him? I thought you preferred working alone."

Will grimaced. "He's new to the department. I'm supposed to show him the ropes."

"So I guess that means you're no longer the new kid on the block."

"Guess so." Will stared straight ahead as he drove out Route 200 toward Sonny's Barbeque. In the dim light of the street lamps and commercial buildings along the main artery of western Ocala, I could see that his jaw was still tight.

Apparently my diversion hadn't completely worked.

"What are your plans for tomorrow?" he asked.

"Sherie's going to help me take my car to the body shop." I was congratulating myself on my innocent tone when he gave me a sharp glance.

Returning his gaze to the road, he said, "Are you crazy or just stupid?"

I stared at him, heat burning in my chest.

Who are you, and what have you done with my boyfriend?

I opened my mouth, then clamped it shut again. I was hardly in a position to claim the moral high ground here.

When I could trust my voice, I said, "At the time I set that up with her, I didn't know some thug was going to try to kill me."

He was silent, glaring out the windshield as if he were that other Will —Will Smith slaying rogue robots in his path.

"Look, I'm sorry. I never intended to make contact with–"

"After a while, *sorry* doesn't cut it anymore."

I pursed my lips, counted to ten.

He's got a point, internal Mom said.

Another deep breath. "Can you let me explain? I had no intention of getting anywhere near Marissa Andrews. I was antsy and decided to take a drive, and see if you all were watching her place. If not, I'd keep an eye on her for you for a while."

"You drove an hour and a half each way, in case we didn't have anyone on her right then. You could have called me and I would have told you whether we did or not."

Yeah, like you would have approved my filling in for you.

I was so far past hungry and my insides were so tight, barbeque no longer had much appeal. "Would you mind if we just went home? All I want is a peanut butter sandwich and my bed."

He looked over at me as we passed a streetlight. The lines of his face had relaxed some. "Okay, sure."

Then the sound of air being drawn in. "I'm ordering a patrol car for in front of your house–"

I opened my mouth.

He held up his hand. "This guy knows where you live now, and Sherie might be in danger too."

I shuddered at the thought of Lenny the Plow coming into Mayfair and maybe mowing down my unsuspecting friends and neighbors.

"Okay."

"And I want you to stay home until we catch this guy." His voice was firm, but with an undercurrent of pleading. "We'll deal with getting your car to the shop after that."

My already unhappy stomach twisted with guilt even as my chest warmed. Will really did love me, and all I did was cause him worry.

But the guilt wasn't enough to make me willing to agree to a short leash for an indefinite length of time. For one thing, I wanted to go visit Becky soon.

I chose my words carefully. "I swear that I won't do anything to interfere with your investigation or anything that will put myself in danger until you get him."

I caught a quick glimpse of his pearly whites. "Good." He reached over and picked up my hand from my lap, gave it a squeeze.

I squeezed back.

~

When I glanced out my window the next morning, sure enough a sheriff's department cruiser was in front of the house. I had to admit that I did feel safer.

But the restless feeling was back. What to do with myself until Stephie got here? She had an early morning shift at the Buckland County shelter.

Were there any leads I could pursue to find out more about that party?

I sure as heck wasn't going anywhere near Marissa Andrews again. I might be reckless sometimes, but I'm not completely stupid.

Will might argue with that, Ms. Snark smirked.

I ignored her. *Stupid* had given me an idea. Frat brothers acted pretty stupid at their parties, but if a young man wasn't too drunk to remember them, they were often the highlight of his college career. Ben still told stories, when our mother and my nephews were out of earshot, about his fraternity's escapades.

I called Shawn Davis. After the opening niceties, I said, "Hey, can you get me a list of the guys who were at that party five years ago?"

Silence for a beat. A horse neighed in the background.

My chest tightened. Was that Niña?

"Lemme go inside and call up the website," Shawn said. "There's a roster of each year's new brothers. I can use that to jog my memory."

"Great. Is there contact info available for these guys?"

"For most of them, although it might not be current." The sound of a screen door slamming. "Let me work on this and send you a list. You think you can find out more about what really happened back then?"

"Hopefully." I gave him my email address. "Oh, and tell me again what you remember from when you woke up next to Marissa to when the police arrived."

He did and I listened carefully, noting what was missing. When he finished, I asked, "Were your pants down?"

A long pause.

I'll bet he's blushing, Ms. Snark said.

I shook my head and waited.

"It's all a bit foggy, other than the details I've repeated so many times. But no, I don't remember pulling my pants up."

"And no memory of a condom anywhere?"

"No. Again, that doesn't mean there wasn't one."

"Okay, thanks. Get that list to me as soon as you can."

"Working on it now," he said.

I put my laptop on the kitchen table and opened my email account.

Then I distracted myself with cleaning out the fridge, while keeping an ear peeled for the ping of an incoming email.

I had just thrown out the second plastic container of unidentifiable fuzz when the ping sounded. I jumped into the chair in front of the computer and started to click on the new email.

Reading the sender's name, I sagged in my seat. It was from my mom. I clicked anyway.

It was only one line. *You still alive down there?*

Yes, I responded. *In the middle of something. Will call soon.*

Another ping. This one was from Shawn.

This isn't a complete list yet, but these guys stood out as ones I'm sure were there. Will send a might-have-been-there list soon.

I scanned down this initial list—eight names, with addresses and phone numbers next to them. There were email addresses too, but I figured face-to-face was best, and a phone call second best.

I started by calling the ones who lived out of state. A couple of them were dead ends, the phone numbers listed no longer theirs. But by the end of the morning, I had reached three of the out-of-town frat brothers, although only one remembered the party in question. Unfortunately, he didn't remember any details that added to what I already knew.

I also had appointments to meet with two of the ones who still lived in north central Florida, both in Gainesville.

Despite the lack of tangible results, I was feeling like a real detective.

Shawn had sent me an extended list of brothers who could have been at the party, but he wasn't sure. I'd tackle them later this afternoon or tomorrow.

For now, I needed to change hats and become a dog trainer again.

A thunderstorm was rolling in so we decided to train inside. Stephie added a pen and a water bottle to the items Patches could now retrieve on cue.

"How would you train him to get the water bottle out of the refrigerator?" I asked.

Our dogs were trained to the specific needs of their future veteran owners, so, as a trainer, she would need to innovate new approaches based on the task required.

She thought for a moment, then picked up the kitchen towel lying on my counter. "May I?"

I nodded.

She looped the towel through the fridge's door handle and wrapped one hand around the ends. Calling Patches over, she waved the ends of the towel in his face. Of course, he grabbed them in his teeth, ready to play tug of war.

Only Stephie let go and Patches's tugging almost landed him on his butt as the fridge door opened. "Good dog," Stephie immediately crooned and gave him a treat.

Next time she said the word "Fridge," as she waved the ends of the towel at him. Soon Patches was quite into this new game of Fridge.

Finally she stepped a few feet away from the refrigerator, her hands behind her back, and said, "Fridge."

Patches immediately grabbed for the towel but only got one end. It pulled off the door handle. He looked at Stephie, then shook the towel as if it were prey he'd caught in the wild.

A snicker escaped before I could catch myself.

She glanced my way, smiled a little, and took the towel from the confused dog.

"Tie it to the handle," I suggested.

She did so, waved it in Patches's face again, and said, "Fridge." After a few successful pulls, she once again stood back and just said the word.

Patches grabbed the towel and opened the fridge door.

Stephie repeated that several times.

Then she rolled the water bottle across the floor toward the fridge. "Go get water," she said.

Patches retrieved the bottle and trotted to her with it gingerly held in his teeth. She repeated that several times, then showed him the bottle, said, "Water," and put the bottle on the bottom shelf of the refrigerator door while he watched.

"Fridge," she said. He grabbed the towel and pulled open the door. "Go get water," she quickly added.

He tilted his head to one side.

"Pull the bottle out and set it on the floor," I said.

Stephie did that. "Go get water."

Patches immediately picked the bottle up and offered it to her.

She repeated all those steps several times, pulling the water out of the fridge herself to sit it on the floor, then having the dog bring it to her, giving treats along the way. "Too soon to try again?" she asked after Patches had successfully jumped through all those hoops for the fourth time.

"Maybe, but try anyway."

The water bottle went into the fridge and the door swung closed. Stephie stepped back and said, "Fridge," followed quickly by "Go get water."

The dog opened the refrigerator and pulled the bottle off the shelf with his teeth.

"Woohoo!" Stephie yelled.

Patches dropped the water bottle, and I chuckled. "You sometimes have to keep your enthusiasm to yourself."

She gave me a sheepish look and then ran Patches through the routine three more times.

She glanced at her watch. "I've gotta go soon. I have a night class tonight."

"Okay. I'll reinforce it a few times this evening and again in the morning. But before you go, tell me the three tenets of dog training that you just used, besides the obvious one of rewarding the desired behavior."

The young woman stared at me, her mouth slightly open. "What do you mean?"

"Stephie, you have great instincts for this, and that's a crucial part. But it's important to consciously understand *why* you're doing what you're doing. That way, at times when you feel stuck, you will know intellectually what to try next. So, what were you just now doing as a trainer?"

"Um, when he didn't understand, we broke it down into smaller tasks."

"Yes. It's called shaping. You also built on what the dog already knew by rolling the bottle toward the fridge, a familiar gesture that he knows goes with the 'go get' command. What else?"

She thought for a minute, then shrugged.

"It's the one you did first, and it's perhaps the most important one."

She shook her head.

"You used something that comes naturally to the dog to get him started in the right direction."

She still looked confused.

"By using the towel like a tug toy."

A smile spread across her face. "I didn't even think about it. That just seemed the most logical way to start."

"Exactly." I smiled back. "Like I said, good instincts. And often making a game of the task is a good way to go."

My smile turned into a half smirk. "Now, how would you teach him to close the door again?"

Stephie laughed. "I guess we do need to teach him that too. How do we do that?"

I shook my head, not inclined to make it that easy for her. "Give it some thought. You'll come up with something."

～

I was trying to decide if I was up for calling more frat boys, when the rumble of Will's pick-up going by my house made the decision for me. If he was home this early, he'd be coming over soon.

I quickly gathered up my list of names and other notes I'd made about the brothers I'd already contacted.

Sure enough Will was on my front porch a few minutes later, with a bouquet of mums in his hand—a nonverbal apology for being so cranky yesterday.

"I managed to get away a little early," he said, "so I could help you get your car to the shop."

"Thanks." I took the flowers. "Did you catch Lenny then?"

"No, but there's a BOLO out on him. It's only a matter of time. And it'll take the shop a few days to get your car fixed."

"Lemme put these in water and grab my purse." I didn't have to fake a cheerful tone. It had been a good day and was shaping up to be a good evening.

"Bring Buddy," he called after me as I headed for the kitchen. "We'll stop at Horse and Hounds for dinner after we drop your car off."

Yeah, definitely gonna be a good evening!

Out on the front walk, Will handed me his keys. "You take the truck. I'm going to drive your car, in case your friend Lenny shows up."

I stopped and put my hands on my hips. "Why is it better for *you* to be in jeopardy rather than me."

Will sighed. "Because *I've* had training in evasive driving. If you see any vehicle getting too close to me, you drop back and stay out of the way."

"Oh." I dropped my arms to my sides. "Okay. I'll make sure your truck doesn't get dinged up."

"Thank you," he said with exaggerated patience.

I settled Buddy in the small backseat of Will's pickup and then climbed into the driver's seat. It took a few minutes to get stuff adjusted so I could reach the things I needed to reach and see the things I needed to see out of the mirrors.

I flashed the lights to signal Will, and he pulled away from the curb in my car.

The switch in drivers turned out to be unnecessary. We drove to the auto body shop on Route 200 without incident and turned my car over to them.

The owner of the shop greeted me by name. I wasn't sure how to feel about that.

The Horse and Hounds Restaurant wasn't too crowded yet, as it was still early. We sat at a black metal-mesh table on the side patio and Buddy settled at my feet. The sun was beginning to sink toward the Western horizon.

I shivered a little as a cool evening breeze floated across a nearby field, bringing with it the scent of freshly mown hay, the first cut of the season. "Should've brought a sweater."

"I'd lend you my shirt…" It was a long-sleeved chambray, one of his favorites, and mine too because it matched his eyes. Will pointed his chin to something behind my back. "But that lady over there is already checking me out."

I intentionally dropped my napkin, so I could lean over and steal a look. Sure enough, a middle-aged woman farther down the patio was staring at us. I couldn't make out her face under the shadow of her table's umbrella, but she seemed vaguely familiar.

I retrieved the napkin, sat up and grinned at Will. "She's got good taste."

Once we'd ordered our food and had drinks in front of us—a beer for him and I'd decided to indulge in a margarita—his face grew serious. "Marcia, I want to ask you something and please think about it for a few minutes before you answer."

Uh, oh. I braced myself and nodded.

"I'd rather be officially engaged, but I understand that you're not comfortable with that yet. But can we agree that we are definitely headed in that direction. Sort of a pre-engaged status."

I opened my mouth, but he held up his hand. "Think about it first."

Okay, if you insist. I'd been about to say yes. I might be resistant to the idea of getting married again, but I knew if and when I ever did, it would be to him. I figured he wouldn't feel encouraged by the "if and when I ever did" part. Best to leave that out.

I opened my mouth again. "When I can get past–"

"Ms. Hanks, is that you?" A woman's voice with a slight twang.

CHAPTER SIXTEEN

Will's eyebrows went up. "Ms. *Hanks*?"

I looked up to find Shawn Davis's mother hovering beside our table. She was accompanied by a gray-haired, rotund gentleman whom I assumed was Shawn's father.

"Hi, Mrs. Davis. Good to see you." I was just being polite. Her timing couldn't have been worse.

"I wanted to thank you for… Wait," she was staring at Will more intently now, "aren't you the detective on the case?"

"The Burrows case, yes," Will said.

"So are you two discussing the case?" Mr. Davis said, his voice gravelly.

"No, we're having dinner." A note of sarcasm in Will's tone.

It apparently went over Mr. Davis's head. "The question is *why* are you having dinner?" he demanded.

His wife shot him a quelling look, which he ignored.

Because we were hungry, Ms. Snark said in my head, but I managed not to blurt it out.

"We're dating." I gave Mrs. Davis a bright smile, intentionally avoiding eye contact with her husband.

Don't look an alpha dog in the eye.

"When did this start?" Davis asked in a belligerent voice. "When you met at our place?"

"No," Will drew the word out some, in a low, irritated tone. "We've been going together for over a year."

Davis took a step forward, nudging his wife slightly to the side. "I don't quite understand this."

His wife tugged at his sleeve. "Everett, please."

He shrugged her off. "How is it that the private investigator working on my son's case to clear him is dating the police detective who's trying to put him away?"

The waiter had arrived with our food and was trying in vain to get past the Davises. "Excuse me."

Mr. Davis ignored him.

Will stood up. He towered over Davis. "Mr. And Mrs. Davis, I will be happy to discuss the case with you," his tone said he wasn't the least bit happy, "either by phone or at the sheriff's department, when I am *on* duty. But at the moment, our food is getting cold."

A rumbling growl came from my feet. I reached blindly for Buddy, not willing to take my eyes off of the tableau in front of me. He'd sat up under the table, his head sticking partway out below the metal-mesh top. I found his collar and held it firmly.

Either the big dog or the big cop, or both, made Davis rethink his belligerence. "Harumph," he muttered and turned on his heel.

"I'm so sorry," Mrs. Davis whispered before hurrying after him.

Will sat back down, and the waiter quickly placed our plates on the table, then scurried off without the usual *Is there anything else I can get you?*

I glanced surreptitiously at the other diners scattered along the patio. Some were staring at us. Others were acting a little too interested in their own meals.

I looked down at my fish and chips, with the "chips" extra crispy, just as I'd ordered them. Unfortunately, they'd lost some of their appeal.

Will was expressing his annoyance with the interruption a bit differently. He slashed his steak knife across the T-bone on his plate and forked a bite into his mouth, then whacked his baked potato in half and slathered each side with butter. His movements were sharp, his gaze on his plate.

"I'm concerned about Buddy," I said. Maybe if I started us on a different subject, I could get things back on track. "He's been doing that more lately, growling when he thinks I'm in danger."

Will looked up at me, his baby blues not exactly icy but not totally warm and loving either. "And that's a bad thing why?"

"Well, that's what I'm trying to decide. Technically, he's breaking training because service dogs are not supposed to be for protection." Will already knew that but I kept blathering, hoping to distract him. "They're supposed to wait for instructions from their owners, rather than react instinctively like that."

"You might not be having this problem if you didn't put yourself in danger quite so often."

Okay, he had a point there.

"I don't do that intentionally." And if I was going to keep doing this P.I. stuff, it might be good to have a big dog ready to go all protective on someone trying to hurt me.

"Not much you don't." Will's tone would have done Ms. Snark proud. "What did Davis mean about you helping to clear their son?"

I took a deep breath. "Look, I'm staying well away from Marissa Andrews and that whole operation. I'm only checking with some of the frat brothers, trying to find out what really happened five years ago."

"You think that party's related to the murder?" Will put another bite of steak in his mouth and cut off a chunk of potato.

"I don't know, but you all aren't looking at that, are you?"

He shook his head, his expression almost back to normal. "Honestly, we don't have the man hours to do that. We're watching Andrews's house when we can and tracking down leads on Gerry Fields."

"You still haven't found him?"

Will shook his head again and shoveled some potato into his mouth. He swallowed, then pointed his fork at my fish. "Something wrong with your food?"

"No." I took a bite of fish and picked up a french fry to nibble on. "So I figured talking to these frat boys wouldn't be dangerous."

"You didn't think looking into young Davis's background for Campbell would be dangerous either."

"True." I finished the french fry and ate another bite of fish.

"Why did Mrs. Davis call you Ms. Hanks? You posing as Tom Hanks' sister these days?"

"Oh, I had this stupid idea early on that I should use a fake identity. So I made it Mary Hanks. That way, if someone found out my real name later, I could pretend that's what I'd said all along, and they misheard me."

Will stared at me for a beat. The corners of his mouth twitched. Then his lips parted, exposing his pearly whites. His grin widened.

"Are you laughing at me?"

He shook his head. "No, not at all." But his baby blues were twinkling now.

"Well, it sorta worked with Shawn. He didn't react when I called him earlier and forgot and said my real name. I guess he and Lexie have talked about me, and she knows me as Marcia. He must've assumed he misheard me when I said Mary."

He was still staring at me, that grin on his face.

"What?"

"One thing for sure," he said, "life is never dull around you."

I reached for another french fry. "Look, I'm sorry I make you crazy–"

He grabbed my hand. "Marcia, *you* don't make me crazy. Putting yourself in danger, that's what makes me crazy."

His face suddenly sobered. "And your name change may have worked with Marissa Andrews. Lenny the Plow would have found you a lot sooner if he'd had your real name."

That sent a chill through my body that had nothing to do with the evening breeze.

"I don't know which way to go with this P.I. thing," I said. "I enjoy the investigating, and I think I'm pretty good at it. But I *don't* enjoy the danger." Being chased by that thug was right up there on my five worst moments of my life list. Just below having a gun pointed at me and just above finding out my ex-husband was cheating on me.

I poked at my fish with my fork.

Will sighed. "Hey, if you want to be a P.I., well, who am I to say you can't. My job is dangerous too."

I glanced up. The loving look was back in his baby blues.

"Yes," I said.

His brow wrinkled in confusion. "Yes, you want to be a P.I.?"

I shook my head. "Yes, I'm okay with being pre-engaged."

By the time we left the restaurant, we were both flying high. Me because of the margarita, plus two glasses of champagne from the half-split Will had ordered to celebrate.

His high was more a natural one, since he'd only had one glass of the sparkly stuff. He still had to drive us home.

We headed for his truck. Buddy growled at the darkness at the far end of the parking lot.

"Buddy! Sheez, now he's growling at shadows." I stopped walking and held my hand out flat. He touched my palm with his nose.

"Behave," I told him.

Will decided to take the back roads. He lowered the windows halfway to let the pleasant night air wash over us, and keep him alert.

We rode in companionable silence, holding hands on the truck's console between us. As he turned onto Highway 42, which led eventually to Mayfair, I glanced his way. With nothing but the dashboard lights to illuminate the cab, I could barely see his profile. But I could make out his pearly whites. He was still smiling.

"Gee, if I'd known getting pre-engaged would make you so happy I would have said yes–"

I never got the *sooner* out. Will was turning his head toward me, when bright lights flared outside his side window.

Before my brain could register what was happening, an engine roared and the lights surged ahead. A dark shadow veered toward the truck's front fender.

My heart leapt into my throat and my stomach hollowed out.

The screeching sound of metal meeting metal rent the night air.

CHAPTER SEVENTEEN

The truck's right tires careened off onto the shoulder. Will wrestled with the steering wheel.

"Call 911," he yelled.

I frantically rummaged through my purse for my phone. When I looked up, we were stopped, a little skewed to one side, but still upright. And the lights of the other vehicle were also stopped, about a hundred yards ahead.

Its backup lights came on.

"I've got a little surprise for you, bozo," Will growled. He reached under his seat and came up with an object. I couldn't make out what it was. He flipped a switch on it and suddenly a blue strobe was pounding against my eyeballs.

"Ack!" I held up my hand to shield my eyes. Heart racing, I punched 911 into my phone and put it on speaker.

Will reached out his window and placed the flashing light on the truck's roof.

The backup lights ahead of us went off.

"Nine-one-one. What is the nature of your emergency?" filled the truck cab.

Will jammed the truck into gear. "Detective William Haines," he yelled. "Marion County Sheriff's Department."

The engine screamed and gravel spewed, some of it banging against my side of the truck. We shot forward.

"I need back up on SE Highway 42, approximately two miles east of 441. Someone intentionally tried to run us off the road. I am in pursuit, headed east on 42."

The dispatcher reported that back-up was on the way.

I looked down the road. Taillights lit up. The vehicle had slowed for a curve.

I expected Will to slow as the taillights disappeared and we approached the curve. "Hang on," he yelled.

My right hand was already curled around the grab bar above my window. I twisted my left arm around as best I could to reach between the seats and grab Buddy's safety harness to help steady him. I think I screamed when we hit the curve at almost full speed.

Buddy whined as centrifugal force tried to throw him off his feet. His weight pulling on my arm threatened to snap it in two.

Blood pounding in my ears, I clamped my mouth shut to keep from asking Will to slow down. I wanted him to catch this guy.

We were gaining on him as we approached the turn off for Mayfair. The guy kept going and so did Will.

Another curve was coming up fast. Will slowed a bit more than last time. I suspected it was as much about Buddy's whining as my screaming.

The taillights ahead disappeared.

"Don't worry," Will yelled over the straining engine and the air blowing through his open window. "I'll catch him on the next straightaway."

But he didn't have to. On the other side of the curve, our headlights lit up the back end of a black SUV, nose down in a ditch across the road.

Will slammed on his brakes. As the truck careened to a stop, he shoved the gearshift into park and jumped out of the truck, almost all in one motion. He was across the road in two strides and yanking on the driver's door, his gun in his hand.

"Get out slow," he yelled. "Hands where I can see them."

A dark pant leg appeared, then a person crawled out after it. The man stood, facing away from me, his hands held in the air. I recognized the silhouette of his broad shoulders and thick neck.

Will tried to get me into the observation area next to the interview room where he and his partner were interrogating the SUV driver. His captain vetoed the idea, but the effort made my heart warm.

I ended up waiting in the detectives' bullpen. I was nodding off in his desk chair when he nudged my feet, propped up on one corner of his desk.

"Is it that Brody/Lenny guy? Did he confess?" I dropped my feet to the floor, forgetting in my fog that Buddy was under my chair.

He jerked back a little. My heel had barely missed his nose. "Sorry, boy." I leaned over to check on him and almost fell off the chair when my head swam. I was exhausted.

Will put a steadying hand on my shoulder. "Come on. I'll tell you all about it on the way home." His voice sounded as tired as I felt.

Once we were all in his now-somewhat-battered truck, Buddy secured in the mini-backseat, Will said, "Yes, he's Leonard Hoffman, aka Lenny the Plow. His uncle owns an auto shop in Ocala. Lenny gets the family package—a small discount, fast work and no record that his vehicle was ever there."

"Did he talk?"

Will's teeth flashed white in the dark cab. "Squealed like a stuck pig."

I smiled to myself. He was beginning to pick up my "motherisms."

"When he realized he'd almost killed a cop, he practically wet himself." Will chuckled, then his voice sobered, "He'd been following your car, but realized you weren't driving. He called Marissa Andrews to report you were with a man. He described me, and she said to take us both out. But she didn't bother to mention that I was with the sheriff's department."

My throat closed. "So I almost got you killed, or you almost got me killed?"

He glanced my way, his expression grim. "I guess a little of both."

"Did he say why he tried to run me off the road before?"

"Only that he was under orders from Gerry Fields to follow you, and if you, quote, 'kept pokin' around Shawn Davis or Marissa' he was to take you out."

I shuddered. "Fields was afraid my poking around would expose his prostitution ring."

Will nodded. "Most likely. Vice flipped Lenny. He's going to help bring them down."

I wasn't sure how I felt about that. The man who'd tried to kill me on three occasions was going to get a lighter sentence because he helped bring down a group of criminals that the police already knew existed.

"He's going to tell Marissa he succeeded in wrapping us around a tree, and we're either dead or in the hospital. Which means I have to keep a low profile and you..." he glanced away from the road to give me a pointed look, "need to keep your nosy self in Mayfair."

I didn't respond, not willing to make a promise I might not be able to keep. "What's 'low profile' mean?" I said instead.

Will grimaced. "That I have to stay at the department while my partner works with Vice. The good news is I'll be able to come home at a decent hour most nights."

Note to self: if I go out investigating, get home well before five.

The next morning, I was relieved to see the sheriff's department cruiser was gone. Apparently Will trusted Lenny to keep his word, and me to stay put. The twinge of guilt I felt about the latter was offset by a touch of anger.

I hadn't wanted to fight with Will about it last night. We were both wrung out.

But I had no intention of canceling my appointments with the frat boys. I felt like I was on the verge of discovering something important.

I was, however, going to take precautions.

Buddy and I went for an early walk and lay in wait for Edna. Today's muumuu was turquoise, with big white lilies on it.

We chitchatted while our dogs played in the field across from the motel. "Say, you wouldn't happen to have any wigs, would you?" I asked, trying to sound casual.

"Might have." Edna glanced sideways at me. "Why?"

"Um, I'm trying out for a part in a play, up in Gainesville."

"Long drive for rehearsals. Bennie, Bo, come here, boys."

They ignored her, but when I called Buddy over, they followed. "It's just a community theater thing." I clipped Buddy's leash back on. "I don't think they'll rehearse more than once a week or so."

Edna and "the boys" led the way to the motel steps. "Had some wigs from when my sister-in-law had...was sick."

She always avoided saying the word *cancer*. She came from the generation that thought if you didn't talk about the "big C" then it somehow wasn't real.

"Not sure what kinda shape they're in though," she added. "They'd been out in the shed."

That explained how they could still be around. The motel had burned to the ground last spring and Edna had lost almost everything she owned.

One of the wigs was dry-rotted. But a short blonde puffy one had been kept in a hat box and was in pretty good shape. "Susanna's mama didn't like that one much. She wore the other one more."

I hid a smile. Edna might not like to talk about cancer but she mentioned her long-lost niece every chance she got, always with a dreamy look on her face. Said long-lost niece had been found and reunited with her family last December, thanks to Will and me. Bringing Susanna back to Edna had finally appeased my guilt about indirectly causing the motel fire.

I tried on the wig.

Edna grimaced. "It's kinda old-fashioned."

I almost laughed out loud. If Edna thought that, it was way beyond old-fashioned and into downright archaic territory.

"Uh, the play's set in the seventies," I said, "so this should work fine." I figured I could work with it and maybe get some of the puffiness out.

"You need other wardrobe stuff as well? Yer about Susanna's size and her wardrobe is definitely stuck in the seventies."

This from a woman wearing a neon muumuu and flip-flops.

She led the way to her niece's room.

Susanna jumped up off her bed where she'd been reading. She was in her early sixties, but she still moved, and to some extent acted like a young woman. "Marcia!" She greeted me with a hug.

"Susie," Edna said, "she needs to borrow some clothes for a play she's tryin' out fer."

"Sure. Whacha need?" Susanna threw open her closet door.

I was glad to see she had gotten over her shyness some, with me at least.

"I need something that says seventies," I said, "without being too flamboyantly so."

"Hmmm." She stared at her clothes for a moment, hand on her chin. Then she pulled out a pale blue peasant blouse. "How 'bout this? You can wear it on the shoulders, or off." She wiggled her eyebrows suggestively.

I laughed out loud. "Perfect. I'll wear it over my skinny jeans and hopefully I'll look like a teenaged girl."

"What's the play?" Susanna asked, her blue eyes sparkling.

"Um, Under the Boardwalk," I improvised. "You know, like the old song."

"Sounds like fun. Break a leg."

"Thanks," I said, praying that wouldn't literally happen. If Marissa Andrews found out I was alive and well and still investigating, she'd send Lenny the Plow after me again.

Or maybe it would be Will who'd break something if he found out what I was up to.

～

I didn't look like a teenager, but I also didn't look like myself as I climbed out of the muddy-mobile in sunglasses and the wig and peasant blouse get-up. I figured the old Bonneville completed the "blast from the past" persona.

If my outfit said I was stuck in the seventies, Harold Long's living room said he was stuck in college student mode. An old saggy couch, a literal orange crate for a coffee table, and some lawn chairs constituted the furniture. The rest of the floor was littered with, well, litter—pizza boxes predominantly.

Buddy sniffed at one. "Leave it," I said. I kept my voice low, even though Harold had left the room to fetch the glass of water he'd offered. He'd offered beer as well, but I figured nine-thirty in the morning was a little early for that.

Buddy looked at me and his big tongue came out and licked his snout.

"We don't know how old that is," I whispered.

Harold came back into the room, a glass of grayish water in one hand and a beer bottle in the other. "Have a seat wherever." He handed me the water.

I pretended to take a sip, then placed the glass on the orange crate as I settled on the couch.

My first mistake of the day. The couch swallowed me up. The peasant blouse slipped off one shoulder as I struggled my way back to the edge.

Harold leered.

I adjusted the blouse and perched on the front of the squishy cushions. Buddy settled at my feet.

Taking off my sunglasses, I said, "So Harold, tell me what you remember about that party five years ago?"

"Call me Hal." He leered again. "As for that party, I don't remember much. I was pretty wasted. But when the cops came... well, let's just say that seeing uniforms tends to sober ya up some."

"So what happened when the cops came?"

"The girl, Marissa, she was Gerry's regular hump."

I winced at his language.

"She was still out of it," Harold-call-me-Hal continued, "up in Gerry's and Shawn's room. But Gerry and that friend of his, Jason, they were hauling Shawn down the stairs. Gerry was yelling, 'Who the H called the cops?' But then Jason said maybe it was for the best, or something like that."

I moved my assessment of this guy's sensibilities up a notch. He'd apparently noticed my wince. I doubted seriously that Gerry had said "who the *H*" at a drunken frat party.

"Then what happened?"

He squeezed his eyes shut. "Guys were scrambling around, hiding stuff, you know, that they didn't want the cops to see. And the girls were straightening their clothes." He opened his eyes.

"What happened with Gerry and Jason and Shawn?"

"Oh, Gerry dropped Shawn's arm and gave Jason a dirty look. Then he went back upstairs and slammed his door."

"So he didn't seem to like what Jason said?"

"Yeah, and he was kinda reluctant when they were telling the cops what happened. Jason did most of the talking, saying they found Shawn on top of Marissa in his bed."

"And where was Marissa at this point?"

"A lady cop had gone up to talk to her. She brought her down a few minutes later. Marissa was crying. They took her to the hospital, I think."

"They being the cops?"

"Yeah. Gainesville PD, not the campus cops, since our frat house was off campus."

"When Gerry and Jason brought Shawn down the stairs, what was the state of his clothes?"

He squeezed his eyes closed for another couple of seconds, then opened them. "His shirt was untucked and I think I remember his belt hanging down on one side."

I paused, giving him time to add something if he wanted to.

"His pants weren't threatening to fall down though?" I asked.

"Nope, I think I would've remembered that." He grinned.

I struggled to keep my face neutral. This guy might be a UF graduate, which meant he had some smarts, but his maturity level was stuck back in middle school.

"Can you remember anything else about the party that might be relevant?"

He shook his head, but then raised his hand. "Wait, I remember thinking Marissa was a bit of a 'ho."

I clenched my teeth and struggled again with my expression. Typical sexist reaction, to blame the victim.

"Why was that?" I said when I thought I could trust my voice to stay even.

"'Cause I'd seen her in another room earlier, with some other guy."

"What were they doing?"

"They were in bed, you know…" He moved his hips in a suggestive way and grinned at me.

I tried not to gag. This guy was a piece of work.

"Do you remember whose room it was?"

He cocked his head, thought for a beat. "Nope, just some bro's room. They'd left the door open even. I watched for a while." His grin was back.

"Did you recognize the guy?"

"Nope, didn't get a good look at him, only his hair and his bare back."

"What color hair?"

"Brown. That's how I knew it wasn't Gerry. His hair's blond. And I'd just seen him, a few minutes before, headed for the kitchen."

"Well, thanks for your time." I put my hand on the edge of the soggy couch. The peasant blouse slid off my shoulder again as I pushed myself to a stand.

He jumped up. "But you haven't finished your water. Wouldn't you like something stronger?"

"No, I'm fine." I took a step toward the door.

He moved into my path.

Crapola! Second mistake of the day.

I'd let Horny Hal get between me and the door.

CHAPTER EIGHTEEN

A low rumble, deep in Buddy's throat. He stood beside my knee, the hair up along his back.

Harold stared down at him. I think he'd forgotten the dog was even there.

He swallowed hard, his Adam's apple bobbing in his scrawny neck. Taking a step back, he said, "Well, I've gotta get to class anyway."

"Oh, you're still in school?" I said pleasantly as I started toward the door. Buddy kept pace with me but watched the man's every move.

"Grad school."

I had to begrudgingly up my assessment of his intelligence. UF was hard enough to get into as an undergraduate—it was even harder to get into their graduate programs.

"Again, thanks." I considered asking him if he still had my number under his recent calls, in case he thought of anything else, but decided against that.

"Sure. No prob." He nodded and quickly got out of Buddy's way.

I suppressed a grin.

The other guy had agreed to meet me for an early lunch at eleven. I got to the fast food place near the mall on Newberry Road at a few minutes before.

Yesterday, I'd told Danny Stevens I had reddish-brown hair so he'd recognize me. That was before Lenny the Plow had tried his plow maneuver on us and I'd somehow ended up under "house arrest." I found a parking spot in the shade and took the wig off.

I made a face in my visor mirror. The only thing worse than hat hair is wig hair. I fluffed it out as best I could, then put my sunglasses back on.

Danny found me while I was standing in line to get an egg burrito—I love fast food places that have breakfast all day long. He tapped me on the shoulder, making me jump.

"Sorry." He jammed his hands into the pockets of his khaki slacks, as if they'd done something offensive. His brown hair was cropped short and he wore a navy golf shirt with the Florida Gators logo on the left shoulder.

"No problem. You want anything?" I said, hoping he wasn't a big eater. I only had fifteen bucks on me.

"Just a Coke, if you don't mind."

He's a breath of fresh air after that other clown. Mom this time. I silently agreed.

I tried chit-chatting with him while I got my food and our drinks. His mostly one-word answers were said in a quiet, almost shy voice.

I gestured toward the door, soda cup in hand. "Let's sit outside so I can get my dog out of the car."

We settled at a table far enough away from the road I figured no one driving by would be able to recognize me. The other outside tables were unoccupied.

Buddy flopped down in the shadow cast by our table on the sidewalk.

"So what do you remember about that party?" I asked, then bit off a big chunk of the burrito. The apple I'd grabbed for breakfast on the way out the door this morning had long since worn off.

He shook his head. "I've been straining to remember more since we talked yesterday. But I wasn't there very long."

My body slumped. It was looking like this trip to Gainesville would be a bust.

"I wasn't that into the drunken parties." He ducked his head. "Weed was more my thing. I had a meet with my dealer that night. When I got back to the frat house, the party was in full swing. I figured I'd have a couple of beers and then go up to my room and...."

He played with his straw, still in its wrapper. "I didn't want to light up in front of the other guys. If they saw what I had, they'd expect me to share, and...well, I'd paid quite a lot for it. So I got out of there as soon as I heard sirens. I didn't want to have to flush it."

Florida had recently legalized medical marijuana, but five years ago, it was still totally illegal. And even today, I doubt the police would buy the story that frat boys were smoking reefers for medicinal purposes.

"I don't do that stuff anymore," Danny quickly added. "I'd lose my job if I got caught."

"Where do you work?" I asked, mostly to be polite.

He tilted his head toward the chain bookstore that anchored the strip shopping center behind us. "I'm the assistant buyer."

"Oh yeah. That sounds interesting."

He gave me a shy smile. "Sometimes it is."

"So what did you see at the party, before you left?"

"I don't remember Marissa being there at all, although I knew her. She often came to the parties with Gerry, her boyfriend." He paused, took the lid off his drink and took a swig. "The only thing I could come up with that might be relevant was something I saw a little earlier."

He looked down and fiddled with the straw again.

I let the silence spin out as I took another bite of burrito. It was *so good!*

"Gerry and his friend were hauling Shawn Davis up the stairs. He'd passed out on the couch in the main room. I assumed they were taking him to bed."

I perked up. This guy might not have been at the party very long, but he was probably the only brother there whose brain cells hadn't been addled by drugs or alcohol, which made him a far more credible witness. "*Up* the stairs, not down?"

He looked up, his brow furrowed in confusion. "Yes, up."

"And the friend, it was Jason Burrows?"

He nodded. "I don't think I ever knew his last name though, back then. Of course, I've seen it on the news, since his murder."

"You saw them taking Shawn upstairs before or after someone called the cops?"

"Before. Like I said, I got out of there when I realized the cops were coming. But it wasn't long before, maybe ten minutes. I remember I glanced at my watch and thought, 'Wow, it's only ten o'clock and already someone's that gone. And then when I was outside in my car, leaving, my dashboard clock said ten-fifteen, and I laughed to myself that it was the shortest party I'd ever been to."

"And the someone 'that gone' was Shawn Davis?"

Danny nodded again. "He was totally passed out. They were pretty much dragging him."

"So they put Shawn in his and Gerry's room?"

He shrugged. "I don't know where they took him. I just assumed it was to his room."

Something occurred to me that I hadn't bothered to ask anyone yet. "Do you have any idea who called the police?"

"Actually, when I was thinking about all this last night, I remembered some girl up on the walkway. The main living room was open, you know, with a cathedral ceiling." He raised his hands and spread them wide. "And there was this walkway, kinda like a balcony, around the upper level, where the bedrooms were. This girl was right by the door to Shawn and Gerry's room and she was crying and pointing into the room. And she had a phone to her ear."

"Did this girl know Marissa?"

"I don't know," Danny said.

"Okay." I did make sure he had my number in his phone. "If you think of anything else."

"Sure. Um, for what it's worth, I remember thinking the next day that it didn't sound like something Shawn would do. He seemed to have more respect for women than that. Gerry and Jason on the other hand…."

I quickly finished off the burrito and wiped my gooey fingers on a napkin. I offered my hand to Danny. "Thanks for your time."

He took my hand tentatively, then dropped his gaze as he shook it. "Not sure I was all that much help."

I gave him a smile. "You can only report on what you honestly remember."

He smiled back and it lit up his otherwise ordinary face.

"You should smile more often," I blurted out.

Danny's cheeks turned pink.

"Thanks again for your time." I hustled Buddy and myself to my car before I could stick my foot in my mouth again.

The wig once more in place, I pointed the muddy-mobile toward home. Even though I knew Lenny the Plow was no longer out to get me, I still glanced at the rearview mirror every few seconds.

Third mistake of the day—not checking on Will's whereabouts before returning to Mayfair. His truck was in front of his house when I drove down our street.

He'd said he'd be home at a decent hour, but one o'clock?

I quickly pulled the muddy-mobile into Sherie's garage and tore off the wig. With Buddy in tow, I snuck across her front yard to my own porch.

Praying he hadn't seen us, I unlocked the door and hurried to my bedroom to change my clothes. I hid the wig and peasant blouse on my closet shelf.

Then I raced to the kitchen and took some chicken out of the freezer to defrost in the microwave. If he had seen me, I'd say I'd only gone as far as the Belleview meat market to get him something nice for dinner.

I was chopping veggies for a salad when I froze, knife mid-air. When did it get so easy to devise lies to tell Will?

Okay, I wouldn't confess if he hadn't seen me, but if he had, I'd tell the truth.

But I wanted to share with him the information I'd gotten. Well, I could pretend I talked to the two frat brothers on the phone.

Oh the tangled web we weave, Ms. Snark commented.

I didn't even bother to tell her to shut up. She was right.

My insides twisted with guilt. It wasn't only the lies. We'd just gotten pre-engaged and here I'd gone off and done exactly what he'd told me not to do.

The word *told* stuck a little bit in my mental craw.

Okay, I'd say I talked to the guys but wouldn't say when or how, unless he asked. Yeah, I could live with that little sin of omission.

I tossed the veggies into my best plastic salad bowl, snapped the lid on and stuffed it in the fridge, along with the defrosted chicken.

I would make him a nice dinner later, but first I'd work with Patches for a while, and at least appease that part of my guilty conscience.

By three p.m., I'd reinforced everything the dog had been taught so far, including the "go get water" command that Stephie had taught him the day before. I opted not to start him on anything new. I'd wait for Stephie, who was coming tomorrow morning.

I took a quick shower and was debating if I should call Will to see what time he wanted dinner, when my doorbell rang. I peeked out the window. Speak of the devil.

He had a key but usually rang the bell, in case I was in the middle of training.

I opened the door, then wished I'd looked a little harder out the window first.

Susanna was strolling down the road toward us. She waved and called out, "How'd the audition go, Marcia?"

Will's brows drew together and he narrowed his baby blues at me.

Busted.

Standing on my tiptoes on the threshold, I waved to Susanna over Will's shoulder. "Great! Thanks again."

"Hey," I said to him, a big fat smile plastered on my face, "I saw your truck earlier. You got home *really* early."

His expression did not soften. "Audition?"

"Oh, I was thinking about trying out for...." I caught myself in mid-lie. Swallowing hard, I stepped back from the door and gestured for him to come in. I began again, "I borrowed a wig and blouse from her, for a disguise, but I told her I was trying out for a play."

He stepped over the threshold and handed me a plastic pie container from the grocery store. *Pecan Pie, made with Florida pecans*, the label announced. My mouth watered.

Then my throat closed. He'd been getting me something sweet while I was out gallivanting behind his back.

I hung my head. "I was careful that I wasn't seen by anyone who could identify me, but I already had appointments set up with two of the frat brothers."

Will's frown deepened and he blew out air. "Marcia, this is not a game. If Andrews or Fields finds out you're still alive and walking around injury-free, Lenny Hoffman's life could be in danger."

I guess I should have felt even more guilty about that, but it pissed me off instead.

"First the guy tries to kill me—three times! And now I'm a prisoner in Mayfair because his criminal buddies might hurt him if somebody sees me." I heard the rising pitch of my voice and stopped to take a breath. Slightly calmer, I asked, "Does that sound fair to you? And why wasn't I consulted before you all decided I had to play dead?"

To my surprise, Will's angry expression deflated. "Look, I don't want to fight with you. You're right, it's not fair, and we should've consulted you first."

Well, stick a pin in our balloon, why doncha? Ms. Snark said inside my head.

Will's temper might flair easily, especially when my safety was at stake, but reason quickly reasserted itself—reason, love and fairness. It was one of the many things I loved about him, normally.

"Oh," was all I could think of to say out loud. "Um," I led the way to the kitchen, "I've got some chicken and a salad for our dinner."

I put the pie down on my counter and turned around. Will had a weird expression on his face. "What's the matter?"

"Nothing." He glanced at his watch, his face still all twisted up funny. "It's early enough we could have some pie now, and it wouldn't spoil our dinner."

"Sure. I'll make some coffee."

"Great!" A big grin split his face, a bit more enthusiasm than even pecan pie should merit.

Feeling slightly off-kilter, I got the coffee maker rolling while he pulled out paper plates, mugs, forks and a sharp knife to cut the pie.

He sat down at the kitchen table, carefully arranged everything at our places, then shoved the pie over in front of me. "Here, you do the honors." His odd, twisty face was back.

Wondering when he'd become such a neatnik, I broke the seal on the clear plastic container and popped the top off. And there smack in the middle of the pie, where the *made with Florida pecans* label had covered it before, was a small candy flower.

And under the flower was a ring.

CHAPTER NINETEEN

"It's *not* an engagement ring," Will said quickly, no longer able to contain his grin.

I just stared at the thing—the silver band and oval blue stone, surrounded by tiny sparkly white chips of something. Probably diamonds.

I hated diamonds, ever since the day I threw the gaudy one Todd had given me in his face, along with my wedding band.

"It's a sapphire, your birthstone." Will's grin was fading.

"What are the white things?" My tone was less than enthused.

"Cubic zirconia. After all, it's *not* an engagement ring." No grin left at all now, and his baby blues were more a worried gray.

He remembered about the diamonds. My chest warmed.

"It's more a, you know, *pre*-engagement thing," he said tentatively, as I continued to stare at the ring.

Suddenly my eyes were stinging and my nose was running and a lump the size of a golf ball had formed in my throat.

I looked up at Will. "It's beautiful," I whispered. "Thank you."

A while later, the chicken was in the oven and we were snuggled up on the sofa. Will had his arm around my shoulders, and since he wasn't willing to relinquish that position, I was feeding him bites of pecan pie, alternating with taking bites of my own.

"How'd you get the ring inside the sealed container?" I asked.

"I told the lady at the bakery counter what I wanted to do. She unsealed it, stuck the ring on there with that sugar flower. Then she put a fresh label on it."

I glanced at my watch. "Bet she's just now getting home and telling her husband about the sweet guy who came by her counter today."

Will chuckled. "So I made two women happy today."

I held up my left hand to admire the ring. "Yes, you did."

I fed him his last bite of pie.

He chewed and swallowed, licked his lips. "So did you find out anything interesting from the frat boys?"

"Not much. I got a few more random pieces about the party, but I'm not real sure how they fit together yet." I actually had an inkling, but I really didn't want to talk about all that right now. "I'm going to call the other guys on the list tomorrow."

"Okay, but can you put off meeting anyone else in person," he gave me a pleading look, "until after we pull this sting off?"

"Sure, since you asked so nicely. When's the sting supposed to happen?"

"Friday night. Vice has a guy undercover who's playing the high roller, giving a huge party for his business associates and wants the whole stable of girls to be there."

"I gather the business associates will be cops?"

"You got it."

"Slick. So they can gather them all up at once."

"Ideally, but they'll probably have a few slip through the net. They're less concerned about the girls though. It's the leaders and the muscle guys they want. Most of whom already have long rap sheets. Derek's hoping to get some equally long sentences that will keep them off the streets for a while."

"Does Florida have a three-strikes law?" I asked.

"Yup. Mandatory minimum sentence if they're convicted of three separate felonies within five years."

"Do you think you'll be able to find out anything more about Jason Burrows's murder after the sting?"

Will grimaced. "Hard to tell. If Marissa knows anything about it, she may use that to get a lighter sentence on the trafficking charges. But there's no evidence that she's had any recent contact with him or that she knew anything about his blackmailing Davis."

I sat up a little and turned to face Will. "Did I tell you I saw Marissa at Shawn's place, the first day or so I started investigating all this? I didn't even know who she was, but she was yelling at him."

Will shook his head. "No, you didn't. What did she say?"

"I only caught a couple of words. One of them was *money.*"

"You think Marissa was in on the blackmail?"

"I did at the time, but Shawn said no, that she'd said money wasn't enough, that she was going to make him pay a different way."

Will had a thoughtful look on his face. "It's not uncommon for prostitutes to have child sexual abuse in their histories."

It sounded on the surface like a *non sequitur,* but I suspected where he was going with the thought. In graduate school, I'd taken an elective course on trauma recovery. Sexual abuse was far more common than most people thought, and it had far-reaching repercussions for many of the survivors. It was the reason behind all too many teenage runaways. And all too many of those runaways ended up as prostitutes.

"But one assault," I said, "wouldn't be likely to turn her into a hooker. And isn't she helping to run the show?"

"She was one of the girls originally, according to Derek. Early on, she was the only one, and Gerry was her pimp."

My stomach tightened and suddenly I wished I hadn't eaten such a big piece of pie. "How could they go from college sweethearts to that?"

"Could have been other nasty stuff in her history," Will said.

"Yeah, that would make more sense psychologically. If you're taught from early on that's all you're worth ...." I shuddered. "That would explain the intensity of her reaction to what happened at the party." I'd already told him about Lexie's and my speculations about the missing condom.

"But what has stirred all that up for her recently?" Will said, "Something had to have happened that triggered her going over and confronting Davis."

He pulled his arm from around my shoulders and pushed himself to a stand. "You got your list of the frat brothers?"

"Yes, it's in the kitchen."

"Okay, let me get my case file from the house. Derek gave me a copy of the phone dump for Marissa Andrews's cell phone for the last couple of months. There were about a dozen numbers the electronics guys couldn't trace back to owners. They figure they're disposable cells. Let's see if any of them are on your list."

"You really think they will be?" I asked.

He shrugged. "It's just a hunch, but hunches sometimes develop into solid leads."

Ten minutes later, Will and I were at the kitchen table, stacks of papers in front of each of us. "Wow, she makes a lot of calls," I said.

"And receives even more." He winked at me. "That's why they're called 'call girls.'"

I rolled my eyes. "We've got half an hour before the chicken's done."

"We're only concerned about the ones circled in red. Those are the ones that couldn't be traced."

I shuffled through my pages. There were seven circled numbers. "Okay, let's compare them against this list first." I put the sheet with Shawn's first list, the brothers he was sure were at the party, in between us.

With an index finger under one of the red-circled numbers, I scanned down the frat boys' list. Nope.

By the time I got to the fourth circled number on Marissa's phone call list, something was niggling at the back of my brain.

I scanned Shawn's list of frat brothers at the party again. This number wasn't there either.

I stared at the number. It looked familiar. The niggling thought popped to the forefront. "Hang on." I got up and ran to the living room to get my phone out of my purse.

Scrolling through my contacts, I walked back to the kitchen. I held out the phone in front of Will's face.

He read the name of the contact. "Roger Campbell."

I pointed to the circled number on my sheet.

"Well, son of a gun," Will said.

"How much you wanna bet Roger's the one who got Marissa stirred up again?"

Will nodded. "I need to go have a chat with Mr. Campbell tomorrow."

The oven timer dinged.

Will stood and gathered up the phone dump sheets. "By the way, if anybody asks, you never saw these. Can I get a copy of your frat boys list? I'll have someone at the department go over them tomorrow and see if there are any other matches."

The fact that he'd trusted me with the phone call list, that probably even he shouldn't have—he'd have no way to get a subpoena for them when Marissa wasn't *his* suspect—made me feel all warm and fuzzy inside.

"Sure. I can print another list out from Shawn's email." I started to move toward my laptop on the far end of the kitchen counter, next to my small wireless printer.

Will grabbed me around the waist, the papers still bunched in one of his hands. He pulled me close. "And then we'll forget about all this depressing stuff for tonight. Let's eat dinner and then celebrate our pre-engagement some more."

"What, eat more pie?" I said with mock innocence.

He bent down and kissed me, long and tender. My insides melted.

He broke the kiss and, blue eyes dancing, said, "That too."

The next morning, Stephie came over to do some training. She worked with Patches while I looked on. He was beginning to get the hang of the first two parts of the cover task, turning and sitting every time Stephie stopped.

"He is so smart," Stephie said, flashing a proud-mama grin.

I grinned back. "Let's put them in their service vests and take a walk, see if he remembers to turn and sit outside of my yard."

Stephie stopped at three random spots as we walked from my house to the motel. Without being prompted, Patches turned and sat two out of the three times.

Good progress.

As we turned the corner to pass in front of the motel, my phone pinged in my pocket.

I dared to sneak a peek. It was a text message from Will, telling me he had to go into work and would probably be late tonight. He'd "caught a related case."

Not sure what that meant, I swallowed my disappointment and plastered on a smile for Stephie's benefit. But when I looked up, my smile quickly faded.

Charlene Woodward, in jeans and a green tee shirt, was coming out of the motel's front door onto its mock-Victorian, covered porch. When she spotted us, she rushed to the top of the porch steps. "Marcia Banks, how dare you keep parading that vicious animal around town."

Stephie and I stopped, exchanged a look. Both dogs turned around and sat.

I tilted my head toward Patches. Stephie leaned down to give him a treat while I put my hands on my hips. "Charlene, what is your problem?"

She glared at me. "That dog, obviously. It's endangering the citizens of this town!"

Grinding my teeth, I glanced down at Patches, sitting serenely with his back to Stephie. Then I looked at Charlene again. "This dog? Seriously."

The motel's front door opened and Edna appeared in the doorway, in a purple blouse and black stretch pants, her official motel manager outfit. She'd even made an attempt to comb her wayward gray hair.

"Charlene, stop caterwaulin' out here in front of my motel. Yer disturbin' my guests."

Susanna's pale face, framed by blonde-gray wisps, appeared briefly over her aunt's shoulder. Then a flash of pink clothing as she scuttled away. She hated confrontation.

"What guests?" Charlene made a point of sweeping her gaze over the empty parking lot.

"The ones I'd have if you weren't standin' around shoutin' at folks. Now go on with ya. I'll talk to Marcia."

Charlene harumphed and stomped down the porch steps. "We'll see about this," she hissed as she passed us, although I noted she didn't get too close.

Patches turned his head and stared after her but otherwise showed no interest in viciously attacking her.

When I looked back at the motel, Edna was standing on the top porch step gesturing for me to come over.

Buddy and I complied. Stephie told Patches to stay and rewarded him with another treat when he obeyed.

I smiled. This dog was definitely coming along. I needed to call Mattie again and see if she was willing to give me another veteran to work with, especially since I wouldn't get the full fee for Patches if someone else had to do the last part of the training with Roger Campbell.

Edna took another step down. I shaded my eyes to look up into her face and my stomach dropped. Her expression was downright grim.

"Charlene's plannin' on bringin' it up with the Chamber of Commerce to ban certain dog breeds from Mayfair."

"Oh for Pete's sake," I said.

"Well, don't get too het up about it yet," Edna said. "I'll talk to Sherie before the next meetin'. We'll probably be able to back her down, but we gotta give her a chance to have her say."

Stephie had closed the gap between us. She stood next to me. Patches turned and sat but she ignored him.

I cleared my throat and tilted my head in the dog's direction.

She ignored me too. "If you all do that," she said to Edna, "Marcia could sue the town. You'd be interfering with her ability to make a living."

What's she studying in school, pre-law? Ms. Snark commented internally.

I mentally shushed her and raised a hand to stop Stephie from saying more too. "I've got this. Edna, first of all, a Chamber of Commerce is not a town council. They can't pass legislation or put restrictions on citizens. And second, you know all this hoopla about the bull terrier breeds is nonsense."

"I know that. But Sherie and me, we got responsibilities as co-chairs of the Chamber. We can't seem like we're only listenin' to our friends."

I rolled my eyes and shook my head, wishing I'd never suggested to Edna that we use the grand re-opening of her motel as the kick-off for an effort to attract more tourists to Mayfair. That suggestion had led to the forming of the Chamber of Commerce and several hare-brained schemes since, such as an aborted attempt to build an ice-skating rink in central Florida.

Now it seemed every dispute between neighbors was going to end up becoming a brouhaha at a Chamber meeting.

"Next meetin's Monday night," Edna said. "Can ya be there?"

I sighed. I'd already known about the meeting, had been debating whether or not to go. Now it looked like I'd better. "Yeah, I'll be there."

Stephie stood up straighter. "And so will I!"

Edna glanced at her, gray eyebrows in the air. "Ya can't vote," she said in a dead-pan voice, "if ya don't live here."

I held up my hand again. A budding idea was forming in my brain. "Good that you can come, Stephie. We'll have you put Patches through his paces." The things he could already do would impress folks. And I'd make the point that Stephie was a novice trainer. If she could "control" Patches, anyone could. We should take him out in public more though, so the crowd wouldn't throw him. A trip to Belleview or Ocala this week would be a good idea.

Then I remembered I was supposed to lay low until after the sting operation on Friday. *Crapola.*

I faked a smile. "By all means, add Charlene's concerns to the agenda, but make sure you allow time for a demonstration of exactly what a service dog can do."

Edna nodded and turned. Hand on the railing, she half climbed, half pulled herself up the steps. Suddenly she looked every one of her eighty-some years.

My chest ached. I felt queasy at the thought that my neighbors, people I'd assumed were friends, might actually try to curtail what breeds I could train. And if I didn't win them over at the Chamber meeting, my only recourse might be legal action, which I could ill afford.

I wanted to cry.

Edna had gone inside. Dexter stepped out onto the porch, his face pinched. "I was listenin' at the window. Don't worry, Marcia. Aunt Edna won't let 'em do nothin' against ya."

He sounded like *he* was going to cry.

"Thanks, Dexter." He was a brick or two short of a full load, but sometimes he picked up on emotional nuances better than some of the brighter people I knew.

I wished I could share his confidence. Even Edna's response had left me feeling a little betrayed. How could she let Charlene bring this before the Chamber, which had no legal authority anyway?

I justified steering Stephie and the dogs back toward my house with the thought that I didn't want people seeing Patches now and forming an early opinion of him.

But mostly I was shaken to the core.

The dogs in tow, Stephie and I walked back up the street, the silence between us not all that comfortable. As I tried to think of something to say to break the tension, my phone rang.

Lexie Campbell the screen read. Apparently she'd added some minutes to her phone. I didn't feel up to talking to her right now, so I let it go to voicemail.

By the time we got to my porch, I was feeling guilty for not taking the call. I stopped and checked the voicemail.

At first, I couldn't make out words, just that she sounded very upset. I listened to the message again.

To Stephie, I said, "Can you work with Patches on the go-get command for a while? I need to return this call."

"Sure." She opened the front door and paused on the threshold. "Sorry I jumped in there."

I waved a hand in the air. "Not a problem. And I appreciate you being willing to come to the meeting."

She nodded and took Patches inside.

I sat down on the edge of the porch and called Lexie back.

"I'm sorry to bother you but Shawn said to call you." Her voice was frantic.

"Why? What's happened?"

"They found Gerald Fields's body."

That sent my heart into overdrive. I was glad I was sitting down. "Oh," was all I could think of to say.

That must be Will's related case.

Some sniffling sounds. "It had been there for a while."

That conjured up an unpleasant mental picture that made me wish I'd never watched *Bones* or *CSI* on TV. "Where?" I asked.

"In one of the Davis's hayfields, in a shallow grave." Louder sniffling. "They've arrested Shawn."

CHAPTER TWENTY

Lexie said she was out driving around. "I've got no place to go," she wailed and begged to see me.

I'd promised Will I'd stay close to home, so I suggested she meet me at the Mayfair Diner. I gave her directions. Turns out she was less than ten minutes away.

I disconnected, wondering why she was only ten minutes away. Mayfair was pretty much out in the middle of nowhere.

After a quick check in with Stephie, I grabbed my purse and Buddy, and we headed back up the street.

The diner had originally been built in the 1960s and made to look like a real train car, even though there were no train tracks within fifty miles. The new owner, Jessica Randall, had given it a pink paint job and put plastic shutters, bright purple, on either side of the two big plate glass windows looking out on Main Street.

Out back, the diner was a bit shabbier, but Jess had installed three picnic tables under a huge live oak tree. Buddy and I settled at one of the tables. I'd told Lexie to come around to the back.

But Susanna Mayfair showed up first. "What can I get you, Marcia?" She wore a pink uniform and poised a pencil over an order pad.

"You're waitressing here now?" I asked, unable to keep the stunned note out of my voice.

She nodded. "Aunt Edna and Dexter and me have been trippin' all over each other. There isn't enough to keep all three of us busy at the motel. So I told Jess I'd help her out for a while."

Typical. No Mayfair family member was happy unless they were doing something productive.

This must have been where she was scurrying to earlier, her new waitress job. I wondered how much of the confrontation with Charlene she'd heard. But I wasn't about to bring it up. I knew she wouldn't want to talk about it, and neither did I.

"For now, bring a couple of iced teas," I said.

"Sweet or unsweet?"

I was pretty sure from her accent that Lexie had grown up in Florida, so she probably liked the sweet stuff that made my teeth hurt. "One of each."

Susanna and Lexie passed each other at the corner of the building. Susanna gave her a big smile. "You must be Marcia's friend."

Lexie's worried expression didn't change. She nodded slightly, looking my way. She wore jeans and another knit top, peach-colored.

I waved her over, anxious to hear what was going on.

Unfortunately, she didn't know much about the body or the police investigation. "Some boys came running up to the house this morning, yelling that they'd found a body. One of them had already called 911 on his phone."

"Wait, what house?"

"At Clover Hills." Lexie ducked her head. "I've been staying there the last couple of days. Roger kicked me out."

"What?" For the second time that morning, I ground my teeth.

"I refused to break up with Shawn." Lexie waved her hand in a dismissive gesture—that wasn't what she wanted to talk about. "Mr. Davis told us to stay at the house, but Lucinda and I followed at a distance."

I assumed Lucinda was Mrs. Davis. Interesting that Lexie called her by her first name but not *Mr.* Davis, not even when she was staying under his roof. Interesting but not all that surprising. I'd only met the guy once, but he hadn't inspired a desire to get chummy with him.

"A couple of deputies got there as Mr. Davis and the boys were approaching the body. They shooed him away and we all went back to the house."

"The boys too?"

"No, the deputies kept them there. They were asking them questions. About an hour later, those detectives showed up at the house."

"Detectives Haines and Brown?"

She nodded. "They asked us a bunch of questions that we didn't know the answers to. Then they went looking for Shawn."

"He wasn't there."

"He left early this morning to check out some breeding stock at another farm."

"And they arrested him there?"

She nodded again. "Mr. Davis and Lucinda had to go pick up his truck and the horse trailer. They were leaving right after Mr. Davis made me pack up and go."

"He threw you out?" Third teeth-grinding moment of the day. At this rate, I'd need dentures by dinnertime.

Lexie started crying softly, just as Susanna arrived with our iced tea. She whipped out a wad of paper napkins from a pocket of her uniform and gave me a dirty look.

I stared at her, trying to convey that I hadn't made the girl cry.

Susanna must have gotten the message. Her face softened. She patted Lexie wordlessly on the shoulder and walked away.

She hadn't brought me any sugar—I do add some to my tea—but I wasn't about to call her back.

Lexie picked up a napkin and blew her nose.

"Have you talked to Shawn?"

"Yeah." She still sounded a little stopped up. "But only long enough for him to tell me to call you."

"Does he have a lawyer?"

"Lucinda said she'd get him one."

"So why did Mr. Davis make you leave?"

Staring down at the table, she said, "He's never really liked me. Lucinda had to insist that they'd take me in. This morning, he said it was my fault that all this got stirred up again, because my brother had hired a detective to find dirt on Shawn."

"I had that guilty thought myself at one point, but then I realized that Shawn was being blackmailed long before I came on the scene." I suspected her brother had done a lot more than hire me to stir things up, but didn't know that for sure yet.

I took a swig of tea, forgetting that it had no sweetener in it at all. I swallowed quickly.

Lexie was rubbing a napkin across the picnic table surface, ostensibly to mop up condensation from her glass. "Mr. Davis, he, um...." She glanced at me, then quickly broke eye contact again. "He said some mean things about you, and something about you playing both ends instead of being in the middle."

"Playing them *against* the middle." It was one of my mother's favorite expressions, usually aimed at the TV when a politician was giving a speech.

Lexie gave a one-shouldered shrug that said, *Whatever.*

I intentionally laid my left hand out flat on the table. "Lexie, do you know that Detective Haines and I are dating?"

Her eyes went wide. She stared first at my ring, then at my face.

"That's what Mr. Davis was talking about," I said gently. "He thinks I'm not really trying to help Shawn because I've got that connection with the sheriff's department. But I *am* trying to help, like I promised I would. I'm looking into some things that the police don't have the manpower to pursue."

She was still staring at me, her mouth slightly open.

"And now that I've gotten into it, I've realized how time-consuming it is." Shawn's list of possible party attendees was long. But an idea had been forming in my mind. "Would you like to help?"

She closed her mouth. "Um, yeah, sure."

"I can put you up, for tonight at least."

She ducked her head and it dawned on me that this had been her agenda all along. I was very glad I'd added the "for tonight at least."

Her gaze still on the table, she nodded. "Okay, thanks."

I stood up. Buddy slithered out from under the table.

Lexie's head jerked up. "I didn't even know he was there."

He shook himself and then cocked his head to one side with his what's-up look.

I smiled at him. "He's very well behaved."

Rather than mess up Lexie's backseat with black dog hairs, I suggested Buddy and I walk home and Lexie follow in her car.

When we got back to my house, Stephie was on the front porch, just leaving. "Patches is in his crate. We added keys and glasses to his go-get list."

"That's great."

Lexie had climbed out of her car at the curb. She walked to the porch. I introduced her without explaining why I'd brought home a stray.

Stephie gave me a curious look but didn't ask any questions. "I've got a big test Friday so I won't be able to come back until Saturday."

"Okay," I said. "We'll take the dogs to Belleview. See how Patches does when there are more people around."

Stephie nodded and left.

Once inside, I showed Lexie to my "guest room," the tiny second bedroom that I used mostly for storage. I pulled the foldaway cot out of a back corner, got her some sheets and left her to make up the bed and get settled in.

Meanwhile, I went into the kitchen to call Mattie.

"Hey Mattie, how ya doing?" My effort at a fake cheerful tone was wasted.

"Roger Campbell's back on the waiting list," she said in a clipped voice. "For the time being. I talked to his counselor. She couldn't say too much but she did admit that he missed his last two appointments with her. And she didn't know he was drinking again but didn't seem too surprised."

"Again?"

"Apparently he's had trouble with booze in the past."

Not a huge surprise, but my chest ached a little. I didn't like the guy, and perhaps he had contributed to Shawn's current problems by stirring the pot, but still I hadn't wanted him to be deprived of his service dog. And I hated to think that he was going into a downhill spiral.

"Did he seem attached to the dog?" Mattie said in my ear as I paced across the kitchen floor.

"Not particularly."

"Good. I'm going to assign Patches to a female veteran who's close to the top of the list, pending her approval of the dog. I'll set up a meeting for you to go talk to her."

I breathed a small sigh of relief that I would get paid the full amount for training Patches. "Okay, but maybe we're being a bit hasty with Roger."

The *we* really wasn't accurate. I had no say in the matter, but I felt bad that I had started this particular ball rolling. "I'm not totally sure he was drinking when I was there last time."

A beat of silence. "I went to talk to him, about you. He was most definitely drunk. I doubt he even remembers the conversation." Her tone was neutral. Too neutral.

Butterflies fluttered in my chest and stomach. Was she still pissed at me?

Might as well find out.

"Um, can you assign another veteran to me as well? Patches is coming along great, and with Stephie helping, I'm ready for a second dog."

Another beat of silence. "Okay, I'll take a look at the list."

I began pacing again. "And Mattie, I'm sorry about what happened with Roger. If I do pursue becoming a P.I., I'll steer clear of our clients." I turned at the far end of the kitchen to pace back the other way.

Mattie's answering grunt barely registered.

Lexie was standing in the doorway, wide-eyed and pale. "What happened to Roger?"

CHAPTER TWENTY-ONE

"Nothing. He's fine," I quickly reassured her. That part was easy, but how to tell her the rest of it?

I gestured toward the kitchen table. "Um, have a seat."

We sat down across from each other and I tried, as gently as possible, to explain what had happened.

"But that's horrible," Lexie exclaimed. "Roger needs his dog."

"I know he does and I feel bad that he's not going to get one right away, but we can't leave a dog in his care if he might not be responsible about taking care of it. Has he ever been abusive–"

I was about to add *toward animals* but stopped when tears sprang into Lexie's eyes. She was suddenly staring down and off to the side, at the floor.

"Has he ever hit you?" I asked gently.

She shook her head, still studiously examining the old-fashioned black and white tiles on my floor.

"But he has a temper?"

She nodded. Her shoulders began to shake.

"So he might harm an animal, without meaning to, if he was drunk?"

She finally turned her tear-stained face toward me. "Yeah," she said, barely above a whisper. Then in a slightly stronger voice, "I need to go home. Roger needs someone to take care of him."

A part of me wanted to let her go. I didn't need her family's drama in my life. But I couldn't help myself. This could be a crucial turning point in this young woman's life.

I reached out and grabbed her hand lying on the table. "Lexie, have you ever been to an Al-Anon meeting?"

She froze for a second, then nodded her head slightly. "A friend took me to one once."

"Have you heard of the term *enabling*?"

She nodded again and swallowed hard.

"There's a fine line between helping someone and enabling. I'm not sure where that line is in this case, but I hope you'll give it some thought before you run back home."

And he kicked you out, remember? Ms. Snark added in my head.

After a moment, Lexie squared her shoulders. Pulling her hand loose from mine, she used the back of it to swipe at her cheeks. "What do you need me to do to help Shawn?"

I divided up the list of frat brothers who still needed to be called, and we discussed possible openings and questions to ask. Lexie used my grocery list pad to take notes.

She pulled out her phone, in a pink case with bright yellow flowers on it. I hid a smile. She was such a girly-girl, but I was discovering that she also had a backbone.

"Hey, don't use your minutes." I handed her the cordless phone for my landline—which my mother paid for because she was convinced I needed one, but I almost never used it.

Lexie punched in the first number from her list, and I went into the living room to start making my own calls.

Three hours later, we had finished our lists and were both starving. I called out for a pizza, half sausage for me, half extra cheese for her. I fed the dogs while we waited for it to arrive.

We ate at my kitchen table and compared notes. Most of the frat brothers barely remembered the party, other than recalling that some girl had accused some guy of assaulting her. Three of them had remembered seeing Gerry and Jason hauling Shawn up the stairs at some point during the evening. Four others recalled that they were bringing him downstairs when someone said the cops were coming and chaos ensued.

Nobody remembered the state of Shawn's clothing, but one brother had noticed the crying girl on the phone near Shawn and Gerry's room.

And another brother recalled seeing a young woman and a guy through an open doorway. They'd been on a bed and the guy was shirtless, so he'd quickly looked away and went on about his business. He couldn't remember if he'd seen their faces but said he hadn't recognized them.

"So you think it was this other guy who actually attacked Marissa?" Lexie said.

"Or she had consensual sex with him."

"Under her boyfriend's nose?"

I gave her a pointed look. "You're in college now, aren't you?"

She nodded.

"Been to any frat parties?"

"No, but I get your point. It's a what-happens-in-the-frat-house, stays-in-the-frat-house thing. So how'd she end up in Shawn's bed?"

I'd been giving that some thought. "Suppose Gerry found out that Marissa cheated on him. Maybe he wanted to play a trick on her, and/or Shawn."

Lexie dropped a half-eaten piece of cheese pizza on her paper plate. "So he set it up to look like Shawn had assaulted her."

I nodded. "With a little help from his friend Jason. Which would explain the lack of a condom. And it all went horribly awry when somebody called the police, maybe the girl outside their room who'd heard them say Shawn had attacked Marissa."

Lexie's face tightened. "Why didn't they fess up when the cops got there? How could they let him be charged?"

"Maybe they would have confessed, if the charges hadn't been dropped. Do you know if there was any reason why Gerry would have it in for Shawn?"

"No. They weren't besties but I think they got along okay, from what Shawn has said. I got the impression, though, that Shawn and Jason didn't like each other, even back then."

"Thus Jason's willingness to blackmail Shawn for a crime he knew he didn't commit."

Lexie sat forward in her chair. "It all fits, but Gerry and Jason are both dead. So how do we sell it to the sheriff's department?"

"Um, let me give that some thought."

My chest hurt. I didn't have the heart to tell her that while our theory might lift an emotional load off Shawn's shoulders, it probably wouldn't help regarding the murder charges, and it might make things worse.

"You have *who* in your spare room?" Will said.

"Shh, you'll wake her." I grabbed my purse.

Buddy was lying in the middle of the living room floor. He opened one eye and looked at me, as if to say, *Seriously? You're up this early?*

"You stay here and keep Lexie company," I told him.

Probably only *stay* registered, but that was good enough for him. He went back to sleep.

"Come on," I said to Will, who'd stopped by to ask me to breakfast at the diner, before another long day began for him. "I'll bring something back for Lexie."

We walked out to his truck so we could drive the short distance to the diner and he could go on to work from there. I winced at the sight of his banged-up fender. My car was still in the shop, and I wondered when we'd have time to deal with his.

Once in the truck, I glanced sideways, noting how handsome he looked in his navy suit and pale blue dress shirt. I left him to his thoughts as I tried to organize my own. How to present our theory to him?

At the diner, we settled at a formica-topped table. Susanna came by with much-needed coffee and took our orders.

I waved at the diner's new owner through the wide pass-through.

Probably about my age, Jess was a small dark-haired woman, no more than five feet. She was standing on a stool at one of the shiny new stainless steel counters in the kitchen. She waved back and returned to rolling out biscuit dough. The fragrance of baking biscuits drifted out to the tables.

My mouth watered.

"Hey Susanna," I called after her. "Add a biscuit to my order, please."

She smiled back over her shoulder. "You bet."

I took a big gulp of coffee, then clasped my cup between my hands to warm them up. This time of year in Florida, business owners had to make an educated guess in the morning as to whether they would need heat or air conditioning later in the day. Jess had apparently opted for AC this morning. The diner was a bit chilly.

Leaning forward, I quickly spelled out, in a low voice, what Lexie and I had found out. "So we think either someone else assaulted Marissa or she had consensual sex with them, and Gerry found out and was playing a trick on her, with Jason Burrows's help." I sat back, rather pleased with my succinct presentation.

"A very plausible theory," Will said.

Warmth spread through my chest.

"We can't necessarily prove it," he continued, "but it definitely makes sense. So I need to find out if Davis knew that Burrows and Fields had set him up, and if so, *when* did he know it." He took a sip of his coffee. "Burrows was definitely the blackmailer. Monthly deposits of a thousand dollars were made into his account."

It wasn't surprising news, but it confirmed that Shawn had a strong motive.

Our eggs were delivered, mine with a freshly-baked biscuit on the side. I ordered an egg sandwich to go for Lexie.

"And you can forget Fields as an alternate suspect for Burrows's murder," Will said as he picked up his fork. "M.E. says Fields died roughly eight hours before Burrows did."

"That doesn't make any sense."

Will took a quick bite of toast. "No, it doesn't. But we'll figure it out eventually."

While he shoveled in his eggs, I plucked off a piece of biscuit and popped it in my mouth. I closed my eyes to savor it. The warm flaky goodness practically melted on my tongue.

"You're assuming the same person killed both of them?" I asked.

Will paused between bites. "Not assuming, but it's likely. You know what else I discovered yesterday?"

"What?"

"Burrows had two calls four months ago, from that same untraceable phone number."

"Hunh? Roger's number?"

"Yup." Will picked up a strip of bacon and chomped half of it off.

"He put Burrows up to the blackmail."

"Either that or he called Burrows to get information about the party, and that gave Burrows the idea."

I nodded. That made more sense. "Lexie told me they switched to disposable phones because Roger didn't like what their cellular carrier was charging them. I thought it was a rather skinflint reaction at the time—"

"Skinflint?" Will gave me a teasing grin, his baby blues twinkling a bit.

I pretended to ignore him, but that dimple of his had me melting a little. "Roger *wanted* his phone number to be untraceable."

Will nodded and devoured another strip of bacon.

I ate a couple of bites of scrambled eggs, along with another heavenly chunk of biscuit. "Did you talk to Roger yesterday?"

"No, the new corpse and tracking down Davis took priority. It's on my to-do list for today, but first I need to talk to Davis again. Before Lexie somehow gets the word to him about what you all figured out."

I took another bite of egg and then of biscuit, rolling my eyes in pleasure.

"That was good detective work," he said. "You came up with a lead that even we hadn't thought of, and you diligently pursued it."

"Thanks for the compliment."

"I mean it. You could be a detective, if that's what you really want to do."

My chest warmed again at his support. "I don't know. My brain may be able to master the skills required." I thought about poor Shawn, now in jail for two murders. "But I'm not sure my heart can take the roller coaster ride of emotions."

He smiled and patted my hand. "Unfortunately, I need to get going." He flagged Susanna who brought him the check and me a box for the rest of my eggs and biscuit, plus Lexie's egg sandwich and a plastic bag to put it all in.

Outside, Will gave me a quick kiss. "I'll text or call later, to let you know when I'll get home."

Feeling kind of warm and fuzzy, I watched him climb into his truck and drive off.

What's so different between this and being married? My mother's voice.

Good question. I was trying to think of a good answer when my phone rang. I didn't recognize the number but it was a Gainesville area code.

"Hello?"

"Hi, this is Danny Stevens. You asked me to call if I remembered anything else."

My heart rate kicked up a notch. "Yes?"

"About four or five months ago, this guy came into the bookstore. I was unpacking some boxes of books, checking them against the delivery slip. He saw the Gator logo on my shirt and got me talking about UF and then fraternities and then that party."

"That didn't strike you as odd?" I'd started walking slowly toward home, the plastic bag of food dangling from my elbow.

"No, because he said he was a freelance reporter doing an article for the *Gainesville Sun*, on UF fraternities that had gotten into trouble." The words were coming fast, his pitch high with excitement. "We talked about a couple of other ones first, like one that got closed down because they were selling drugs out of their frat house. Then he brought up our fraternity getting expelled for a year and… well, he asked a lot of questions about the party but he was subtle. They were thrown in between other questions about the other fraternities. He seemed like a real nice guy and I wanted to help him out."

I walked past Sherie's house. "Our talking about the party the other day didn't jog this memory?"

"No, I thought of it this morning when I stopped to get my paper on the way to work. I'm old fashioned about my newspapers. I like real paper and ink, not something online."

I rolled my eyes. *Get on with it.* Since when did Shy Danny get so talkative?

"As I was reaching for the paper in the bin, the thought popped into my head that I'd never seen the guy's story show up in the *Sun.* And then it hit me that he was probably an investigator like you."

"Yes, he probably was." And I had a pretty good idea who'd hired him.

I'd reached my house. Instead of going inside, I put the bag of food down and sat on the edge of the porch. "Did this guy give you his name?"

"Yeah, but I don't remember it. He gave me his card even. I looked for it in my desk but couldn't find it. It might be at home."

"Can you check later and let me know if you find it?"

"Sure thing."

"Thanks so much, Danny. This is a big help."

"No problem." I imagined him blushing on the other end of the line.

We disconnected and I stared into space, not really seeing the cleared lot across the road where the aborted ice rink was supposed to have been built.

The pieces were falling into place, or at least most of them were. I wasn't the first detective Roger Campbell had hired. And the other guy had followed pretty much the same leads as I had.

He'd found out about the party and Marissa's attack and no doubt got contact info for Roger on all the key players.

Did he figure out that Shawn wasn't really Marissa's attacker?

Roger contacted Jason first, trying to stir things up. But instead of bringing the whole mess out into the light of day again, Jason had decided to make a few bucks off of keeping quiet.

So then Roger had contacted Marissa herself. What did he tell her that got her riled up?

And he'd hired me, hoping my "amateurish" stumbling around would...accomplish what?

Was he just slinging mud around, hoping some of it would stick to Shawn, or did he have a more organized plan?

Had he intended Jason and Gerry would be killed so Shawn would be framed? Had he killed them himself?

I found that hard to believe since he was housebound at this point. He couldn't drive yet, although his file had mentioned a plan to equip a car with hand controls once he had his service dog and felt more comfortable going out on his own.

I pushed aside the twinge of guilt mixed with pity.

He could hire someone to take him places. Or hire someone to kill for him.

My stomach rumbled, protesting that the rest of my breakfast was getting cold, and so was Lexie's.

My eyes came into focus on the empty field again. And it finally registered that Lexie's car was missing from in front of my house.

I jumped up and unlocked my front door.

Buddy was standing in the middle of the living room, his head tilted to one side. Patches, in his crate, was also giving me a cocked-head, what's-up look.

"Wish I knew, guys."

I took the bag of food into the kitchen and spotted a note propped up against the salt shaker on the table.

Going to Clover Hills to tell Lucinda about what we figured out. Want to see her face! Back later, Lexie.

"Uh, oh," I muttered. I didn't want her getting Mrs. Davis's hopes up that our discovery would help Shawn beat the murder charges against him. I found Lexie's number in my contacts on my phone.

It rang twice and connected. I waited for her *Hello*, but instead Lexie yelled, "Hey, give that back." Then rustling noises, a grunt, and Lexie calling out, "Marci–"

An odd gurgling sound, then nothing.

I raced back toward the front door, grabbing my purse and Buddy's leash along the way. "Come on, boy," I yelled to him. He ran after me.

Lexie had sounded downright terrified.

CHAPTER TWENTY-TWO

Fortunately, I didn't have to go looking for Sherie. She was again on her front porch, in her green terrycloth bathrobe, watering her hanging plants.

I ran down my steps and paused at the bottom of hers. "Gotta borrow the Bonneville again," I said, a little breathless.

She scowled at me, hands on her hips. "I promised Will I wouldn't lend it to you a–"

"It's an emergency." Lexie's scared words replayed in my head. "Maybe a matter of life or death."

Sherie relented and went to get the keys.

While I waited, I called Will. It went straight to voicemail.

Crapola! I left a frantic message.

As I drove to Clover Hills Farm in the muddy-mobile, various scenarios ran through my head. None of them seemed all that plausible. One was of Shawn's parents attacking Lexie. Unlikely. I couldn't imagine even his dad doing anything that would upset her so. And Shawn certainly wouldn't.

I was trying not to think about my worst fear, that she had encountered the killer.

My foot stomped down on the accelerator.

The muddy-mobile coughed and bucked and then surged ahead onto the highway. Today, I was grateful that pretty much everyone speeds on I-75, but I wanted to go even faster. I veered in and out of traffic, as much as one can in a tank, and prayed I wouldn't be too late.

Once off the highway, I risked rummaging in my purse for my phone and called Will again. Voicemail again.

I gritted my teeth. *Double crapola!*

He was probably at the county jail, interviewing Shawn. I left another message, a bit more coherent than the earlier one, even though it was unlikely he'd get it in time to help.

At the farm's entrance, I slowed and moved carefully up the drive, scanning the pastures and barns for signs of life. All was still.

Buddy and I got out of the car and I snapped on his leash. We headed for the main horse barn.

Niña stuck her head out of a stall and whinnied softly. I paused to stroke her soft nose, listening. All was quiet, except for an occasional stomping sound coming from Diablo's end of the barn.

I dropped Buddy's leash and pointed to the other side of the barn's aisle. He went over and sat against the wooden wall of a stall. "Good boy. Stay," I said quietly.

I headed Diablo's way, but stopped in the open doorway of the stall next to his. The straw on the floor was stirred up, like someone'd been dancing in there.

Or wrestling. My heart thudded in my chest.

I stepped into the stall, looked around. A pitchfork was leaning against one wall, but otherwise the stall was empty.

I turned to go back out into the aisle, and saw it.

Lexie's phone, in its pink and yellow-flowered case, was in the half-full water bucket.

A sound. *Whimpering?*

It seemed to be coming from the next stall over.

I went to that door and opened the top half, jumping back when Diablo's head lashed out, his teeth snapping. He barely missed my arm.

"Whoa! Easy, boy. It's just me." I took a half step forward and reached out my hand, flat, palm up, wishing I had a carrot or sugar cube.

I was fighting off some serious *déjà vu*, my stomach churning with dread. Was I about to find yet another body?

I glanced Buddy's way. He was still sitting where I'd told him to stay, his head tilted in that questioning way of his. "Stay, boy," I repeated, even though it wasn't necessary.

The whimpering sound again. I managed to crane my neck far enough to see past Diablo's sleek black rump.

Lexie was cowering in the back corner of the stall, a bloody gash on her forehead.

"Hold still," I said, in as calm a voice as I could muster. "Give me a minute to calm him down and I can get him out of the stall." I wasn't as confident in my abilities as I sounded.

Diablo was much more riled up this time, the whites of his eyes showing as he bobbed his head up and down and shrieked out a long, eerie whinny.

Lexie shuddered.

"Be still," I told her again. I took another half step forward, my hand out as if offering a treat. "Easy, boy. It's okay. Sh, sh, sh."

He seemed to calm a little. His velvet lips snuffled at my hand.

Praying he wouldn't bite it off when he discovered it was empty, I brought my other hand up slowly and reached for his halter.

He shook me off like I was a pesky fly.

I ran to the stall that was used as a feed and tack room. Sure enough, there was a small fridge in one corner. Inside were little bottles of medicines, and eureka, a bag of carrots.

I grabbed four, breaking them in half and stuffing them in my jeans pockets as I went back to the stall.

Lexie was still cowering in the corner.

"Here, boy." I held out a half carrot. Diablo took it and quickly crunched it down.

"You're such a good boy," I murmured as I offered another carrot with one hand and went for his halter again with the other. Slowly,

slowly, caressing the side of his head first, then gently latching onto the leather strap.

He let me hold onto the halter this time. I fed him another piece of carrot, crooning "good boy," over and over.

I slipped a hand down inside the door and unhooked it. "Come on, boy. Let's move you over one stall, okay?"

I held a carrot out in front of his nose and led him to the stall next door. I fed him the carrot, then bolted out of the stall, slamming the bottom half of the door shut behind me.

He raced around in a tight circle twice, screaming out his eerie whinny again.

I risked slipping a hand inside the opening and snatched the phone from the water bucket. I suspected plastic and lithium batteries would not be good for his digestive tract.

When I returned to the other stall, Lexie was crouched down in the corner, crying into her hands. "I thought I was going to die."

I took her by the forearms and gently lifted her to a stand. "Are you hurt anywhere, besides your head?"

She pulled an arm loose and gingerly touched the gash. "He hit me," she whimpered.

"Who hit you?"

"Me." A male voice from behind me.

CHAPTER TWENTY-THREE

I whirled around. Leonard Hoffman stood in the stall door opening.

Ms. Snark jumped to the forefront. "Sheez, Lenny. You're really stuck in a couple of ruts here. You need to add more techniques to your killing repertoire."

He looked confused for a moment, but then his face cleared. He curled one side of his lip up in a lopsided sneer. "Well, I got this." He glanced down.

I followed his line of vision as he lifted a gun to his waist level and pointed it right at my heart.

Said heart was racing. *Get him talking.* I didn't know where *that* voice came from, but it's what people did on TV shows all the time, when staring down the barrel of a gun.

"I thought you were helping the cops now. Didn't they flip you?"

He sneered some more, took two steps toward us. "Yeah, that's what they think too. But I got too many outstanding charges against me, in a bunch of different jur-is-dic-tions." He exaggerated each syllable in the last word, his accent saying he was originally from New Jersey.

"Better to do one last job, get a stake, and disappear." He waggled his gun up and down. "Now, both of youse, move! You're goin' in the stall with the black horse."

"No, Lenny, you're going in the stall with the black horse."

We all whirled around.

This is getting old, Ms. Snark said in my head.

Marissa Andrews stood in the stall door opening, a pistol in one hand. The other hand, encased in a rubber glove, was wrapped around the handle of a pitchfork, low, near the tines. She brought the handle down on Lenny's head.

His eyes went wide, rolled back a little, but he was still standing.

Marissa brought the handle down again, harder. Lenny toppled forward, his gun making a dull thud on the packed dirt floor of the stall.

I lunged for it.

"Freeze, or I shoot the girl."

I froze and looked up. Marissa had her pistol pointed toward Lexie, not me. I put my hands in the air and rose slowly.

Marissa tilted her head. "Kick it over to the other side of the stall."

I did as I was told. Lenny's gun klunked against the wooden wall. Diablo kicked the wall from the other side.

"Now drag him out here," Marissa said.

I made eye contact with Lexie and nodded.

Get her talking, my inner voice hissed.

Okay, okay! My body was having trouble maintaining its adrenaline level. My stomach felt queasy and my knees were wobbling.

Lexie and I stooped down and grabbed each of Lenny's thick arms. Huffing and puffing, we moved him a few inches at a time as Marissa backed out of the stall, keeping her gaze and her aim on us.

"So you weren't just one of Gerry's girls," I said, between huffs. "You were running the show."

"No, Gerry was in charge," Marissa said, "until I found out what he'd done."

"Set you up to think you'd been assaulted by Shawn."

"No, he set me up to be raped by that friend of his."

My head jerked up and I stopped pulling on Lenny's arm for a second. "Jason?"

"Yes." The word came out as a snarl, but her face looked like she was about to cry. For a second, I felt sorry for her. Then I remembered the whole holding-a-gun-on-us thing.

"Gerry drugged me so I could hardly move, but I knew what was happening. Afterwards, they put me in Shawn's bed and I passed out." She waggled her gun.

We resumed yanking on Lenny's arms, dragging him a step or two at a time.

A piece of the puzzle fell into place with a loud internal ka-ching.

Quit mixing your metaphors. My mother's voice this time.

Not now, Mom!

"Jason paid for you," I said. "Was that the first time Gerry pimped you out?"

"Yeah, only I didn't know it at the time. For years, I thought it was Shawn who'd turned me into a worthless...." Her voice broke.

I was tempted to point out that lots of rape survivors don't become prostitutes, but now was not the time.

Another couple of pieces fell into place. Gerry wasn't paying back a cheating girlfriend or playing a trick on his roommate. He was covering for the fact that he'd sold his girlfriend to his friend.

Had he then thrown Shawn's alleged attack up in her face whenever she needed reminding of her lack of worth? That would be the kind of ploy a pimp might use, to maintain control.

I ground my teeth. My already tense muscles tightened even more, my fingers digging into Lenny's fleshy arm.

"Then I got a phone call," Marissa said, "from some guy named Roger."

A sharp intake of air. I glanced over at Lexie. She was staring at Marissa.

I softly cleared my throat and shook my head slightly. She glanced at me, then dropped her gaze. We dragged Lenny a few more feet, out into the aisle.

"He said he knew all about the party and that Shawn and Jason had both…." Marissa's voice broke. "It all came flooding back." Tears were running down her face. "I confronted Gerry and he admitted Jason had paid fifty bucks to…." Her voice broke again, but then her face morphed into an angry mask. "He laughed about it. That was the last time he laughed."

A chill ran through me.

Marissa waved her gun back and forth.

We slowly dragged Lenny toward Diablo's stall.

A low rumbling off to my right. I was careful not to look Buddy's way. When the timing was right, I hoped he would offer a distraction.

"So you framed Shawn for the murders?" I said in a loud voice, to drown out his growling.

Marissa smiled. It was not a pretty sight.

Lexie dropped Lenny's arm and made to move toward Marissa. I stepped in her path and held out my arm in front of her. "Easy, girl," I said softly.

"You." Marissa pointed her pistol at me. "Get the horse over to the other side of the stall so we can get Lenny in there."

"What are you going to do with us?" I asked as I moved to the stall door.

"We're going on a long road trip to the Everglades. By the time they find your bodies, I'll be in the Bahamas, with a whole new stable of ladies."

She stepped toward Lexie, stroked her fair cheek with the back of one finger. "Maybe I'll take this one with me. You'd bring in some good money."

Lexie batted the hand away, and Marissa backhanded her.

Lexie flew back a couple of steps and fell to the floor, slumped against the door of the next stall over.

A louder growl and Buddy was across the aisle. He jumped up, his front paws landing on the side of Marissa's hip. She staggered sideways. He grabbed the jacket sleeve of her gun arm.

She screamed an obscenity and tried to twist her sleeve out of his grasp. Failing that, she grabbed for the gun with her other hand.

I yelled, "Leave it!" and threw the latch on the stall door.

Buddy let go of Marissa's sleeve and jumped back as I yanked the door open. Diablo bolted out of his stall and ran right over Marissa. Her pistol went flying.

"Get Lenny's gun," I yelled to Lexie.

"Diablo!" Lexie jumped up and, eyes wide, pointed at the horse bolting down the barn aisle. "Shawn's gonna kill us."

"He won't go far. This is home. Get the gun!"

I glanced down at Marissa. She was out cold. I quickly scanned the barn floor, located the gun farther down and in the middle of the aisle.

"Buddy, go get gun." I pointed at it. He'd never been taught the word *gun*, but like most dogs who'd lived with humans for years, he understood pointing. He trotted in that direction.

Lexie came out of the other stall, carrying Lenny's gun between two fingers, held out from her like it was a dead fish. I scrapped my original plan of having her hold it on Marissa while I checked for a pulse.

Taking the pistol from her, I held it in my left hand. My heart pounded as I crouched down to touch the woman's neck. I found a pulse.

Thank you, Lord. I didn't like the woman, especially since she'd tried to kill me multiple times, but I didn't want to be responsible for her death.

Buddy trotted back with her gun. I took it and jammed it in the waistband of my jeans. Then I held my free hand out.

Buddy touched his nose to my palm.

"Good boy. Big steak for you tonight! Now go lie down." I pointed to the spot on the other side of the wide aisle. I wanted him well out of the way, in case Marissa came around and had some fight left in her.

She was still unconscious but Lenny was starting to stir. I stepped back a couple of paces so I could aim the gun more or less at both of them. Pulling my phone out of my pocket, I handed it to Lexie. "Call 911. Tell them to send an ambulance as well as the sheriff's deputies."

Ms. Snark took over. "And ask them to call Detective Haines and tell him his fiancée caught his killers."

CHAPTER TWENTY-FOUR

Will and I stood in the sunshine just beyond the shadow of the front of the horse barn. He'd herded Buddy and me outside, no doubt so we could talk privately. But so far, he hadn't said anything.

The EMTs wheeled out their gurney, with a still unconscious Marissa on it. "She gonna be okay?" I called over.

"Her vitals are stable," one of them said over his shoulder.

I was relieved, more for Diablo's sake than hers.

"Have the doc call me as soon as she's conscious," Will said, then turned back to Buddy and me.

I was trying not to smirk.

Okay, I wasn't trying all that hard.

His expression said that he couldn't decide if he should frown or smile.

He seemed to have no such conflict where Buddy was concerned. While the EMTs loaded the gurney into the ambulance, he crouched down and gave the dog a good ear and back scratch. "Thanks for saving her bacon, boy."

When he straightened to a stand, his navy slacks were covered with black dog hairs and a few were sprinkled across his rumpled shirt. He'd ditched the suit jacket, but his tie was still in place.

I knew he wished he could loosen it. One of the few things he hated about being a detective again, instead of a county sheriff, was that he had to wear a suit and tie.

I cocked my head toward a sheriff's department cruiser, where Lenny the Plow was handcuffed in the back. "He should probably get medical attention too. No doubt he has a concussion."

"His hard noggin can wait until they get him to the jail infirmary." Will stepped in closer and looked down into my eyes. His expression had relaxed.

"You realize, don't you, that you announced our engagement to the whole department. Might have been nice if you'd let me know first."

I swallowed hard and looked up at him. That's when I noticed his baby blues were sparkling with amusement.

He broke out a grin and opened his arms.

I stepped into them and relaxed with a sigh against his solid chest.

He kissed the top of my head, then moved his mouth to beside my ear. "Sorry I missed your calls," he whispered. "You should've waited for me."

I leaned back a little in the circle of his arms. "If I had," I said in a soft voice, "Lexie might be dead now."

He nodded and kissed my forehead.

"Were you interrogating Shawn?"

"No, at his arraignment. It's the only time I turn my ringer off. Judges frown on cell phones going off in their courtrooms."

Those warm lips of his were headed toward my own, when I caught sight of Lexie running toward us.

"I've gotta find Diablo." Her voice was frantic.

Will let me go and I grabbed the young woman's arm. "This is his home, where he's fed. He won't go far. He's probably in some back field pigging out on grass."

She tried to shake me off. "I've gotta find him. Shawn will kill me. He raised that horse."

I held on tight. "Lexie, listen to me. You're not a horse person, and even I'm rusty in the dealing-with-horses department. Neither one of us should go after him. He'll just run away from us, which will make it that much harder for the Davises to catch him." I looked around. "Where are they anyway?"

Will shook his head. "They don't seem to be home."

Behind him, I spotted a silver Mercedes pull into the lane. It moved to the side to let the ambulance by, then roared back onto the asphalt and raced toward us.

"They were at their son's arraignment this morning," Will continued, apparently oblivious to the approaching car. "I overheard a whispered but heated conversation between them. Davis apparently wanted to let his son rot in jail. Something about teaching him that actions have consequences."

Lexie's face fell even as her eyes blazed with anger. "Sounds like Mr. Davis. But why hasn't Shawn called me?"

I opened my mouth to remind her that her phone had been drowned, probably about the time that Shawn was being released, when the Mercedes screeched to a halt in front of us.

Lucinda Davis jumped out. "What's going on here?"

Will turned around and I watched him shift into cop mode, his body straighter, his face neutral, his eyes missing nothing. He took a step toward Lucinda. "Where have you been?" His tone was firm.

Lucinda blinked up at him. "At the lawyer's office, discussing Shawn's case."

Will nodded. "Marissa Andrews sent her underling here. We don't know why yet, but he tried to kill Alexis by putting her in a stall with your stallion."

Lucinda's face turned pale under her tan. She grabbed Lexie's hands and seemed to notice for the first time the Picasso painting of dried blood on the girl's forehead and cheeks. "Are you okay?"

Now that's a stupid question if I ever heard one, said Ms. Snark, but thankfully not out loud.

The girl nodded.

Lucinda brought a packet of wet wipes out of her purse. She started to pull one out, but Lexie took the packet from her. Apparently her desire for a mother figure did not reach the level of allowing her face to be cleaned by another woman.

Will resumed his report. "Andrews followed him here apparently and then tried to kill him, along with Alexis and my fiancée." His lips twitched up on the ends, despite his best efforts to maintain cop mode.

"Marcia's dog distracted Andrews." I noted the use of Marissa's last name now. She was no longer a crime victim or even just a prostitute, a crime that he thought really shouldn't be a crime. She was now a full-blown perp in Will's mind.

"Marcia opened the stall door," he continued. "The horse ran Andrews down and took off."

Lucinda's hand flew to her mouth. "Where is he?" she screeched.

Lexie burst into tears. "We don't know. I'm so sorry."

Lucinda took off for a golf cart parked near the far corner of the barn.

I wrapped my arms around Lexie. "Shh, it's not your fault."

But she was having none of my comfort. She pulled loose and ran after Lucinda. "Where's Shawn?" she called out as she ran.

Lucinda was climbing into the golf cart, hampered a bit by her tailored suit with its pencil-thin skirt. I had trouble visualizing her catching Diablo and bringing him back to the barn in that get-up. But even an expensive suit was far less valuable than that horse.

"He took off for your place," Lucinda yelled back, "after I told him his father had kicked you out."

Lexie stopped in her tracks. I was pretty sure she'd intended to go with Lucinda to help find Diablo. But now she turned and raced the other way, toward the spot where her car and the muddy-mobile were parked.

She crammed her hand in her jeans pocket and came out with keys.

Will bolted after her, Buddy and I following.

Will reached her before she could close her car door. He grabbed it with one hand and her arm with the other. "You shouldn't be driving. You might be concussed."

"Where are you going?" I said at almost the same time.

"Let go!" Lexie turned pleading eyes on both of us. "Shawn! Roger will kill him."

She didn't mean literally, of course, but I could understand her concern. It would be quite the confrontation.

"I'll take her," I said to Will.

He stared at me for a beat.

"Hey, I just fended off two killers with guns. I think I can manage one angry vet–"

Will cut me off. "Are there any guns in your house?" he asked Lexie.

Her eyes went wide. "We have a revolver that was my dad's. I hid it after… Roger would have these bouts of depression. I was afraid he'd try to hurt himself with it."

"How well hidden?" Will asked.

"It's in my room, under some stuff in a drawer. Roger never goes in there."

Will looked at me again.

Lexie used the distraction to pull her arm loose. She jammed the keys in the ignition.

"Lexie, wait," I said, then to Will, "You can't really make her stay, so it's better if I drive her."

Will stepped back, worry in his eyes. "Be careful." Then the cop part added, "I'll get your formal statements later."

I nodded and pointed toward the muddy-mobile.

Lexie jumped out of her car and climbed into the passenger side of the Bonneville. I quickly hooked Buddy's safety strap to his harness and settled in the driver's seat.

Once we were rolling down the driveway, I said, "You still got the wet wipes?"

"Yeah."

"Use them."

She flipped the passenger side visor down and gasped at the sight of herself in the dusty mirror.

～

At her front door, Lexie held her finger to her lips.

I frowned at her. *What the heck?*

She inserted her key and turned the knob.

The house was its usual dark and gloomy self.

"Nobody seems to be home," I said, even though we'd seen Shawn's car out by the curb.

"Shh." Lexie's eyes were wide. She moved quickly down the hall.

Buddy and I followed.

The great room was empty. Lexie kept moving.

The slider to the lanai was sitting open. She crept down the wheelchair ramp and turned out of my sight.

We hurried to catch up.

She was standing on the lanai, staring at a wooden door in one end of a longish, stucco outbuilding. The door, slightly ajar, was adorned by a wrought-iron silhouette of a wine bottle. An open padlock hung from a sturdy hasp on the doorframe.

A male voice, muffled, yelling something from inside the building.

I couldn't make out words but apparently Lexie could. "No!" she screamed and bolted for the door.

We ran after her, into the building.

A quick impression of windowless walls and a long oak table—wineglasses, an almost empty dusty bottle, and a corkscrew scattered across its smooth top. Then my attention was riveted to something else.

Roger in his wheelchair, his back to us, in front of an open doorway. His foot rested on a pile of dirty old pants and shoes in front of him.

Except the pants and shoes still had legs and feet in them. Apparently Lexie *had* literally meant her brother would kill Shawn.

Lexie ran past the testing table and grabbed the chair's handles. She scrambled backwards, hauling the wheelchair away from Shawn.

Roger's torso lurched forward. He almost tumbled out of the chair. "What are you doing, you stupid little fool?" he screamed. "I have to do this. To protect you!"

But Lexie's eyes weren't on her brother's red face.

I followed her line of vision.

Shawn's inert body was covered with dust. A clean trail across the tile floor showed where he had been rolled to the open doorway.

I gestured for Buddy to lie down and raced toward Shawn's body, colliding with Lexie. I let her stoop down to check for a pulse.

I was too busy staring down the steps in front of me—at another section of tile floor, rows of wine bottle racks on either side. There were dark stains in the grout around the tiles right at the bottom of the stairs.

I glanced down at Lexie, crouched beside Shawn. "Is he alive?"

She nodded. "His pulse is strong." Indeed, he was starting to stir.

I blew out a sigh of relief, then my throat closed as my brain processed what my heart had already figured out. "Lexie, how did your father die?"

Tears streaming down her cheeks were her only answer. "Help him."

Somehow I knew she didn't mean Shawn.

The squeak of rubber tires turning sharply on terrazzo. My head jerked up.

Roger was headed for Buddy, lying near the open door to the lanai.

"Buddy, come," I yelled.

The dog jumped up and scrambled out of the way, then trotted toward me.

Roger's chair picked up speed, through the open doorway.

He's getting away, my inner voice yelled. It dawned on me that he wouldn't get far, with no means of transportation other than a wheelchair.

But I hadn't anticipated his next move.

The door slammed shut behind him.

CHAPTER TWENTY-FIVE

I ran for the door but I was too late. The knob turned, but the door wouldn't budge.

I whirled around.

Lexie was staring at the door, her mouth open.

"What's he planning to do?" I asked. Blood was pounding so hard in my ears I could barely hear my own words.

She closed her mouth, swallowed hard. "I don't know."

Shawn moaned and stirred.

I shoved my fears aside for now and went over to them. Lexie and I each took one of Shawn's arms and helped him to his feet.

Lexie ran her hands down his sides, checking for injuries. "Did he hurt you?" Her voice was choked.

Shawn shook his head, but the grimace that followed said otherwise.

"Hold still." I stood on tiptoe behind him and examined the back of his head, gently touching a small lump.

He pulled away. "Ouch!"

"He didn't hit you?" I said.

He started to shake his head again, then winced. "No. I probably hit my head when I passed out."

"What happened?" I asked.

At the same time, Lexie said, "We've gotta get out of here." She sounded a little frantic.

"You have my cell phone?"

She patted her pockets. "No, I must have dropped it."

I looked down at Buddy, who was panting softly. "Do you have any water in here?"

Lexie shook her head. Her eyes were wide, darting back and forth. "We gotta get out of here," she repeated.

Shawn took a stumbling step closer to her and put an arm around her shoulders. "Shh, it'll be okay."

With his free hand, he patted his own pockets. He gave me a desperate look. "My phone's gone too."

Of course it was. Roger wouldn't want him to be able to call for help, should he survive the initial fall down the stairs.

Lexie's head frantically swiveled back and forth. "Look for something to pry the door open. Maybe the corkscrew."

"Shh, shh." Shawn squeezed her tighter against his side. He glanced at me. "She's claustrophobic."

Okay, that explained a lot.

"Her dad used to lock her in here when he was mad at her, and turn the lights out."

That explained even more.

"Look," I said to Lexie, "Will is going to come looking for us eventually, when he realizes we aren't back at my house and I don't answer my phone. Or Roger will relent and come unlock the door."

She shook her head again, but she seemed slightly calmer. "He said when we had that big fight that I had to choose between him or Shawn. I tried to tell him…" Her voice caught on a half sob, then she gathered herself. "I said it didn't have to be that way, that I loved both of them and he'd like Shawn if he just gave him a chance."

Shawn swayed a bit beside her.

I went behind the table and dragged out one of the two dusty, wooden chairs back there. Testing first to make sure it was sturdy, I gestured for Shawn to sit down.

"Lexie," he said, being a gentleman.

I frowned. "She doesn't have a golf ball sticking out of her skull. Sit."

I started for the other chair, but Lexie sank down on the floor, cross-legged at Shawn's feet.

I did the same, facing them in a tight little circle. Buddy dropped down beside me and rested his head on my knee. I stroked his ears.

He had stopped panting, but I was still worried about him. Humans can go several days without water, but dogs get dehydrated much faster than that.

I recalled seeing several large live oaks shading this building. The room was a little stuffy, but it probably wouldn't get any hotter as the afternoon sun beat down outside.

I leaned my back against the table leg. "We've got time to kill, so we might as well fill it. Shawn, what happened?"

"I came here to apologize to Lexie for the way my father behaved." He looked down at her.

She took his hand and tilted her head to gaze up at him.

His eyebrows flew up. "What happened to your forehead?"

"I'm okay," Lexie said, at the same time as I said, "We had a close encounter with the killers."

His eyes went wide. "What? What killers?"

Lexie and I took turns telling him what had happened at the horse farm. "You never did assault Marissa," she concluded, "and you've been cleared of the murders."

Shawn blew out air and slumped in his chair. "What a relief." He turned shiny eyes toward me. "Thank you, Marcia."

I shrugged and felt a touch of heat rising in my cheeks. "You're welcome. Actually, some of it was dumb luck."

But most of it was good investigating. Will's voice in my head. My chest warmed.

Hiding a smile, which seemed kind of inappropriate at the moment, I asked again, "So what happened here?"

Shawn nodded. "I was gonna leave when I realized Lexie wasn't here, but Roger said he'd had second thoughts, that he wanted to get to know me. He asked if I liked wine."

He gestured vaguely toward the door. "He even left the door open. I feel like such a fool. I never suspected a thing. I was so relieved that he seemed to be coming around and was going to give me a chance."

I felt like saying he wasn't alone in the fool department.

"He kept topping off my glass," Shawn said, "while he just sipped at his. I felt kinda lightheaded and thought, 'Wow, this stuff is strong.' And that's the last thing I remember."

"He must've slipped one of his sleeping pills into your glass." Lexie's tone said the comment was more than speculation.

"Is that what he did with your father?" I asked gently.

Her head jerked around and she stared at me. Finally she said, "No."

"What did happen?"

Lexie was silent.

Shawn squeezed her hand. "You might as well tell her, Lex."

She sighed. "Where to start?"

"Try the beginning, like I said, we've got time."

She sighed again and was silent for a moment. "The beginning is one of my very first memories. I was four. It was the day of the 'unveiling,' as my mother called it." She made air quotes. "The day she gave my father this wine cellar as a birthday present. It was the last time everybody in the family was happy at the same time."

What followed was a sad but all too common story of a child watching her drunken father beat her mother on a regular basis. He started locking the mom in the wine-tasting room, or sometimes in the cellar itself, usually with the lights off.

"Roger would sneak out after Daddy had passed out and let Mommy out. The next morning, they would both act like nothing had happened. Roger would stare at me across the breakfast table, willing me not to cry." Her eyes teared up now.

"Finally Mommy couldn't take it anymore. She left when I was six, in the middle of the night. For a long time, I didn't see her. We didn't know where she was."

Roger would've been thirteen.

"What I didn't know then was that she was in a shelter. It was her money, but Daddy had insisted she put it in a joint account. After she left, he took all the money out and put it in a different account. She fought Daddy for custody, but he claimed all kinds of stuff, that she had beaten us and was an unfit mother."

Another half sob.

Shawn squeezed her hand again. "You never told me all this," he said softly. "Just that she left because he beat her."

I hoped his interruption wouldn't stop her. Despite her upset, finally telling the whole story was probably therapeutic.

Lexie sucked in air and rubbed the back of her free hand across her wet eyes. "I didn't tell you all of that because of the next part. I didn't want you to hate Roger. He was so angry at Mommy for leaving us behind that he backed Daddy's lies. Even as a little kid, I knew that was messed up. I begged him to tell the truth.

"Mommy eventually got half her money back, but she still couldn't get us. Even her visits had to be supervised."

She took another deep breath. "She killed herself a year later. She'd put all the money in two trusts, but she made Daddy the trustee, and Roger was the secondary trustee of mine."

The last part barely registered. My mind was still stuck on the *killed herself* part. Roger had told me only that their parents were both dead.

The next part of the story was again sad but predictable. After his wife's death, the father's drinking got worse and he began taking his anger out on the next best punching bag, his teenaged son.

"He even used to yell at Roger that it was his fault Mommy was dead, that if he hadn't lied on the stand, she'd still be alive."

My heart twisted in my chest. No wonder Roger's head wasn't screwed on tight.

Buddy shifted his head on my knee, gave me a soulful look. He was sensing my distress.

I stroked his silky black ears.

"Roger enlisted in the Navy," Lexie said, "the day after his eighteenth birthday. He was halfway through his senior year, but he said he couldn't take it anymore."

Shawn leaned forward in his chair, his face tense. "And like his mother before him," he said in an angry voice, "it never occurred to him that the drunk might turn on a helpless child."

"He started beating you?" I said softly to Lexie.

She bit her lower lip and nodded. "I managed to hide it from Roger when he came home on leave, but when he got injured and came home for good…."

"He lured your father out here," I said, more statement than question.

But she shook her head. "Daddy was already out here, drinking. Roger came out to confront him. He wanted control of my trust early. I was supposed to get it anyway, when I turned twenty-one. But Roger wanted it so we'd have enough money to move out of the house and get a place of our own. He didn't want me to have to work while I was still in school.

"Daddy stood up and began pulling off his belt. He yelled something about taking care of Roger once and for all. I was terrified." She stopped, gulped air.

"You were there?" I asked.

She nodded, tears streaming down her cheeks. "Just outside the door. I remember thinking, 'How can you do this? How can you beat a man in a wheelchair?'"

Buddy's gaze had shifted to Lexie's face. He looked back at me and whined softly. I gave a small nod.

He sat up and licked the salty wetness off her cheek.

Lexie's face relaxed some and she patted his head. "Daddy swayed and keeled over before he even had the belt all the way loose from his pants. Roger wheeled over to him and started nudging him toward the other end of the tasting room with his foot. I didn't know what he was going to do but he was muttering, 'We'll see who takes care of who.'"

"Wait, with his foot?" I said.

"Yeah." She made a sniffling noise. "He was controlling his leg with his hands. He'd lean forward and grab his calf, and push forward to hook his foot under..." She let go of Shawn's hand and demonstrated on his leg next to her, wrapping her hands around his calf and angling it forward.

Buddy cocked his head to one side. I imagined him thinking, *What the devil is she doing?*

I gestured for him to lie down again. He did, but this time his head was on Lexie's thigh.

"Then he'd lift the leg up." She slipped a hand under Shawn's knee and bounced his leg up and down. "Daddy would flop over and...." Her voice broke.

Buddy shifted his weight so he was lying firmly against her leg.

She cleared her throat and rested one hand on his head. "Roger told me to go in the house and I went. They found Daddy at the bottom of the stairs the next morning."

"Who found him?" I asked, keeping my voice gentle.

"The police. Roger called them, saying he couldn't find his father and was afraid he'd wandered off and was lying hurt somewhere." She stared at me. "He sounded so convincing on the phone with them, that I almost believed him myself."

I leaned back against the table leg and blew out air. It was one heck of a story, but I believed every word of it. Lexie had no reason to lie.

"I've gotta help him."

I stared at her. Was she kidding?

"Please don't tell anyone what he did today, or what I just told you." She put her hands together as if praying. "Please! I'll get him into rehab. When he's sober, he's a nice guy."

"Lexie," I said as gently as I could. "It's gone too far."

The truth of my own words hit me. If it had only been the father, I might have looked the other way. After all, Roger was trying to protect himself and his sister from a drunken abuser. And no doubt the death had already been officially ruled an accident.

But attempted murder of Shawn, and now imprisoning all of us in this room? No, the man was too dangerous.

"And I'm engaged to an officer of the law." Who hopefully would be here soon to rescue us. "I can't lie to him."

Lexie opened her mouth but before she could say anything else, the lights went out.

She screamed.

Sheez, can this get any worse?

It could.

A muffled crack, then another.

It took a second for their meaning to register.

My hand flew to my mouth, stifling a scream. *My God, not Will. Please, not Will!*

CHAPTER TWENTY-SIX

Something raked across my knee. My already pounding heart jolted up another notch. Then I realized it was Lexie's fingernails.

I leaned forward and blindly felt around for her. The back of my hand brushed against Buddy's coat. My fingers found Lexie's, and she held on so tight I thought my bones would be crushed.

I could hear her breathing rapidly in the total darkness.

"Lexie, stop! You'll hyperventilate. Stop and take a deep breath."

I felt around with my other hand for Buddy. It connected with soft furry warmth. I scooted forward a little bit on my butt.

The fast breathing had stopped. Had Lexie passed out?

The death grip on my fingers said no.

"It's okay, baby." Shawn's voice, soothing, from just above my head.

Sobbing noises.

"It's okay." His voice rose in pitch, more hysterical than soothing this time.

The chair scraped across the floor. Buddy must have shifted out of the way because I lost contact with his fur.

Air movement in front of me. Shawn's voice, soothing again and at my eye level. "Come here."

Lexie, still sobbing, let go of my hand.

Suddenly I felt adrift in the sea of blackness. I'd never been anywhere that was this totally dark. For a moment, I wasn't sure which way was up or down.

I laid my palms on the cool tile floor and pushed myself back against the table leg. Taking my own advice, I sucked in a deep breath.

I could hear Buddy panting. "Come here, boy."

He whined.

"Right over here." A warm rough tongue licked my cheek. I felt immensely better.

Sirens in the distance, squealing sickly to a halt.

Why are they stopping so far away?

Realization dawned. They weren't far away. The sirens were being muffled by the walls of the building.

But if I could hear the sirens at all, those walls were not completely soundproof.

"They're here," I said, praying Will was with them and hadn't come ahead of his back-up, that he wasn't lying somewhere bleeding.

I shoved that thought aside before it could threaten my already shaky sanity.

"We should take turns yelling," I said.

It seemed like a year went by. We were all hoarse well before we heard someone call out, "Back here!"

"Help!" the three of us croaked in unison.

"Somebody get a bolt cutter." Will's voice, outside the door.

I sagged with relief, losing contact with the table leg. Cool air replaced Buddy's warmth beside me. My head swam.

A woof from across the room—Buddy reacting to Will's voice.

"Come here, boy," I said in a shaky voice, as I scrabbled around and clutched the smooth square of the table leg.

And it was in that ignoble position that Will found me, my eyes scrunched closed against the blinding light from the open door and clinging to a chunk of wood like it was my blankie, my dog licking my face.

Will led me out into the sunshine. I opened my eyes a tiny bit. The light still hurt but I made myself leave them that far open.

Buddy brushed against my knee. I blindly reached down and found his head.

I glanced around, looking for my fellow prisoners. They were clinging to each other, both with the same squinty-eyed pained expression that was probably on my face.

A uniformed deputy pulled them apart. Lexie let out a small scream.

The deputy spun Shawn around and started to handcuff him. Shawn's face went gray-green.

"Stop," I yelled. "He was the victim."

Will looked up. "Booker, turn him loose."

"Sorry," Deputy Booker said, then jumped back as Shawn bent over and vomited on the deputy's shoes.

I heard hysterical laughter. Will put his arm around my shoulders. "Easy, girl." I realized the laughter was coming from me.

I shot Shawn an apologetic look, but he was smiling sheepishly. Lexie actually giggled, and I smiled at both of them.

I felt lightheaded, giddy. *We're free! We've been rescued.*

Air whooshed out of my lungs. I looked down. Buddy was panting harder now. I tugged on Will's sleeve and pointed to the dog.

"Somebody bring a dish of water," Will called out.

Another deputy appeared with three water bottles in his hands.

If I hadn't been hanging onto Will, I would have grabbed the guy and kissed him.

"We can't get a dish right now, Detective," someone else said from behind me.

Will looked past my shoulder and nodded, his expression grim. He let go of me, stooped down and cupped his hands.

The deputy handed two of the bottles to Lexie and Shawn, then leaned over and poured water into Will's hands.

Buddy lapped greedily. The deputy poured more for him and then straightened and handed me the bottle.

I took a long pull. It was tepid but still tasted heavenly.

Will stood and wiped his hands on his suit pants, which were definitely going to need a trip to the cleaners after this day.

They didn't take us through the house. "It's a crime scene," Will said, his tone grim.

Instead, they led us to a side gate in the privacy fence around the large backyard, Will and I in the lead, his partner and poor Deputy Booker herding Lexie and Shawn along behind us.

"What time is it?"

Will checked his watch. "Two-forty."

We'd spent the better part of three hours in that building. My stomach rumbled, protesting missing lunch.

Will grinned. "Good sign you're already getting back to normal."

We stopped on the sidewalk in front of the house. His partner led Lexie and Shawn past us and over to a waiting ambulance. My gaze followed them. They'd been through a lot, but they were going to be okay.

I turned back to Will. He was still grinning.

"Okay, you get to smirk now. You've earned it." I might have caught his killers earlier, but he'd still had to come rescue me in the end, as he had at least twice before. Or maybe two and half times. Once he'd shown up right after somebody else had rescued me.

Then I remembered the gunshots. I braced myself. "We heard two shots, a few minutes before the sirens."

His face fell, and my stomach dropped. *Crapola!*

"Campbell must have found the gun in Lexie's drawer. He tried to kill himself, but he wasn't successful. We found him slumped over in his chair, next to the open breaker box in the kitchen. That's how I figured out where you were. The only breaker that was switched off was marked wine cellar."

A strange mix of relief and sadness washed through me. Buddy leaned against my leg. I stroked the top of his head.

"You didn't hear us yelling?" I asked.

He shook his head.

Great, so I had a sore throat now for nothing.

I glanced over to where Detective Brown was talking to Lexie and Shawn. She started looking frantically around, like she had in the wine-tasting room. Pulling loose from Shawn's arm draped over her shoulders, she darted toward the front porch.

Two EMTs were bringing out a gurney. Roger Campbell was strapped to it.

A lump made my throat hurt worse. "How bad is he?"

"Hard to tell," Will said. "The first bullet grazed the side of his head. Then it looks like he tried to shoot himself in the heart. That one went through his shoulder."

I shook my head. Had he been so drunk he couldn't shoot straight, or had second thoughts about leaving his sister and us locked in the wine-tasting room made his aim falter?

The EMTs had gotten the gurney down to the sidewalk. Lexie was beside it holding her brother's hand. He seemed to be only half-conscious, moving his head back and forth and mumbling something.

Shawn stepped up beside Lexie. She let go of Roger's hand as the EMTs loaded him into the ambulance. Turning in Shawn's arms, she sobbed against his shoulder.

They're still gonna be okay. Internal Mom that time.

Yeah, but I'm not so sure Roger will be.

"Another veteran attempting suicide." Will's voice was somber.

I sighed. "Sadly this one was screwed up long before he went to war."

"Oh?"

"Long story. Short version. Mother ran away from an abusive husband. The father started abusing Roger instead, then turned his wrath on Lexie when Roger went into the Navy."

Will winced.

I was still debating how much of Lexie's story about her father's death I should or would tell him.

He shook his head slowly. "The misery people create for themselves and their families. Speaking of which, remember those speculations we'd made about Marissa Andrews's background? She was taken away from her parents at age ten after her doctor reported signs of abuse to child services."

My eyes stung with unshed tears. "How do you do it, witness so much misery all the time?

He shrugged. "That was part of the appeal of being sheriff of a rural county, not nearly as much violent crime. But that got boring after a while."

"And now?"

He smiled down at me, his blue eyes soft. "I have you and my wacky neighbors in Mayfair to balance things out." He wrapped an arm around my shoulders. "Come on. I'm taking my *fiancée* and her fearless canine companion home."

The word *fiancée* did not strike fear in my soul, as it once had. Indeed, it sounded reassuring. Maybe even a little exciting.

"Don't you have to stay here and mop things up?"

"Nope." Will glanced over at Detective Brown with a small smirk on his face. "That's what junior partners are for."

EPILOGUE

Will had seriously underplayed how much mopping up would be needed and his role in it. He'd worked through the weekend, helping Vice round up the prostitution ring, interviewing suspects and witnesses and, of course, doing the paperwork, all while still working his other cases.

He'd come home yesterday so exhausted I'd insisted he skip the Chamber of Commerce meeting. He gave me his proxy, but it turned out I didn't really need his vote.

Finally he had a day off. We sat at my kitchen table eating breakfast —egg sandwiches from the diner again; I'm allergic to cooking before noon—and debating how to use our precious day together.

Stephie was taking Patches for an outing, only his second outside of Mayfair. I should be going with them, but she'd reassured me she could handle it. And after their performance at the Chamber meeting, I had total confidence in her.

"So tell me more about the meeting," Will said.

I'd already told him the outcome, that the townspeople had soundly defeated Charlene's proposal to ban certain dog breeds from town. Two things she hadn't counted on. Many Floridians love dogs, and even more of them hate restrictions on people's personal freedom.

"After Stephie demonstrated some of the other things Patches can do, she put a water bottle on a table and told him to 'go get water.' When he brought the bottle to her, she held it up like a trophy and said, 'He can even open a refrigerator to get this, but that was too hard to demonstrate here.' The applause was deafening."

"Bet that improves Chamber meeting attendance, if folks think they'll get a show each time." We both laughed, but then his brow furrowed into a small frown. "You've probably made an enemy of Charlene though."

"Not my intention, but I had to fight her on this. Edna told me privately that Charlene's afraid of dogs in general, even her 'boys.'" I made air quotes. "Oh, you'll never guess the other proposal Edna made last night. Instead of an ice-skating rink, she wants to build a riding stable to attract tourists."

Will shrugged. "Edna's had crazier notions. This one might not be such a bad idea."

"You don't seem surprised."

"She mentioned it to me. I told her I'd support it. Anything beats trying to keep ice frozen in Florida, even in December."

I nodded and changed the subject. "So is Marissa Andrews talking?"

Will shook his head, chewing on a big bite of his sandwich.

"One thing I don't get was why Lenny was even at Clover Hills that day."

"He gave us that." Will paused to wipe some grease off his chin with his napkin.

Come on, spill! I thought, but managed not to say out loud.

Finally, he said, "Andrews had decided that Shawn needed to disappear, so we'd assume he was guilty and the case would be closed. Lenny was supposed to grab Shawn without being seen, but Lexie showed up and spotted him. So he figured he'd add her to Shawn's list of crimes, or maybe people would assume she got trapped in Diablo's stall by accident."

Will took another bite of sandwich and chewed.

I plastered what I hoped was a patient look on my face and waited.

"Apparently Andrews didn't trust her underling," he continued. "Maybe he'd let something slip that made her suspect he'd flipped on her. Anyway, she'd followed him. When she saw that you'd shown up too, I suspect it was too good a chance to pass up. She'd get rid of all her loose ends at once."

"And Shawn would be blamed for another death."

"Oh, and that pitchfork handle she used on Lenny?" Will popped the last bite of his sandwich in.

"Yeah?"

He chewed and swallowed. "The lab had already examined one like it from the Davis's barn, since it was the right size and shape to have left the contusions on Jason Burrows's head. But the techs hadn't found anything that first time. It was clean, we thought, except for several sets of fingerprints, including Shawn's. If we could've proven it was the murder weapon, we would've arrested Shawn then. But our captain wanted a stronger case against him first."

Will paused to wipe his fingers on his napkin. He was making me crazy.

"Knowing that Andrews clobbered Lenny with another pitchfork, the lab took a closer look at the first one, checking for more than blood and hair this time. They found some flakes of dandruff in a crack on the handle. The tech sent it off to the state lab. He thinks they can get DNA from it. Bet it'll match Burrows."

"*I'll* bet Marissa was really annoyed when you didn't arrest Shawn after she'd left you the murder weapon, complete with his fingerprints all over it." Curiosity won out over the slight queasiness this discussion was triggering. "But how come it didn't have blood and hair on it?"

"Burrows didn't bleed all that much. All the open wounds were from the horse's hooves, *post mortem*. The two contusions on his head, one was on the side and not all that hard. Probably just stunned him. Or it may have been a second blow that wasn't even necessary. The other," Will touched the back of his own head, "was at the hairline. M.E. says it broke his neck right below the brain stem. He died instantly."

I winced. "Lucky blow?"

Will shrugged. "He was probably leaning over for the envelope that he thought had his payoff in it. She had a clean shot at his head and neck. He may have never seen it coming."

"And then she dragged him into Diablo's stall. She has guts, I've got to give her that."

"She knows horses. The foster family she was with from ten to fourteen had a farm."

"By the way, I never did hear how Gerry Fields died."

Will mimicked being garroted. "Based on the marks, the M.E. said it was probably a man's belt. They're checking all the belts we found in Andrews and Fields's house."

"Why's Lenny being so cooperative?" I asked. "He told us that his deal with you all wasn't worth much, since he was wanted in too many 'other jurisdictions.'" I mimicked Lenny's Jersey accent.

Will smiled and distracted me for a moment with that sexy dimple of his.

"Our DA implied he would fight extradition, as well as give Lenny a lighter sentence, if he testifies."

"And he's going along with that?"

"Yes, because now he's looking at two counts of first degree murder, three of attempted murder and a slew of other charges. The one thing Marissa did say was that it was all Lenny's doing. That he killed Gerry and Jason, and she knew nothing about it until afterwards."

I snorted. "Which leaves him holding the bag unless he cooperates. How much of a lighter sentence will he get?" My whole body tensed at the thought of Lenny the Plow back out on the street any time soon.

"Life sentence without parole but the death penalty comes off the table. The DA's relatively sure the other states with outstanding warrants will go for that. Lenny will be put away forever and they don't have to spend any money on trials."

I nodded. My stomach relaxed and happily accepted the last two bites of my sandwich.

"You know," Will said, "You've got good instincts. You really could be a good detective, if that's what you want to do."

I shrugged. "I haven't decided yet."

"Are you still worried about Buddy breaking training to go all protective on you?"

I shrugged again. "I guess not. He's not a true service dog anymore. And honestly, I've taken him with me lately partly *because* I wanted a big intimidating dog along, not just for his company."

"Well personally I'd prefer that he be protective, and that you have him with you as much as possible. Whether you become a P.I. or not, you do have a propensity for finding trouble."

I might have been offended by that, if it weren't for his teasing grin and its accompanying dimple.

I playfully stuck out my tongue. His grin widened.

"I may train him to do some things on command, like head-butt people's knees to knock them over. I don't want him grabbing limbs like he did Marissa's arm. If he bites someone, even while protecting me, I could have the county saying that he's dangerous and should be put down." My heart pounded at that thought.

"I can help," Will said. "I'll borrow some padding from the department's K9 unit. So back to what to do today—"

"We could lay around all day." I wiggled my eyebrows suggestively.

"I don't know. It's a pretty day." His tone was nonchalant. "Let's go for a drive and stop somewhere for lunch later."

I was a little surprised he wasn't taking me up on my offer, but we had all day. We could "lay around" later.

Once Stephie had picked up Patches, Buddy and I climbed into Will's truck.

Will took back roads, headed in the basic direction of Ocala. Windows lowered, we enjoyed the spring air. March is, in my opinion, the most beautiful month in central Florida. April's weather is iffy, and by May, we're definitely moving into the heat of summer. But today, the air was a pleasant seventy-six and the humidity was about as low as it ever gets in Florida.

I sat back in my seat and watched the scenery skimming by. For the first time in a couple of weeks, my whole body was relaxed.

Maybe the tension of being a P.I. wasn't worth it. And as it had turned out, I'd barely broken even. The bill for my banged-up fender had been six-hundred and eighty dollars. I'd opted not to submit it to the insurance company, for fear they would drop me. That left one-hundred and twenty dollars of what I had received for the "case," which worked out to $4.80 an hour.

That reminded me of Roger Campbell. Thoughts of his attempted suicide sobered my mood. I'd never really liked the guy, and had suffered some guilt over that. Bottom line, he wasn't a nice person and, from the sound of it, hadn't been even before his military service. Still, it was sad that he'd never had much of a chance for a normal, healthy life.

Last I'd heard, he was being released from the hospital to a rehab facility for veterans. When he'd recovered from his self-inflicted wounds, he was facing attempted murder charges.

Shawn had asked if he could drop the charges, but Will had gently pointed out that attempted murder wasn't quite the same as shoplifting or swinging a fist in a bar fight. Prosecution was up to the DA's office.

And then there was the father's death. That case had been reopened after I'd told Will about Lexie hearing her brother and father fighting the night before he was found dead.

I'd left out her description of how Roger had rolled the man's inert body across the floor, and I hoped she had the good sense not to fess up to having witnessed that. It could make her an accomplice in the eyes of the law.

I was also hoping the courts would go easy on Roger, but not too easy. Ironically, he was the one, not Shawn, who needed to learn about consequences for one's actions.

"If you do become a P.I.," Will broke into my thoughts, "you need to watch your tendency to assume your clients are always good people. That will get you into trouble every–"

I laughed. "Were you reading my mind? I was just thinking about Roger Campbell."

"Case in point," he said. "I interviewed him yesterday. He admitted to calling Andrews. He was pissed at Burrows because he went the blackmail route, so he told her both Burrows and Shawn had assaulted her."

"And ironically he was closer to the truth than he realized."

We fell silent for few moments.

I glanced Will's way. "Actually, I'm leaning away from becoming a P.I."

His eyebrows shot up but he kept his gaze on the road. The corners of his mouth twitched. I knew he'd prefer that I kept leaning in that direction.

A green and white sign flashed past my side window, and Will slowed for a right turn. Into Clover Hills Farm.

"What are we doing here?"

"I thought you might want to visit your old friend, Diablo?" Now Will was full-blown grinning.

"Not really." I spotted Lexie's white sedan amongst the farm vehicles parked outside the barn. "But I wouldn't mind seeing how Shawn and Lexie are doing."

Will nodded and swung the truck in beside the cars, trucks, and a golf cart that were lined up along one side of the paved area in front of the barn.

I hesitated as we got out. "I'm not sure I want to see Mr. Davis though."

"I don't think he'll be around. I got the impression that his wife kicked him out."

"Really? They seemed so...." I trailed off. *Devoted* didn't sound quite right, but they'd been together for a long time. "She did seem unhappy with the way he handled Shawn's situation."

Will took Buddy's leash from me, something he almost never did, and wrapped his other arm around my shoulders. We walked toward the barn.

"Yeah," he said, "It's one thing to apply tough love when your kid's getting himself into trouble, but this time, Shawn's mess wasn't of his own making, and the stakes were a lot higher."

I glanced around at the paddocks and barns. "I hope they don't have to sell this place. Shawn loves it."

Will shook his head. "I, um, was curious so I looked up the land records. The farm is in her name only. Turns out it was a wedding gift from her parents, many moons ago."

I mentally scolded myself. *Banks, ya gotta stop making sexist assumptions about who has the money.*

"Why were you so curious?" I asked.

Will ignored the question and nudged me forward into the barn. "Isn't that the little mare you've become so fond of?"

Sure enough, Niña had her delicate black head sticking out over the bottom half of her stall door. She whinnied softly as I approached.

A fist squeezed my heart. I stroked the mare's velvet nose.

She mouthed my hand, looking for a treat.

"I'll get you a carrot, girl." I figured Shawn wouldn't mind.

I turned toward the tack and feed room and jerked backward. The aisle of the barn was full of people, all grinning at me.

"Surprise!" they yelled.

Diablo kicked his stall door farther down the barn. Shawn laughed. "Easy, boy," he called out.

I was still blinking at the crowd. Lucinda and Lexie I'd expected to see here eventually, but why were Edna and Susanna and Sherie here?

Shawn walked over to me and touched something on the half door of Niña's stall.

I looked where he was pointing. A small brass plate read *Niña, out of Belladama by Diablillo.* I translated her dam's and sire's names in my head, *beautiful lady* and *little devil.*

Shawn gave me a lopsided grin and moved his hand away. On the next line was *Owner: Marcia Banks.*

My mouth fell open and I went numb for a second. Then bubbles erupted in my chest. I screamed and threw my arms around Shawn.

"Wait!" I jumped back. "Did you buy her?" I said to Will. I wasn't sure how I would feel about such an expensive gift, even from my "fiancé."

My mind automatically put mental quotes around the word. I guess I wasn't as over my marriage skittishness as I'd thought.

Fortunately I didn't say any of that out loud, because Will shook his head.

Lucinda Davis stepped forward. "She's your fee for clearing Shawn's name. But I'll be happy to write you a check instead."

My head was shaking so hard, my ponytail flew out of its scrunchie, even as an image of all the outstanding bills sitting on my coffee table flashed through my mind.

But my heart was made up. "How are we going to pay for her board though?" I asked Will.

He was already grinning so wide I was amazed that the grin could get any wider, but it did. "You just said *we*."

So I had. I made a mental note to call my counselor, whom I hadn't seen in months, also due to finances. But I desperately needed a session or two, or three or a dozen, to sort out my feelings about marriage once and for all.

"You're keeping her here, for now," Shawn said, "for free. She's an easy-keeper."

Meaning she didn't have a big appetite. Good to know.

"That is until...." Shawn trailed off and looked at Edna.

She was wearing her hotelier outfit and, in deference to the more formal attire, black flip-flops with glitter on them, and she was also grinning at me. "Susie's gonna run the stable for me. She needs somethin' to do. But she don't know 'nough about horses just yet. So I'd like to give you free board for your filly, if you'll help her out."

My first thought was that I didn't know enough to run a stable either. But I probably did know enough to ask the right questions and find the people with the answers. Such as Shawn.

I started to nod, but the surprises weren't quite over. Lexie elbowed her way to the front of the group and threw her arms around me. "I have another question for you. Will you be my maid of honor? Shawn and I are getting married next month."

I grinned at her, and then at Edna. "Yes and yes."

AUTHOR'S NOTES

If you enjoyed this book, please take a moment to leave a short review on the book retailer's site where you downloaded it (and/or other online book retailers). Reviews help with sales, and sales keep the series going! You can find the links for these retailers at the misterio press bookstore (http://misteriopress.com).

If you'd like a complete list of my books in this series and others, please flip back to the Table of Contents and click on "Books by Kassandra Lamb."

Also, you may want to go to http://kassandralamb.com to sign up for my newsletter and get updates on new releases, giveaways and sales (and you get a free e-copy of a novella for signing up). I only send out newsletters when I truly have news and you can unsubscribe at any time.

We at *misterio press* pride ourselves on providing our readers with top-quality reads. All of our books are proofread multiple times by several pairs of eyes, but proofreaders are human. If you found errors in this book, please email me at lambkassandra3@gmail.com so the errors can be corrected. Thank you!

Let me spread some gratitude around and then I'll chat with you a bit about some of the elements in this story. A big thank you to my beta readers, Marilyn Hiliau, who consulted on the overall story but also on service dog training details, and my amazing daughter-in-law, romance writer G.G. Andrew, who again assessed the overall story but particularly keeps me in check re: how younger people talk and act.

As always, my eternal gratitude to my editor, Marcy Kennedy. I would not be where I am today without you. Big hugs!!

Also *muchas gracias* to Kirsten Weiss and Gilian Baker, two of our wonderful *misterio press* authors who critiqued and proofread this story. And always also, to my partner-in-crime at *misterio*, Shannon Esposito. Health issues have kept her from critiquing this story, but nonetheless, she is one of the main reasons why I am a published and successful author today.

And last but never least, to my wonderful husband who does the final proofread to make sure I've dotted all my i's and crossed all my t's. Any errors you may have found are not his fault. I cannot resist tweaking my stories until the last possible moment, so I tend to introduce new typos after his 'final' read-through.

There are several ironies in the back story behind this novel.

Two years ago, based on a stock photo I'd stumbled upon and fell in love with, I had chosen an American Staffordshire Terrier as the breed of dog who would be featured in this story.

And then we suddenly lost our sweet and elegant rescue dog Lady last fall. We had only had her for two years but her mellow personality had blessed our home with tranquility.

We adopted yet another rescue dog. He *seemed* mellow in the kennel at the Humane Society. He was a Hurricane Irma dog, as in nobody knew squat about him, because he had been found wandering in Marion County during the early stages of that storm.

We named him Dr. Watson. (Get it? I'm Sherlock and he's Watson). And he has turned out to be far from mellow. He is a very energetic young man.

As I have researched his potential pedigree, lo and behold, I discovered that he is probably at least half American Staffordshire Terrier.

But I was advised by my veterinarian to always list him just as "mixed," to avoid prejudices regarding the bull terrier breeds. And sadly, as I was searching the local shelters for our new furry friend, I saw way too many Pit Bulls and Pit Bull mixes in need of loving homes.

All that inspired me to address the prejudice issue via Charlene, the postmistress. (Unfortunately for poor Charlene, I plan to put her through even more grief in the next story, *The Legend of Sleepy Mayfair*.)

Now, I'm not saying that Pit Bulls are always virtuous but they are definitely getting a bad rap overall right now.

And on the subject of bad raps, I hope no members of the Navy or their families take offense that I have portrayed Roger Campbell as unstable and not a very nice person. I wasn't trying to pick on the Navy. It was just overdue as the represented branch of the military, since I have had a Marine, an Army nurse and a member of the Army Corp of Engineers so far. (Air Force will be next.)

The reality is that members of the military potentially run the whole gambit of mental health and personality types just as the general public does. Not all are necessarily noble, good, and sane people before they go into service, and while the military does do psychological and personality screening of new recruits, some bad apples will slip through.

As the series progresses, we will see that the lessons Marcia learned in her dealings with Roger Campbell will impact how her trust issues play out.

And I will stop there so as not to spoil anything.

Back to the ironies. The second one was that I had planned the basic plot of this book well before the #MeToo movement took root in this country. As a retired trauma recovery specialist, I most definitely support this movement and the brave women who have come forward to expose the sexual misconduct and outright abuse that is rampant in our society.

But I also know from my experience as a therapist in the trauma recovery field that false accusations do sometimes happen. And these may not necessarily be due to malice by the accuser but rather a result of the dissociation that can occur as a defense against the emotional trauma and/or as a result of drugs or alcohol that may have been part of the scene, either taken willingly or unwillingly.

Ironically (again), this very evening, just before I sat down to write these author's notes, I watched an episode of *Law and Order, SVU* in which a young woman was drugged, without her knowledge, and then assaulted. And the drugs led to her falsely accusing someone else for her attack rather than the true rapist.

I have tried to handle the issues around Marissa's accusations with sensitivity. I certainly do not want to imply that rape survivors should not be believed! I most definitely feel strongly that there is no excuse for anyone forcing sexual activity or taking advantage of another's incapacitation to seek sexual gratification at their expense.

My editor commented that she didn't quite understand why Gerry Fields set Shawn up in the way that he did. I did add a few things to help explain his motivations. But after having been a college professor for two decades and living in a college town in retirement for fourteen years now, I didn't find his actions hard to believe.

College students do dumb things. In the spur of the moment, half drunk and egged on by his friend Jason, I can easily see Gerry setting up his roommate for what he would think of as an "innocent" prank, which would also serve to cover up what he'd done to his girlfriend.

And once things got out of hand and the police had been called, yeah, he would have most likely let things pan out. If Shawn had been prosecuted, he probably would have come forward—I tried to show that he did have some remorse at the time—but when the charges were dropped, self-interest prevailed.

My apologies to fraternities everywhere. There are a lot of good things about them. My husband was in a fraternity at UF and the camaraderie and support of his brothers very much helped him make the transition from home to college life.

The downside is that the late adolescent brain is not fully mature, and fraternities can sometimes magnify that immaturity.

Brain research is now helping us understand the late adolescent mindset. While so many other parts of their brains are fairly well developed, the areas that connect behavior to both moral ramifications and real-life consequences are the last to fully develop.

Which brings me to the next installment in the Marcia Banks and Buddy's saga, a holiday novella, *The Legend of Sleepy Mayfair, A Marcia Banks and Buddy Mystery Novella*:

Service dog trainer and part-time defacto stable manager, Marcia Banks is about to pull her hair out. Due to the efforts of an anonymous prankster, construction of the new Mayfair Riding Stable has taken forever. And no sooner has she installed her own horse in one of its stalls than the stable's owner and town matriarch, Edna Mayfair decides to turn the barn into a haunted house for Halloween.

Meanwhile, Mayfair's postmistress seeks Marcia's help to track down the parents of her visiting "nephew," leaving Marcia confused, and not just because she and Charlene aren't exactly buddies. Is the boy a runaway?

Juggling spooky decorations, online searches and dog training, as well as her new role as godmother to adorable twins, Marcia tries to focus on the most important mystery—identifying the "prankster" whose escalating vandalism is disrupting the town's tranquility and its budding tourist trade. There's one bright spot at least; she and her police detective fiancé are more in sync...most of the time. But as Halloween approaches, evil forces from the outside world threaten to destroy everything new and wonderful in Marcia's life.

ABOUT THE AUTHOR

Kassandra Lamb has never been able to decide which she loves more, psychology or writing. In college, she realized that writers need a day job in order to eat, so she studied psychology. After a career as a psychotherapist and college professor, she is now retired and can pursue her passion for writing fiction. She spends most of her time in an alternate universe with her characters. The portal to this universe, aka her computer, is located in north-central Florida, where her husband and dog catch occasional glimpses of her.

Kass is currently working on Book 10 of the Kate Huntington mystery series and Book 6 of the Marcia Banks and Buddy cozy mysteries. She also has four novellas out in the Kate on Vacation series (lighter reads along the lines of cozy mysteries but with the same main characters as the Kate Huntington series). And she writes romantic suspense under the pen name of Jessica Dale. (https://darkardorpublications.com/).

To read and see more about Kassandra and her characters you can go to http://kassandralamb.com. Be sure to sign up for the newsletter there to get a heads up about new releases, plus special offers and bonuses for subscribers. (New subscribers get a free e-copy of a novella.)

Kass's e-mail is lambkassandra3@gmail.com and she loves hearing from readers! She's also on Facebook (https://www.facebook.com/kassandralambauthor) and hangs out some on Twitter @KassandraLamb. She blogs about psychological topics and other random things at http://misteriopress.com.

Please check out these other great misterio press series:

Karma's A Bitch: The Pet Psychic Mysteries
by Shannon Esposito

Multiple Motives: The Kate Huntington Mysteries
by Kassandra Lamb

Maui Widow Waltz: The Islands of Aloha Mysteries
by JoAnn Bassett

The Metaphysical Detective: The Riga Hayworth Paranormal Mysteries
by Kirsten Weiss

Dangerous and Unseemly: The Concordia Wells Historical Mysteries by
K.B. Owen

Murder, Honey: The Carol Sabala Mysteries
by Vinnie Hansen

Blogging is Murder: The Jade Blackwell Mysteries
by Gilian Baker

To Kill A Labrador: The Marcia Banks and Buddy Mysteries
by Kassandra Lamb

Steam and Sensibility: The Sensibility Grey Steampunk Mysteries
by Kirsten Weiss

Bound: The Witches of Doyle Mysteries
by Kirsten Weiss

Made in the USA
San Bernardino, CA
14 August 2019